The

Billboard

Bride

MONICA MYNK

Scripture quotations in this book are taken from
the New King James Version ®
Copyright © 1982 by Thomas Nelson.
Used by Permission. All rights reserved.

Cover and interior images:
http://www.depositphotos.com
Mother Cow & Calf: @rghenry
Beautiful Young Girl in a Wedding Dress: @kamenuka
Portrait of a Beautiful Young Bride in Nature: @ Yevgeniya131988

Published in the United States of America by
Prodigal Daughter Publishing
416 Wellington Way
Winchester, KY 40391

Dedication

To my special daddy, who taught me so many things.

I am so blessed to have been raised by a man with such deep faith.

And to God, whose promises are new every morning.

OTHER BOOKS BY MONICA MYNK

The Cavernous Trilogy
Cavernous
Cocooned
Conceded (November 2017)

The Goddess to Daughter Series
Pandora's Deed
Medusa's Hands
Athena's Baby (2018)

Ungodly Clutter (Women's Bible Study)

Chapter One

Melanie Turner clenched her fist around the glittery button that held the right side of her train to her sequined white dress. She snatched it free, her teeth gritted so tight it pained her forehead.

Her well-timed harrumph sent all the bridesmaids skittering backward. The same crowd of girls had thrown her a twenty-sixth birthday bash last October. Now it was June—the sunny month of romance and weddings and honeymoons. But not for her. Nope. She'd be stuck here in Milton. She was doomed to a hot Kentucky summer of tears, sweat, and misery.

She raised her manicured hand to her shoulder and flung the button across the toddler classroom into a tower of empty baby wipe tubs. As the poorly-stacked containers toppled, she ripped the left button free and let the train fall to the floor.

Mama planted a blue satin heel in front of the train. "Melanie. We paid good money for that dress."

"Leave me alone, Mama." She shoved her gaping bridesmaids aside and stormed into the church lobby, missing prim and newlywed Audrey Harris by mere inches. Audrey had taunted Melanie at the birthday party that she'd never be a bride. Melanie had fired back that the wedding was on. And it was... until five minutes ago.

A line of elderly church ladies, sun-dressed girls, and distant cousins parted as she pressed into the auditorium. She marched to the end of the aisle, crunching dried roses beneath her white satin pumps. With a sharp pivot, she faced the dead-silent crowd. "Y'all need to mind your own business."

"Pun'kin." Daddy lunged forward, making a swing for her arm as she hiked up her wedding dress.

"Don't you dare 'pun'kin' me." She loosened the small linen bag she'd tied to her garter and clutched it in her white-knuckled hand. "Did you take me for a fool?"

The collective hum of whispers prickled her arm hair. She wrinkled her nose, twisting her lips to the side. "Did y'all take me for a fool? Why didn't someone—anyone—bother to tell me he was a lyin', cheatin' creep?"

She stalked to the altar. Her hands quivered as she shook the linen bag, letting her thirteen dimes fall to the rose-covered fabric.

They bounced and rolled between the silvery unity candles while the crowd sat in stony silence, wrinkles covering their kind faces and—no! Not pity. Please, not pity.

Melanie's green eyes blurred as the door to the baptistery room opened. Lyle Mullins strutted out, and she dodged him. No way was she letting him talk her into marrying that stupid son of his. It was over. Period.

Lyle ventured forward. "Babe."

Babe? Seriously. Ugh. Like father, like slimy son. She straightened, ripping her veil from her carefully coifed light brown hair and tossing it to his feet. "You tell that low-down bottom dweller I said he can take his thirteen and shove it where the sun—"

"Melanie!" Mama shrieked as she stormed her way to the front of the church, her glittery black dress hanging loose on her wispy frame.

A collective gasp filled the room.

"Melanie Dawn!" Mama's voice came out a rasp. "I never raised you to talk like that."

Melanie clutched her chest and drew her gaze across the room. "Sorry. Mama did teach me better. And for it to be in a church and all…" She bit her lip. "But Lyle, maybe you didn't teach Stephen any better. Anyway, tell him he can have his thirteen, and I'm leaving."

Lyle tugged at his bowtie. "Thirteen what, Melanie?"

"Stephen was always good with numbers." She took ten paces forward, to the end of the front pew in the right-side section. "He'll figure it out."

Three more paces put her next to the fire exit. Thirteen.

"Melly, wait!" Lizzie's shrill twang echoed over the whispers. "I didn't mean ta—"

"Pun'kin." Daddy inched closer.

"Leave. Me. Alone." Five more paces and a good shove of the side door took her to the parking lot. She kicked off her satin heels and fled barefoot across the scalding parking lot to Daddy's extended cab Ford. As the bottlenecked bridal party trickled out of the church, she fished a hunting rifle out from behind the backseat.

"Let's talk about it, Melanie." Lizzie's high-heeled shoes clacked across the asphalt.

Melanie wasn't talking about anything. No way. Not now. Far too late for that. She faced the three fuchsia-clad, up-do-sporting girls and lifted the rifle to her shoulders. "Y'all need to leave me alone."

Lizzie stepped forward, and Melanie pressed her eye against the sight. "I mean it, Lizzie. Not another inch closer. I love ya like a sis and all, but I need to be by myself right now."

While Anna Kate and Mari Beth stood frozen, Lizzie retreated, hands on her hips. "Melly, your poor mama spent thousands on this wedding. And the guests all think you're crazy."

"I don't care about guests. That snake-in-the-grass Stephen has been cattin' around with girls all over Milton, and you..." She swung the rifle and pointed at the gaping face of Anna Kate Roberts. "You!"

Anna Kate ducked her head, her stiff curled ponytail staying fixed in place. "I'm sorry, Melly."

She was sorry? She'd better be sorry. "You knew all along." Following another rifle swing, Melanie retreated further. "Everybody did. Why didn't any of y'all tell me before it came to this?"

"What are you doing, Melanie?" A groan followed the deep voice that so often soothed. But not today.

She spun, her brow furrowed so tight it loosened a couple tendrils from her intricately woven hairdo. She aimed the rifle at his breast pocket. "Stephen."

He'd been tugging at his wavy black hair the same way he always did when he got frustrated. It sat in a bunch atop his forehead, like a mini Mohawk. The veins in his neck throbbed in overdrive.

"C'mon. Let's go inside and talk about it."

"What's to talk about?" She cocked the hammer and straightened her elbow.

Stephen unclenched his fist, which he'd pressed at his sides. "You were misinformed. Now get in this church and let's get married."

"Misinformed? You have to be kidding me. Apologize." She jerked the rifle toward her bridesmaids. "They've all done ratted you out."

His three brothers emerged from the gazebo behind the church, toting booze, and wearing goofy smiles with their tuxes. They strutted toward her then stopped in their tracks.

"Put the gun down, Melanie." Stephen stretched out his palm.

"Any closer, and I'm going to shoot ya in that golf hand." Keeping the rifle fixed on his pocket handkerchief, she backed toward the six-foot fence separating her from the woods behind the church.

"I love how you go all country on me when you get mad." He winked, taking another pace forward.

Ugh. Did he have to always be right? The country twang she'd fought so hard to lose had crept right back in with her fury. "Well, Milton *is* in the country. If you don't like it, maybe you should leave Kentucky and go back to Texas. You and your slime ball dad." She sidestepped him. When she brushed against the gate, it shifted a few inches, allowing her to slip inside.

She kicked the gate shut with her foot, lowered the gun, and lifted the unlatched padlock free from the staple. While Stephen edged nearer, she secured the lock with trembling hands. "Y'all get away from me."

"Melanie Dawn." Mama peeked between the slats. "Come out of there right now and get back in the church."

Dodging Mama's narrowed baby blues, Melanie slid behind a thick-trunked tree. "No way I'm marrying that no-good, lyin', cheatin' fool." She took a breath. Time to calm herself and stop sounding like a hick. "This wedding is not happening. Didn't any of you people hear what Lizzie said? He spent last weekend at a cabin in Cincy with Tricia Billings. She even posted pictures of them on the web. On the web, Mama."

Mama's eyes moved to the next space between slats. "But the money, Melanie, and the food. All these people."

"I'll pay you back every dime." Melanie slung Daddy's rifle over her shoulder. "But that money on the altar? That's for Stephen. Thirteen dimes, Stephen? That ring a bell?"

"Melanie, please." Stephen's perfect, smooth fingers gripped the top of the fence. "You don't know the whole story."

More tears stung her already saturated eyes and she withdrew into the trees. "I know enough. What was it you told me? Truth ain't worth a dime? Well, it is to me. Thirteen, Stephen."

"She wants some space, y'all." Lizzie's shrill voice grated on Melanie's spine. "Let's give her a little time to calm down. Everybody head back into the church, and I'll talk to her."

"Crazy fool." Stephen slapped the fence. "I'm done with this. Y'all enjoy your party. I'm going to Jamaica."

The landscape distorted through tears as Melanie retreated farther into the woods. She hiked over roots and stones, making her way to a small brook. A trickle of blood covered her toe. She should have kept on her shoes.

He was the thirteenth guy she'd dated. Why couldn't it have worked out?

She dropped to a large boulder, the green moss tainting her pure white gown as she sat and propped her chin with her elbows.

Thirteen lies. Thirteen reasons she'd never trust anyone again. Thirteen promises never kept. More like thirteen-hundred. Thirteen million excuses, and thirteen months of wasted time. She'd been cursed by thirteen. It was supposed to be her lucky number. But not anymore.

As the water flowed between her toes, her breathing slowed to a normal pace, and the constant trickle of tears dried up. They'd come looking for her soon. Drag her back to the church and make her apologize to everyone. But she wasn't doing it. No way, no how. Stephen could make the apologies.

Rustling leaves followed a hiss to her right. A small black head poked out of a decaying log and slid its long, slippery body toward her.

Melanie grabbed the rifle and struck the snake. She jumped as it coiled around the barrel, two feet of its body twisting and hanging free, and bludgeoned the thing's head against a sharp rock. Then she hooked it with the end of her rifle and flicked it downstream to the opposite bank.

Across the brook, a monstrous pine loomed above the nearby trees. With its thick, low branches, it offered not only solace, but an easy climb to see into the church lot.

Melanie raised her dress and waded in a diagonal path across the water, sidestepping globs of mud that clung to sticks lodged in the riverbed. She climbed onto the bank and watched the slithering creature writhe, considering another bludgeon even though it was good and dead. If only she could eliminate Stephen that easily.

A shudder overcame her as she clutched the lacy neckline of her dress. Poor snake. It sure didn't deserve her fury. And even at his worst, neither did Stephen. She'd known what she was getting into when she met his sorry act. Everyone had warned her. Even Tricia Billings.

She squeezed between the pine needles to the center of the tree, planting her feet on the lowest spot and gripping the thinner, higher branches. If she stayed close to the trunk, they'd support her. Shoulders squared and teeth bared, she climbed, higher and higher until the church lot rose over the privacy fence.

A well-dressed line of guests formed at the reception table, surrounding the thirty white tables Mama had so carefully arranged on the lawn. Were they seriously going ahead with the party?

The irony of the white calla lilies struck Melanie—she'd chosen them to represent her purity. Though she wasn't religious, she prided herself in saving her sexuality for marriage. Stephen had mocked her. Of course, he had. How had she been so foolish to trust him?

Look at them all—Lizzie, Anna Kate, and Mari Beth laughing and having a good time with Stephen's brothers. Did they even care? Probably not.

A truck engine revved in the wide span of immaculate green behind her. Cows trailed each other across fenced-in fields and rows of corn covered two-thirds of the landscape. An old gray truck stirred up a trail of dust as it sped down the long gravel drive.

Melanie rested her head against the trunk of the tree, filling her lungs with the scent of pine needles. She sneezed, wincing as the rifle tumbled and caught a few branches below.

As she descended to its level, she came even with a rust-tarnished ladder surrounding a thick metal pole. She inched closer, propped one foot on the ladder, and reached for the gun.

Once its strap hung safely over her shoulder, Melanie leaned toward the ladder again and launched herself toward it. Sharp, rusted edges dug into her palms, but she gripped the rung tight. About fifteen feet higher from the pole, a three-foot steel deck jutted out from the base of a long billboard. Perfect.

She climbed higher, dizzy from adrenaline, and pulled herself onto the deck. Behind her, a family of four smiled from a vinyl billboard advertisement. *Milton Church of Christ. Come join our family. Make God's house your home.*

Home... Where was home, since she and Stephen were no longer making one together? No way could she go back to living with Mama, and that big empty house Stephen rented could rot for all she cared.

Her cell shook itself loose from the band securing it around her leg and rattled on the deck. She grabbed it seconds before it tumbled to the mossy rocks below. Daddy. He'd have to wait.

The phone buzzed again. Groaning, she fished her way through lace and sequins to the Bermuda shorts she'd worn under her gown. She slid the cell into her pocket and blinked away tears.

Another buzz, and she banged the back of her head against the vinyl sign. She'd have to talk to him sometime. Gritting her teeth, she dug through the satin once more and tapped the icon to answer the call.

"Hey, pun'kin." Daddy cleared his throat twice, a sure sign he was raging. Was he mad at Stephen, or her? "Where are you? Come on back to the church and we can talk about this."

"I need to be alone right now, Daddy. I can't face all those people after hearing about Stephen and that...they'll be gossipin' all over Milton."

Melanie gripped the rail. Triple towers several miles away released pristine white smoke plumes that broke up the clear blue skyline. Treetops staggered with the hills and valleys in the distance, and a handful of cars trickled down the bypass past People's Choice Bank where she'd worked until last Thursday—the very spot where Stephen had proposed six weeks ago, at her insistence.

"Melanie Dawn? You dragged me into this church. Now come on down here and get married, or at least tell everyone you're not gonna."

"Daddy, I need some time." She ended the call, eased the strap free from her shoulder, and squinted through the rifle sight. Two clear shots to the ropes securing the east side of the food tent, where all

12

her supposed friends sat in a circle, probably laughing like her heart had never been seared.

Shame she'd left the ammunition in Daddy's truck.

Kyle Casey gave another futile tug then dropped his arms to his side, scowling when the aggravating cow gave a snide moo in response. "Stupid animal. How am I supposed to feed you if you won't come with me?"

He moved to the rear, throwing his six feet and 210 pounds of muscle into shoving Bessie from behind, then jumped back when she rewarded him with a squishy wet pile of... ugh. "Disgusting." Good thing he put on his grandpa's old muck boots.

With a grimace, he grasped the rope he'd wrapped around the beast's neck and tugged again, then grinned when she took a small step. He lunged, trying to drag her toward the wide boards he'd propped against the bed of Pa's old truck. Sneezes seized him, and he braced himself against Bessie, sending her backwards a foot. In all his twenty-eight years, he'd never met such a stubborn creature.

"Now Bessie, come on, girl." He pushed his brown bangs back with a sweaty palm and rubbed his goatee. Then he jerked back, grimacing at Eau de Bovine he just spread all over his face. Sweat and dirt covered his red T-shirt. And stink. He aimed his brown eyes underneath the cow's body. She was a girl, wasn't she?

A truck door slammed, and he jumped. Hadn't even heard anyone pull up.

"Son, what are ya doin'?"

The deep country voice sent chills down his spine. He faced a tall, rugged man with a salt-and-pepper mustache matching his slicked-back hair. The man sidestepped the cow pile and gave Bessie a couple good pats.

"Did you come over the fence?" Squinting, Kyle dropped the rope.

The man brushed dust off his navy suit and unpinned his lily boutonniere. "Nope. Drove up. Wayne Lee Turner."

"Kyle Casey." He hastily wiped his palm on his jeans and shook the man's extended hand. Past the stranger, bluegrass from Pa's hayfields danced along the horizon. The long, gravel road stretched between them. How had he not seen the bright red extended cab barreling toward him? Or heard it?

"What are you doing to the poor cow, son?" Wayne stuffed the boutonniere in his suit pocket and folded his arms across his broad chest.

"I'm trying to feed the stupid thing." Kyle inwardly groaned. If the aggravating cow wasn't enough, he now had this sleek man assessing him. "But these stubborn animals refuse to come back to the barn."

"Cows aren't stupid." Wayne stroked Bessie behind her ear. "But people sometimes are. Did you honestly think these boards would support their weight?"

Bessie kicked a hoof toward the nearest board and made a snort-like sound. Guess she agreed.

Kyle shoved the plywood into the truck bed and slammed the tailgate. Could the day get any worse? He held his temper in check and addressed the suited stranger. "I don't know. I put the hay out, but how exactly am I supposed to get the cows to walk to it? Pa—well, that's my grandpa's—instructions said to set it out, but how do I get them to eat it?"

"So you're Pa Casey's grandson." Wayne let out a roaring laugh. "Kylie, right?"

"Not Kylie. Kyle." He held his breath. Would Wayne recognize him? Judge him? "Pa took off on his honeymoon, and tricked me into taking care of his farm. Pretty slick for an old guy. I'm no farmhand, I—"

"So you're no farm boy, huh?" Choking on his guffaws, Wayne waved toward Pa's truck. "Get in and we'll drive back through that field to the barn."

"But I don't—"

"Trust me. Now get back in that truck and head toward the barn. Take it real slow."

Kyle shrugged and headed to the driver's-side door. He popped the locks and climbed in, and when he turned the key, Bessie tossed him another snide glance. "That stupid cow hates me."

He wiped dust from the dashboard as Wayne climbed into the passenger seat, curling up the right side of his mouth. "I told you. Cows aren't stupid. In fact, she's a pretty smart cow to not climb up that contraption."

"Well, that *smart* cow hates me. And I'm not that fond of her, either."

"You must be Denny's boy. The oldest."

Kyle met Wayne's piercing blue eyes then pressed his foot against the pedal. "The *only*. Mikey died in a car accident five years ago, Caden is an overseas missionary, and Drew... well, let's say he's not in the family anymore."

"Sorry to hear that. I used to work with Denny several years ago. On this very farm, when we were teenagers." Wayne crossed his dirt-covered lace-up Docker loafers and leaned his head back against the seat. "What's he up to these days?"

"He and Mom run this Bible college in the Michigan boondocks. They've poured everything they own into the place." Kyle crept the truck across the weed-covered field, but it bumped and shook them like one of those old wooden roller coasters.

"Check your mirror, son."

Sure enough, Bessie followed right behind the truck. A few feet away, a white spotted cow and a smooth-coated black one raised their chins and joined in the march.

15

Kyle shook his head. It worked. "Thanks, man. I feel like the pied piper. But why are they following the truck?"

"Your Pa trained them well. They know you're headed toward the food." Wayne coughed into his elbow then lifted his gaze with a sly grin. "So I helped you. Now, maybe you can help me."

"I can try." Kyle winced as the truck jostled over a deep puddle. "What do you need?"

"My daughter. Have you seen her?" Wayne held out a picture of a leggy brunette dressed in camo, holding some kind of dead bird. "My Melanie came through your gate about an hour ago, and I'm sure she's still out on your farm somewhere. She has my gun."

"I don't understand. Why is she on the farm with a gun? Did she come to hunt?" Kyle wiped sweat from his chin with the collar of his T-shirt. Maybe she'd kill the stupid cows.

"Nah. Although she might shoot her fiancé if she finds him." Wayne clenched his jaw. "Melanie was supposed to be getting married right now at the church next door to your property. She was all dressed up and ready, and then one of the bridesmaids marched in and told her the lowlife had been cheating. Saved the day if you ask me."

Wayne's words packed a punch in the gut—a well-deserved punch. Kyle grimaced, as if the hollow-faced redhead he'd walked out on three weeks earlier had delivered the blow. "So you think your daughter is in that wooded area way over there?" He stopped the truck and drew his hand across the horizon. "Like up by the front fence?"

"I do." Deep creases spanned Wayne's brow. "Can you help me find her?"

Great. Another perfect opportunity to show off his ineptitude. "I suppose I could try. But I'm not very good at this farm stuff. I don't know much about Pa's property. And I still have to drive around that field to get to the barn. Don't know if the cows will keep following me."

"They will." Wayne gestured behind them to about fifty cows plodding behind the truck.

"Guess you're right."

"How long you been back in Milton?" Wayne stroked his mustache with a callused hand.

"Two days. Like I said, I have nothing to do with farms or any of this. But Pa said if I helped him out, he'd—" he shrugged.

"No problem. I can give you some pointers." Wayne leaned out the window. "Now, you see that gate over there. Look at the cow path leading into it. I guarantee if you open that gate, they'll all march right in to get to the hay."

"Why couldn't Pa have told me that?" Kyle started to open the door, but Wayne grabbed his arm.

"Don't get out, drive right up to the gate. You don't want the cows to block it."

Kyle drove up and hopped out to open the gate. He stared a few seconds. How was he supposed to open it?

Bessie and the others picked up their pace, half running toward him. He dashed away from them, back to the driver's side door, dodging Wayne's twinkling eyes.

"Uh ..." He shook his head. He was such an idiot. "How do I open it?"

Wayne laughed heartily. "So why'd your Pa pick you for this job anyway? Seemed he might have had better options."

Was this guy mocking him? Kyle frowned. "I got this letter in the mail saying to come home for Pa's funeral. But when I got to the church—last minute, of course—there stood Pa in the flesh, grinning like a toddler on Halloween. I guess he knew I wouldn't have come back for a wedding." The thistle recoiled, one of the thorns snagging his hand. He jerked it away. "Pa told me I'd have to take care of things while he was on his honeymoon. I was the only one available. And then he said he'd be gone two months."

Wayne got out and shuffled through the mooing cows over to the gate while Kyle trailed behind him. "Two months? So what about your job? Will you be moving back or driving back and forth?"

Kyle scrunched his brow. Maybe he hadn't been recognized, after all. "Don't have a job to quit. The company I worked for… um… let me go. I wasn't planning to come back here, though. But Pa told me he planned to give me my inheritance while he was still alive. He said if I wanted it, I had to work on the farm, and I had to take it now. Otherwise, he'd write me totally out of the will."

Wayne snorted. "That sounds like your Pa."

"Yeah. So here I am. He said he'd let me watch the farm while he traveled and then we'd do the paperwork later. When I got here, all I found was a note on the table with a few sparse instructions. I seriously have no idea what to do." All these bellowing cows pushing around the truck made him claustrophobic. Would they trample him to get through the gate?

"I see." Wayne examined the gate. He freed the chain from the nail holding it, and pushed the rusting metal open wide enough for the truck to pass through.

"Are you kidding me?" Kyle shook his head. "How did I not notice that?"

"You didn't know what to look for."

Once the cows plodded through the gate, Wayne tugged it closed, secured it with the nail, and half-skipped back to the truck.

Kyle slid into the driver's seat and accelerated, the wheels dropping into the deep grooves left by years of Pa's plodding through the muddy soil to the back of the farm. A ride like the ones they'd taken together so many years ago.

The cows forged their path behind him, trickling one by one into the field where Kyle had set out the bales of hay. Once he made it to the barn, he raked filthy hands through his hair. "I don't know if I can do this for two months."

"You did fine, son." Wayne grinned. "Now you can help me corral my daughter."

"Give me a second. Let me run by the house and wash some of this muck off."

"Alrighty."

Ten minutes later, Kyle met Wayne on the porch of Pa's dusty white farmhouse.

"Melanie came through the gate on the northeast corner." Wayne nodded to a line of towering pines separating the front edge of the farm from the church property next door. "I think there's a brook there, and an old trail that leads to a small cave."

"Yeah." Kyle snickered as they got back in the truck. "I used to get in trouble for hiding in that cave when I was a little boy. Think maybe she's there?"

"I doubt it. She's more of a tree kind of girl." Wayne pulled out his phone. "I tried to call her, and she hung up on me. She probably thinks I'm mad at her, poor thing." He locked the screen and tucked it back into his suit pocket. "I should have beaten that loser when I had the chance."

Swallowing the memories back hard, Kyle drove through the cornfields to the edge of the woodsy area where his family had camped when he was a child. Wayne sounded like Lacey's dad, the girl whose heart he'd just shattered. He'd better help find Melanie and get him off the farm. "This shouldn't be too difficult if she's up in a tree. A woman in the middle of the woods in a wedding dress ought to stand out."

Wayne chuckled. "You don't know my Melanie."

Chapter Two

Any other time, Melanie might have laughed at the city boy following Daddy through the woods. Tall, tan, and muscular, but clearly not a hiker.

She peered between cracks in the steel deck as they retraced her path from the church. Daddy marched along with his sure, confident gait. City Boy took cautious steps with his head down and jumped every time a branch snapped back at him.

Sweat rolled down her neck and behind her ears, and she brushed it aside with the back of her hands. Oh, to be closer to hear what they were saying.

They disappeared beneath the canopy of trees that shaded the brook. Every so often, City Boy's red T-shirt appeared between the branches.

Melanie gathered her dress. She hiked the skirt over her Bermuda shorts and bunched it at her waist. Hunting was the only thing Wayne Lee Turner could do better than strumming a banjo. With the bulky wedding gown, he'd surely spot her within minutes, although City Boy might slow him. Either way, she wasn't making it easy.

The horn from a train blared, and the billboard deck shook as the cars raced behind the church and followed the fence line around the property. Maybe she could fly down and land on the roof of one of the trains like she'd imagined as a little girl. Ride along to nowhere, or anywhere. Anywhere but here.

How could she face all those people? Daddy's bluegrass buddies, the bigwigs at the bank who'd never give her job back since she'd quit on short notice, all her friends and their parents, and Stephen's rotten, boozing family. They'd snuck so much alcohol in the church it was more like a dive bar than a place where people... where people did what?

She wrinkled her nose, facing the billboard. *Join us*, the caption said, *weekly. Nine and ten on Sunday mornings, six o'clock on Sunday nights, and seven o'clock on Wednesday nights.* Why would anyone want to go to a church four times a week? What could they possibly find to do there?

A woman's bright eyes stared back at her with a glossy smile. A genuine smile. The woman clutched her two children, and her husband rested his hand on her shoulder.

Come meet our family. A picture of perfection—but was it?

Certainly not the picture she'd have taken if she'd gone through with marrying Stephen. They would have probably divorced before children entered the equation.

Stupid Stephen. New tears stung her cheeks. This was all his fault. Daddy hadn't done anything wrong. It was wrong to make him so worried for her.

And Mama. Down in the parking lot, playing perfect hostess. Her hand on a suited shoulder, guiding a man toward the food tent.

A few feet from Mama, Lizzie backed her boyfriend against the chocolate fountain table, her finger waving in his freckled face. Anna Kate stood at the corner of the church building with one of Stephen's lousy brothers, making sweet talk, no doubt. Her turn would be next. And Mari Beth sashayed around in her bridesmaid dress like a peacock.

Melanie flared her nostrils. Not a single one of them gave her any mind at all.

Heat from the mid-afternoon sun pounded down on her face. She should have changed out of her gown. Or at least brought her bag, where she had sunscreen... meant for the beach. Sweat poured down her forehead, mixing with her five layers of makeup. As rouge-streaked tears dripped on the white satin dress, she found Daddy through the cracks.

His broad shoulders slumped. He knelt at the spot where she'd cut her toe, and wiped his fingers over the blood.

She shot him a text. *Don't worry. I'm fine. Give me some time to sort my thoughts.*

"Where are you, Melanie?" His shout echoed through the trees.

She'd given herself away. Daddy knew she was close enough to see him. He spoke to City Boy, and they both laughed. Using her phone camera, she zoomed in on their faces.

Who was this guy? He looked more like an Abercrombie model than a farmer, with wispy brown bangs pointing in all directions. And a scruffy goatee. Who kept a goatee with long bangs? Huge muscles loomed underneath his red tee. Broad shoulders matching Daddy's shook with laughter.

Her cheeks warmed. No way was she coming down now. They could climb up and get her if they wanted.

"Melanie, come on."

She shifted her weight, accidentally brushing off a branch that had fallen onto the deck. It tumbled straight toward City Boy, who jumped about a foot when it settled at his feet. Daddy guffawed from his chest.

She shrunk back against the billboard and scowled. How could he laugh at a moment like this?

"Pun'kin, I need my gun back. C'mon, girl. It's my good huntin' rifle."

She should climb down and let Daddy drive her back to the church. Maybe apologize to all those people and confront Stephen. Instead, she clung to the rusty steel as though it generated her lifeblood. Like Anna Kate's mama always said, *should don't mean do.*

She drew in a deep breath, filling her lungs with the savory, buttery scents she'd been smelling all day. Was this divine punishment—for the smell to have drifted all the way to the billboard? Her stomach rumbled. Earlier, she'd been too nervous to eat. Now, she'd give anything for a plate of the salmon or steak. She should have at least scrounged the dessert table on her way out. The chocolate-covered strawberries and grapes would have eased her aching heart, at least a little.

Daddy peered up at the trees. He'd find her any minute. But she wasn't coming down. Not in front of some city boy who thought she was a joke, and not until someone got ahold of stinking Stephen and made him come up to apologize.

Kyle broke off a long branch blocking his path and tossed it aside. In front of him, the tall pines parted into an overgrown clearing, and the crystal-clear creek meandered around it, gently rolling over multi-colored stones. A circle of picnic tables surrounded a charred fire pit with enough room to seat about forty people. Now, why would Pa have a place like this on the property? It hadn't been here years ago.

Wayne crossed the clearing in three long strides. "Like I said, my Melanie loves to climb trees. That would be my best guess." He shielded his eyes with his callused hand.

"What is she, ten?"

"She's a huntress, and an excellent marksman. She gets up in those high tops and spots her prey from way back. Girl aced every one of her qualified shooting courses. Can't miss a target, my Melanie." He reached down for a long weed, twisted it, and tucked it in his mouth. As he chewed, a wicked grin spanned his face. "That girl can take a deer out in mere seconds, from almost any angle. She's got a spot, about 2.75 inches above the tear ducts, right in the center of its brain. A clean shot, very little splatter, and very little blood."

Kyle fought to suppress the involuntary spasm of his face. This, right here, the reason he supported gun control. A crazy, angry woman sitting in the top of a tree—in a wedding dress, to boot—with sharpshooter talent. In fact... he took a shaky step back toward the truck. Maybe they needed to get out of the woods good and fast.

"She don't shoot people, son." Wayne slapped a heavy hand on Kyle's shoulder. "Only animals we plan on eating. Maybe next time you can come along. Ever had squirrel?"

No. He'd never had squirrel, and he didn't intend to. "I'm not much of a hunter." Heat covered his cheeks. Pa had tried hard to teach him as a youth. Pa'd wanted to teach him a lot of things. Life lessons, he'd called them. Kyle winced. Maybe if he'd listened, Pa wouldn't have left him in this predicament. Well, he wouldn't have gotten himself into it, anyway.

He searched the canopy of trees at the edge of the clearing, his gaze coming to rest on the old billboard sign advertising the church next door. White satin billowed over the metal deck. "I think I found your girl."

"Yep. There's Melanie." Wayne pointed to the ladder. "Why don't you climb up and talk 'er down?"

"Me?" Kyle jerked back, then picked off a pinecone from a nearby tree and tossed it over a high pine. "She's your daughter. She'd probably do better if you talked to her."

Wayne whistled. "That's a forty-foot tree you cleared." Then he lifted his pant leg. Two long purple scars crisscrossed over his knee. "Can't. Cow kicked me last spring. Had to have the thing replaced a couple months ago."

Kyle's eyes widened. So Bessie wasn't just stupid—she could maim a man. Maybe he'd lock those cows in the barn and never let them out.

Wayne lifted an eyebrow.

Kyle crossed his arms. "So you want me to climb a tree, talk to a girl I've never met, and convince her to... wait. She has a *gun*. You want me to convince her to not shoot me and come down. Right."

"Told you, she doesn't shoot people." As he stroked his mustache, Wayne's lips turned slightly upward. "Thought I was helpin' you out with some cattle."

Kyle grimaced then tossed his hands in the air. "Fine."

Wayne at his heels, Kyle crossed the field, lumbered over to the poles supporting the billboard and reached up, his hands landing several feet shy of the lowest rung. "Can I even get up there? How did she do it?"

Wayne grinned. "I bet she shimmied up that tree and jumped over. C'mon. It's not that high. Not even two full stories. You're a strong guy."

Ten minutes later, Kyle eased across a branch, caught a rung of the ladder, and scrambled up. He stopped when he met the barrel of a hunting rifle.

"What are you doing?" The sweet, chirpy voice sounded almost sardonic, the kind that might sing like a siren before sending him to his death. A sweet, fruity aroma hung in the air between them.

Kyle took a step lower. Between the cracks in the deck, he peered into her intense green eyes. "Your dad sent me to talk to you."

"Not talking, not coming down." She tucked a loose tendril of her brown hair behind her ear.

"Melanie!" Wayne waved from the ground below.

"I'm sure you mean well." She slipped the gun strap off her shoulder and passed it over the deck to him. "Take Daddy his gun, and tell him I'll come down after Stephen climbs up here and explains why he felt compelled to cheat on me. And not a second before."

"You want me to climb down and carry that thing at the same time?" Kyle narrowed his eyes at the gun. "I'll shoot myself."

"Oh, good grief. It's not even loaded." She launched the rifle toward the tree. It caught on a low branch and Daddy scrambled to it.

"Listen." Kyle advanced a few rungs and poked his head through the hole where he could climb onto the deck. "Your dad is worried. You can't stay up here all day."

"Then you need to go find Stephen."

"Stephen, your fiancé? The guy who cheated?" Kyle snorted. "I'm sure he's bolted by now."

"Oh, he's still there. See that creep with the gangster hat standing in the middle of all those guys?" Melanie pointed to the parking lot, where hundreds of people streamed toward cars. In the center, a group of twenty-something guys in tuxes scrubbed at the white letters scrawled across the windows of Stephen's truck. Only the "i" had completely faded, leaving an eerie *Just marred*.

"I'm sorry you're hurting. And I'm glad to help you find Stephen or anything else you might want. But let's get you down first."

"Not coming."

"Fine." He climbed up beside her and sat against the billboard, propping his crossed legs on the railing. "I'm Kyle, by the way."

"Melanie." She flicked a piece of tiny gravel across the steel deck at him. "But I'm not climbing down."

"Your dad wants you to." Kyle touched his thumb to his middle fingernail, placed it next to the gravel, and flicked back. "He says there are a bunch of people who care about you that are worried."

"Ouch!" She rubbed her arm where the gravel struck.

"Oh, sorry!" Kyle reached over quickly, but she slapped him away.

"Yeah. That's why they're all sitting around eating our food and having a good time. I mean, look at them. It's like it never even happened."

"What did happen, exactly?"

"Long story."

Kyle shrugged. "I've got time."

"I always kind of knew Stephen was a slime ball, but I'd hoped he changed for me, you know. I tried so hard."

Another pang sliced his chest. Lacey had said the same thing, and he'd crushed her heart without giving it a second thought. "Look. You stay up here a few more minutes and then come on down. I'm going to go tell your daddy you're fine, and you need a little more time."

"He don't listen. I mean, he doesn't. I already told him that, and he refuses to listen."

Wayne's shout interrupted them. "Aren't you hungry, pun'kin?"

Kyle snickered as her lips quivered. She was good as down. "Yeah, pun'kin. Aren't you hungry?"

"It's Melanie." She blushed as her stomach growled loud enough to break the sound barrier. "And yes, I'm hungry. But I'm still not leaving this spot. You can tell Daddy to go find stinking Stephen and make him get up here and apologize. I'm not coming down until that happens. Not even if I starve."

"Suit yourself." Kyle shimmied down the ladder till it ended and the soles of his boots hovered about three feet from the ground.

"Jump, son." Wayne stepped closer to the sign pole. "Now, what about my Melanie?"

"She's fine." Kyle let go, landing smoothly on the moss-covered ground. "But she's not coming down."

Chapter Three

Beads of makeup-stained sweat dripped to the steel deck, making a flesh-colored puddle by Melanie's head. She sat up and shifted her aching shoulders. As she traced her hand over her face, her fingers found the imprint left from the pattern of the metal beams. She must look a sight.

Lying down had been a mistake, even though it let her view the ongoing reception without anyone knowing she was watching. Maybe they were celebrating that the wedding *didn't* happen. Doubtful. They probably only stayed for the shrimp cocktail and bacon-wrapped weenies.

With the parking lot thinned and the food mostly gone, the caterers dragged carts from their van to the tent and loaded them up. Tables disappeared inside the church and Mama stood by the side door barking orders at the cleanup crew. Stephen huddled with his groomsmen in their boyish camaraderie like nothing had gone wrong.

Melanie stood and fished under her dress for her shorts pocket, retrieving her phone. With her photo app, she zoomed in on Stephen's face. Sharp nose, chiseled chin, high cheekbones. Feathered bangs and long skinny sideburns made him look more like the lead singer of a boy band. How had she not pegged him a player? And that smirk… not even a hint of remorse.

Kyle's smug face came to mind. At least Stephen didn't have a stupid goatee.

She leaned forward.

Stephen cocked his head and whipped his cell out of his suit pocket. After a quick glance toward the screen, he scowled and tapped it with his middle finger. "What?"

Melanie lip-read the words she could as his snarl deepened. Where was she? Right up here watching, her heart in a sinkhole.

He tilted his face toward the patch of trees next to her, and she lowered her phone, balancing it against the deck rail so she could stay zoomed on his face.

His nose twitched, causing his eyes to lift closer to his brow line, which dipped between them at an almost sinister angle. Pure meanness. How had she never seen this side of him before? Was it even possible that he was the same guy she'd loved for the past thirteen months?

The guy next to Stephen spoke. He pointed. He laughed. What was his name? Marcus or something. A guy she'd never more than tolerated, but who Stephen seemed to think could do no wrong. After a brief exchange, Stephen glanced toward the billboard and shielded his eyes from the sun.

Melanie's heart caught as he nodded toward her and his friends all exploded into guffaws.

Well, let them laugh, especially him. It made him look like even more of a jerk. Folding her arms, she plopped back down on the deck, wincing as the steel creaked beneath her. Was she even safe up here?

Didn't matter. She wasn't moving.

Bluegrass music blasted from her phone, a notification covering the camera screen. Stephen stalked away from his friends and held his phone to his ear, pacing the lot beside his truck.

As his name faded from her screen, fresh tears welled in her eyes. It appeared once more, and she tapped to decline the call.

It rang again. She declined.

And a fourth time. She declined. When would he get the picture?

Then, a ping. Two words. *Answer me.*

Clicking off the text, she found his face with the photo app again, her breath catching. Who was this beastly, hateful man, and what had he done with her love?

Last night at the rehearsal, he'd leaned over her as everyone snapped their pictures, resting his hand on one of the brick columns in front of the church. Love shone through his eyes like...

"Like he had gas." A bitter chuckle escaped her lips as Grandma's words came back to her. She'd called his look a pained expression and told him to smile. Had Grandma known, too?

Another ping. *Babe, I'm sorry. Come down and we'll talk about it. Fix this. We can still get married if you want to.*

Babe. She gripped the phone case tighter. Like that no-good father of his. And no, she didn't want to still get married, thank you very much. Was he out of his mind?

She huffed, dragging the hem of her dress through the makeup-stained puddle as she scooted to the other side of the deck. Daddy must have called Stephen. But where had he gone?

There, at the end of a far, grassy field, beside one of the blackest barns she'd ever seen, Daddy had parked his truck. He clung to the frame of the cabin of a tractor that pulled a sickle bar mower, his left foot dangling off in space out the open door. Crooked mowing lines trailed behind it.

She squinted. Was that Kyle driving?

Despite her angst, a giggle bubbled in her chest. That boy had no business on a farm.

She turned back to Stephen and tapped the messaging app on her screen. *Come up here and apologize, and I'll think about it.*

Holding her finger above the send icon, she narrowed her gaze at him. He'd already turned back around, engaged in lively discussion with his groomsmen. He didn't deserve her response.

As she deleted the text, she let out a low groan. Why had she given Daddy his gun back?

Kyle kicked off his boots and sweaty socks and padded across the slick hardwood floors to the kitchen. He opened the fridge, welcoming the blast of cool air. He'd half-forgotten the sticky humidity of a Kentucky summer. The sprinkle of rain they'd had the night before had added to the sauna effect.

Wayne marched in behind him, his dirt-covered loafers leaving a trail of dust. His grandma would have chased him back to the door, had she been alive. Sometimes it didn't feel right being in the old farmhouse without her and Pa.

"Want a drink?"

"Sure." Wayne cleared his throat. "Son, I've done a lot for you today. We'll have our drink, but then you need to keep up your end of the bargain. Go talk that girl of mine into coming down." He scooted the oak chair away from the table and sunk into it. "And I'll come back in a day or two and help you rake and bale the hay. Teach you how to do it all yourself."

Kyle grabbed the filtering pitcher and poured two glasses of ice-cold water. Every muscle in his body burned from using them in ways they hadn't been used in years. "I appreciate all your help. Can't believe Pa left me to handle all of this." He handed Wayne one of the glasses then gulped his down while standing.

"Mind if I grab a quick shower? I smell like cow. She'll be shoving me off that billboard with this stink. Won't take long."

"Go right ahead, son." Wayne grinned and leaned back in his chair.

Kyle reappeared a short time later in a button-down shirt, clean jeans, and neatly-combed hair. He'd even put cologne on. He grabbed another glass of water and sat opposite Wayne at the table.

"Well, well. You sure clean up good."

Kyle squirmed. He wasn't trying to get a date or anything—just get the girl off the billboard. Those days were behind him.

Wayne took several long sips. "Your pa is a great man. I bet you miss him."

"Pa was a great grandfather when I was little. The best. Always taking me out on the tractor and showing me cool things. But after I lost interest…" He tapped his fingers on the table. "Well, I guess we ran out of things to talk about. And then, I got busy with sports and school. So we haven't really talked in a while."

Wayne nodded. "I remember seeing you boys on that tractor before you could even walk." He peered through his glass toward the fridge, still covered in family photos from when Grandma was alive. "I wouldn't mind running into your pa again, or your daddy, for that matter."

Kyle slugged half his water and set the glass down hard. "Good luck with that."

"What do you mean?"

"Dad hasn't been home in ages. We don't even have a place here anymore."

"That's a shame." Wayne loosened his collar button and tugged his shirt away from his neck. "I've got so many good memories from when we were young. Did your Pa tell you the story about your dad, your uncle James, and the cats?"

Kyle refilled his glass and the ice clinked against the side. "Nope. Pa tells a lot of stories, but I've never heard that one. Or at least, I don't remember it if he did."

Wayne folded his hands on the table and leaned forward. "Well, it's a good one. Seems your uncle wanted a pet cat about eight years old, and your dad, as the ever-loving big brother, decided he was going to help him."

"Sounds like Dad. Always the benevolent one."

Wayne snickered. "Turns out an old cat lady down the road passed away and her daughter shooed every one of those cats onto your Pa's farm. You know, that two-story brick house back behind the church. It backs up to the very corner edge of the property."

"Yeah." Kyle unscrewed the cap from the salt shaker and used a napkin to dig the crystals out of its threads. He tapped the lid against the table and salt spilled into a pile. "Let me guess. Dad caught one of them and hid it."

"Oh, no." Wayne flicked away a few stray crystals that had landed next to him. "Better than that. He got in your Pa's freezer—now, Pa had a beef processed a few hours earlier, so it wasn't even frozen yet—and your dad packed a whole bag of beef to lure the cats out of hiding. I'm talking T-bone and sirloin steaks, chuck roast, hamburger meat, you name it. He grabbed a butcher knife, took it to the barn, and chopped the fresh-cut steaks into dozens of little pieces. It's a wonder he didn't cut off a finger."

Kyle brushed the salt into a pile. "How much meat?"

"Probably about twenty steaks' worth. Enough to charm every one of those cats back to the barn."

"No way." After catching the salt in a napkin, Kyle stretched and dropped it into the trash can behind him. "Did he spread the steak out over the field?"

"He left a trail from the field straight into the barn, where the door was open only a crack. Just enough for cats to get through."

"Did he get all of them?" Kyle chuckled.

"Every last one, best we could figure. They walked right past the meat and hid in the barn. Denny was watching to make sure no dogs came around. As soon as he went to close the door, those cats came out and meowed at him for more steak." Wayne's shoulders shook. "Anyway, after the meat delivery, your Pa had taken off to Tennessee with your grandma, and he left her sister, Gertie, in charge. By the time he got back, those cats had settled in good. Gertie and the boys had bought them all kinds of special cat food and had them eating out of her hands."

"I guess Uncle James was thrilled."

"You know he was." Grinning, Wayne twisted his wedding ring. "So he got his wish. But, I still haven't told you the best part."

"There's more?"

"Oh, yeah." Wayne slapped the table. "When your Pa got back home, he found all three of us, me, your dad, and James. We sat in a circle, petting one of those cats and letting it eat out of our hands." His grin spanned his whole face. "A real pretty cat, with a long white stripe running from head to tail."

"A skunk?"

Wayne snorted. "Let's say the barn smelled real good for a long time."

"I'll bet." Kyle's stomach rumbled. A steak sounded great about now.

"About Gertie, did you know that every calving season, Pa named a cow after her? Infuriated the poor woman."

"I do remember that." Kyle shook his head. "One time when I was little, she chased Pa around the front barn with a broom while Grandma stood by the silo doubled over laughing. Seems like that's what she was chasing him over. Something about him saying she was a cow."

Wayne took a long drink and wiped his face with his sleeve. "You keep calling that old cow Bessie, but I'd bet you anything she answers to Gertie. Maybe next time you could call her with that."

"Gertie. I'll have to try that. Speaking of steaks, I wonder…" Kyle rose from the table and opened the door to the screened-in side porch where the freezer stood. He started to open it, but found the plug snaked at the base of it. Shaking his head, he stepped back into the kitchen. Pa sure wasn't making any of this easy on him. "Never mind that thought. I'll have to go buy some steaks, I guess."

"Listen, son. I've got a couple friends whose sons are hard up for cash. You could hire them out and get that hay taken care of—"

"No." Kyle slid Pa's instructions out from under the refrigerator magnet and handed it to Wayne. "I'm sure he doesn't want me to hire anyone. He wants me to do it all myself. Said it would be a good learning experience for me." He rolled his eyes. "I can't forfeit my inheritance. What kind of grandson would I be?"

"Well, I reckon I'd better get back over to the church." Wayne patted his pocket. "Wife's been texting me all afternoon. But if there's anything else I can show you, let me know. You can't figure out everything by yourself. Not being a city boy and all. You'll get yourself killed."

City boy. Well, Kyle supposed it was true enough. "There is one small thing." He led Wayne to the side barn, where the dogs made hoarse yelps from their pens. "I need to figure out how to work that water pump system he's rigged up. Poor animals are probably in danger of dehydration."

Wayne bent down, tracing his fingers over the well pump. He jerked the handle up, and water poured at his feet. "This one?"

Kyle slapped his right hand over his mouth. "Tell me you didn't do that." He filled two buckets and carried them over to the dog pen. When he reached to twist the board holding the pen door shut, Wayne grabbed his hand.

"If your Pa still does it the same way, there's a trough in there and you pour the water into it. Go around to the other side."

"Shouldn't I let them out? It's awful to leave dogs cooped up like this all the time."

"Well, normally, yes. But not these girls. They're in heat." Wayne pointed to a white-eared beagle, who lay curled at the back of the pen. "You let those little ladies out and every male dog in the neighborhood will be hunting them down. Didn't your Pa leave instructions about that?"

"Maybe. So what about the males?" Kyle reached through the wire and rubbed the head of a brown-spotted one.

"I don't know, Kyle. Doesn't look like he's had a male for a while. He kept them on the other side, of course. Used to breed them. I'm sure you remember all the pups growing up." A wide grin spanned his face. "Speaking of pups, did your dad ever tell you the story about the time they painted all the pups green for the St. Patrick's Day parade?"

"No, haven't heard that one."

Twenty minutes and five memory-lane stories later, Wayne's truck disappeared down the driveway, stirring up a mess of gravel behind it. Kyle's promise hung in the air. If he wanted Wayne's help, he needed to convince Princess Melanie to get off that billboard.

His stomach rumbled for the hundredth time, and a sardonic grin spanned his cheeks. *Pun'kin* was hungry. Maybe she'd like a burger and some fries. What was it good ol' Dad had always said? Best way to change a stubborn woman's mind was to give her exactly what she wanted.

Wayne's bridezilla would be hopping down that sign pole by dark.

Chapter Four

Thwack!

Melanie jolted upright, dodging the thick twine knot microseconds before it looped around the deck railing. She peered over the edge, her dress billowing like a sponge, and spotted a tousled head of brown hair surrounded by a huge pile of bags, a pillow, and several pieces of PVC pipe. Kyle? And if so, what on earth was he doing?

She stretched and yawned, jerking her hand back as it struck a hot spotlight hanging from the side of the billboard. Getting dark already? How long had she been asleep?

The sun had dipped lower in the sky, its glow diminishing the bright blue to soft purple and orange streaks. What time was it, anyway? Maybe sometime around eight? She grappled for her phone.

No luck. Her hollowed eyes reflected at her in the shiny black screen. Battery must have died a couple hours ago. So much for texting back and forth with Stephen up to the wedding. What a waste.

Shaking her head, she leaned over the edge again, finding Kyle reaching for a high branch on a nearby tree. "Are you out of your mind? You're going to break your neck."

Kyle grinned up at her. "Send me the end of the rope."

"Weirdo." Why would he throw it up there to have her throw it back? She unlooped it and tossed the knot at his head.

He jumped aside, palmed his forehead, and hauled the knot back over the rail. "Let it hang over!" He pointed to a laundry basket, balanced between two branches. "I'm bringing this up."

"Whatever." She slid the end of the knot between the slat and the deck, feeding the rope through until it brushed his shoulder.

He knelt and scooted the laundry basket closer to him, threading the rope through the handles. After stacking the pipes across the top, he tied them to the basket with more twine. Finally, he climbed the tree, hopped over to the ladder, and used the rope to hoist the basket to the top.

Melanie scooted to the far end of the deck. "Tell me what you're doing."

Grunting, Kyle climbed to the deck and lifted the basket over the railing. He took off the PVC pipes and handed her the pillow. "There's a clean pillowcase in one of the bags."

Melanie couldn't help herself from hugging the pillow, even though it faintly smelled like cows. "What are you doing?"

He fitted a few pieces of the PVC pipe into an upside-down U-shape, with an open piece sticking out toward the billboard. "Here," he dragged the assembly to her end of the deck, "hold onto this for a minute."

"Um… okay." She grabbed the pipe while he returned to the basket and dug through the bags. "Why?"

"I've got a plan." He came out with a handful of plastic zip ties and shoved them into his pocket. While she gaped, he joined the rest of the pipe and fixed it to the deck with the ties.

"There. That should hold."

Over her head, the pipe met to join the two u-shapes and form the outline of a box. "What are you trying to make?" She gathered her dress and stepped out of his way, brushing his shoulders. Sporty cologne wafted to her nostrils, but as she moved away from him, she smelled… "French fries?"

He winked. "Pun'kin is hungry, I gather."

Fury shot through her veins. Oh, to have that shotgun… "Don't you dare ever call me that again, City Boy."

"City Boy? Ha!" He wiped a bead of sweat from his forehead with the back of his hand. "No harm meant. I like the way it makes you growl at me. But seriously, I brought you a burger. Go ahead and eat."

"Well, you are a city boy. Chasing those cows around like... I don't know what." That smirk again. He was pleased she'd noticed, no doubt. Well, she'd only noticed because there wasn't anything else worth watching from up here. She knelt beside the basket, where a Styrofoam box warmed her fingers. Beneath it, the lid of a container of makeup removal wipes showed through a translucent shopping bag.

Though her heart still thundered with rage, she took a deep breath. He was being… kind. Infuriating, but kind. Pre-Stephen, she'd have been flattered. Maybe even intrigued. And yes, she would have noticed. Maybe even flirted a little.

Lizzie would have called him "Man Candy" and said something crazy like, "Snatch that boy up while you can." They'd have giggled and passed notes across the teller counter at work about how he was a "Fine Specimen of Man" and other ridiculousness.

But Melanie had outgrown such silliness. Once Stephen came into the picture, he was number thirteen. The one. Period. She was faithful and true, but for what?

How could she have wasted all that time on someone who cheated? And who knew the extent of it? How many times, how many girls? Stephen had a bad habit of hanging out at the bars and getting sloshed. Everyone had warned her about him. But he'd been good to her. Taken her places. Bought her things. Well, bought her a couple things. A nice watch and new floor mats for her car so she could sell it.

Come to think of it, why had it been so necessary to sell the car? Hadn't she been upset with Stephen for taking the money and blowing it on this trip? The Tricia Billings trip? And now, she had nothing to drive. True, it was a pathetic excuse for a car, but still...

He'd also talked her into selling her Boyd's Bear collection and all her crystal dolphins. Where had that money even gone?

"You going to stare at me all day?" Kyle waved his hand in front of her face. "You've been holding that burger in midair for almost five whole minutes. Want me to unwrap it for you?"

"No." Melanie peeled away the wrapping paper and picked the tomato off. "Thank you for bringing me food."

He reached past her and pulled a bag full of plastic packages from the bottom of the basket. Stubble from his goatee scratched her cheek, and she shivered.

"There's a pair of jeans, a T-shirt, and a sweatshirt." He grinned. "And underwear. I had to guess your size."

"Underwear? How dare you even..." She bit her lower lip. Here he was helping her, and all she could do was spit vitriol. Stupid Stephen. It was all his fault. "Sorry, I... um, thanks for the clothes and stuff, too."

"No problem." He removed four shower curtains from the bag. "And, I'm giving you some privacy. Go ahead and eat. It's probably already getting cold."

While he used the twine to stitch two of the curtains together at the top, she dug into the crinkle fries.

"This should give you a space to change where no one can see you. And, you can fold these up over the top when you want more air." He draped the joined curtains over the 3-D rectangle formed by the pipe and stapled the other two curtains together.

She sighed. "I don't know why you're doing all this. Stephen will probably be up here to talk to me in an hour or so."

"Then come down." Kyle slung the second set of joined curtains over the pipes in the opposite direction and returned to the basket. "But if you're not coming down, then I can't have you up here dying of starvation on Pa's property. And being all uncomfortable. So I had to do something. I promised your dad."

Of course. Daddy was behind all this. She sunk her teeth into the best burger she'd tasted in a while. The crunchy sourdough bread oozed melted butter, mayo, and cheese. "This is amazing," she murmured, her mouth stuffed full. Probably three thousand calories. She'd better change out of the dress if she was going to eat a meal like this.

He held his staple gun up to the curtain and clicked it.

"Why are you stapling the curtains?" She dabbed at her mouth with the rough white napkin she'd found stuffed in the box. "That's an expensive privacy closet. And when I come down, they won't be reusable. You shouldn't have."

"You have a better idea, Pun'kin?"

She threw a fry, hitting him squarely between his cocky brown eyes.

"Look. I figure if you're going to sit up here being all crazy then I should at least be hospitable. Help make you more comfortable, at least." He disappeared inside the curtain, the staple clicking intently.

Tears burned her eyes. He thought her crazy. They all did.

"Oh, there's unsweetened tea in one of those bags. Pure Leaf." Kyle's voice had softened. "Wayne said you loved tea. I also got you some bottled water. And, uh," he cleared his throat, "there are a couple of empty bottles if you need to relieve yourself."

"I've got that covered, thanks very much." She spotted the black lid of the tea and shoved bags aside to grab it. A toothbrush and toothpaste spilled out, landing on a box of Kleenex and baby wipes. Beside them, a portable charger blinked on. He had thought of everything.

As Kyle emerged from behind the curtain, she studied his pleased face. "I have no idea what to say."

He dragged his fingers through his hair and slid past her. Whistling, he freed the basket from the twine and tossed the rope to the ground. With a sharp wave, he started down the ladder. "Thanks will suffice, Pun'kin."

Her nostrils flaring, she scrunched her lips and exhaled loudly for twenty full seconds.

He laughed all the way to the ground.

Lights from the city diminished the sky full of stars. Otherwise, it might have been one of the prettiest nights Kyle had seen in a while. Wow, had things changed.

Milton had grown around Pa's farm. First the new high school, then the homes, and now the new shopping center. It wouldn't be a bad place to live, now that they had some business and industry. Maybe he could get a gig as an assistant coach at the high school. With his savings from playing pro baseball for eight years and the payouts from the commercials, he'd never need to work again.

He'd not expected the wave of nostalgia to hit him as he looked over the town from the billboard. It had been incredible to see everything so clearly—the park bench where he'd had his first kiss, the old ball field where he'd hit his first home run, and the hospital where he'd volunteered as a teenager through a school program.

The house he grew up in had been dwarfed by a modern neighborhood, but the current owners had put a pool in the backyard where he'd played catch with his brothers all those years. Maybe coming home wouldn't be so bad after all.

Wayne had surely recognized him, though if he had, he'd been gracious. After all, everyone in town sent him off to the minor—and later the major leagues—with big parties. A couple of those "last-one-out-turn-off-the-lights" kind of events.

They'd kept up with him on social media for the first couple of years, posting selfies at the games with him in the background, and congratulating him on wins.

And then the support waned. People got busy, he supposed. Caught up in their own lives. Ticket sales started declining and people didn't have the money to travel from Milton to Cincinnati anymore.

And thankfully, the people from Milton had been strangely quiet during his big social debacle. The pictures. The video. The press-conference confession. He'd only bet on one game. Mistake of a lifetime, and a huge public downfall—he'd trended on social media for two full days.

Wayne must have known. Wayne knew Pa, and Pa would have still talked about him to anyone in town who'd listen. Pa had been proud. *Had* been.

A tiny jolt struck his heart. He always lied. He lied to his ex, he lied to Mom and Dad, he lied to Pa… And now, he'd lied to Wayne.

He'd even lied about why he'd come home. Even when he thought it was a funeral, Kyle hadn't come home to pay his respects. He'd come for the 1972 Torino he'd had his eye on since he was a kid.

And Pa knew, to make things worse. In his note, he'd said if Kyle could manage the farm, he could have the car. Well, with Wayne's help, he might. If he even deserved it.

He turned his gaze to the billboard, fully lit by spotlights. Princess Melanie sat huddled in the jeans and sweatshirt he'd bought her. They'd probably been two or three sizes too big. She'd tossed the dress into the tree branches and it hung like an eerie white ghost. A trophy to what might have been. Like Lacey's dress had been.

Lacey's freckle-topped smile framed by her sleek red hair seemed to appear in the branches. "How could you, Kyle?" Those four words had replayed in his mind so many times. She'd stayed up all night crying several days in a row.

And Melanie would cry like that, too. No way she could sleep with all that brightness from the street lights. Her pain would be on display for the whole town.

His chest tightened, and he tore his gaze from the window. Why'd he have to start feeling guilty now? Maybe he should text Lacey. Apologize.

He scrolled through his phone contacts for her name. She hadn't even ranked high enough to be a priority number. Why had he led her to believe things were so serious between them?

Lacey? You up?

His phone dinged within seconds. *What do you want?*

To tell you that I'm sorry. I feel awful for what happened.

The text disappeared into the void with a swoosh. Seconds later, the screen faded, and he set the phone on the bedside table. Change slipped through his fingers as he emptied his pockets, bouncing across the hardwood floors and under the wrought-iron twin bed he'd slept in as a child.

You should.

Lacey, I'm sorry.

He swept his arm across the floor, bumping into a metal box. Saliva stuck in his throat. Pa's baseball cards. Hours and hours of discussions about stats and skill. And Pete Rose. Goodness knows they talked about Pete Rose. Charlie Hustle, as Pa liked to call him. The Hit King. His rise to fame, his terrible downfall, and his exile from the sport—way too familiar.

Kyle scooted the box out and set it on the bed, rubbing the dust off with his sleeve. He unlatched the lid and opened it, his heart stopping again when he saw the card at the top of the stack.

His photograph, in a plastic sleeve. The red cap with the big white C. The pristine jersey and shiny black bat. And underneath it, the article that ended his career.

He closed the box and set it next to his phone on the table. Closing his eyes, he reached into his back pocket for his wallet and felt through the receipts for the folded newspaper article that announced his fall from grace. The quote, which he uttered nightly as though it were a prayer. "I bet on the game of baseball, and I bet on my team."

His head hung, he opened his eyes, catching the screen of the phone as it lit up. Lacey's name and a single word. *Creep.*

To quote Pa, he reckoned so.

Chapter Five

A couple beeps and slamming doors jarred Melanie from fitful sleep. She arched her back, reaching overhead, and jumped when her hands struck cool metal. Her eyes flew open, still stinging from tears, greeting the clear, blue sky. Plain white shower curtains were surrounding her.

She scooted back, grasping at the steel deck as she sat upright. The wedding. The billboard.

Another few doors slammed.

The church. She opened the shower curtains. Trucks and cars filled the parking lot.

Daddy sat in a lawn chair beside his truck, his head buried in his hands. Melanie winced. Had he been there all night?

She turned her head side to side, cracking her neck. No. She would have noticed.

A suited man with a protruding belly approached him, shifting a Bible under his arm as he extended his hand to Daddy.

Daddy smiled, pointed up at her, and blew her a kiss.

As the man looked up with his face scrunched, she gave a tiny wave. He must be wondering about Kyle's little contraption.

She grinned, but then it faded. No, he must be wondering about her. What kind of lunatic climbs up a billboard and refuses to come down? People make movies about crazies like that.

Daddy stood and shook the man's hand. Did this guy know him? Probably not personally. He seemed more like a fan. She could imagine the conversation. Wow. *The* Wayne Turner? It always happened.

They talked for a minute, and Daddy followed the man across the parking lot and through the double-oak doors.

Melanie caught her oily, matted hair at the base of her neck. Daddy went into the church? With a preacher? At least, the guy looked like a preacher. But then again, all the men streaming into the building looked like preachers. What had the man said to Daddy? She almost didn't get him to go in for the wedding, let alone a service. Was he staying?

She checked her cell. The charger Kyle had given her worked its magic. Ninety-two percent battery. Maybe Daddy would answer if she texted him.

Are you going in there?

She waited as the lot filled with more vehicles. Melanie expected half of them would stare at her, but they all seemed to be focused on getting in the building. Some carried bags like teachers, and others ushered small children inside. A few elderly folks made their slow way toward the door and a group of teens laughed all the way across the parking lot. And they all looked... happy.

Melanie scrunched her nose. More power to them. Church was a place where someone stood in front of the room for an hour and pointed out your every flaw. Daddy had said so himself.

Bluegrass music erupted from her cell, the special ringtone Daddy had made for her last Christmas. She swiped the screen. "Hey, Daddy."

"Pun'kin."

"You went in the church."

"I did. Checking things out." Daddy whistled through his teeth. "Ready to come down?"

"No." She stared at the shiny oak door. She wasn't coming down. Not until Stephen came up to apologize. Hadn't she made that clear?

"Then I'll catch up with you after services."

"Fine." Her words were lost to the end call screen.

Seconds ticked by, then minutes, as she scrolled through her social media feeds. They'd quoted her and posted pictures, amplifying her crazy to the point that it had gone viral, at least in town. Some took Stephen's side, calling her naïve and stupid. Others named him the slithering snake that he was.

Several girls posted claims of having been with Stephen recently. A couple of them even had pictures. Her heart sank. How humiliating. She hid behind the curtains, just keeping them open a crack.

As the end of the hour approached, still more vehicles pulled into the lot, and families hustled into the building. Still, no one glanced her way.

When two full hours had passed, members trickled out of the church in clusters. A few cast curious glances in her direction, but most herded their families together and drove off. Daddy finally emerged from the building, the preacher at his side, and a wide grin on his face.

He tilted his chin toward her, blew her a kiss, and got in his truck.

As he drove toward town, her blood boiled. He was *leaving*? Wasn't he even going to ask her to come down?

She gritted her teeth and slid into the new sneakers Kyle had brought her. When she'd tied them, she rushed to the ladder. As she climbed down, her heart thundered. Maybe she'd go give Stephen a piece of her mind.

Nature called, and she slipped into a thick cluster of trees. Careful to avoid poison ivy, she took care of business and walked back to the sign pole.

No, Stephen was going to come to her. She wasn't groveling. No way.

Back on deck, she ripped into one of the granola bars Kyle had left for her and peered across the field to the farmhouse. No sign of the old truck he drove around.

Sweeping her gaze wider, she chewed a mouthful of honey, oats, and chocolate chips. Had Kyle gone to get lunch? She hoped so. She hoped so? Was she insane? Expecting Kyle to rush to her like he owed her something. But then again, he had said he'd feed her. That he didn't want her sitting up there starving.

She looked around the farm. There he was. In spite of herself, she giggled. Poor guy stood in the middle of a path, trying to nudge a stubborn cow forward.

She dug through the basket again. Maybe he'd left something else to eat. After patting down several empty bags, she sighed. She'd have to wait.

A receipt poked out of the top bag, and she grabbed it. A hundred sixty-seven dollars? A scowl crossed her face. And thirteen cents. Always stupid thirteen. But he'd spent over one hundred sixty-seven dollars to make her comfortable for what would hopefully be a few more minutes... or hours? What kind of guy would do that? What kind of guy had that sort of money to throw away?

She folded the receipt. On the blank side, he'd scrawled his name and a number. Kyle Casey.

She unlocked her phone and opened the browser. Maybe he was on Facebook.

Three seconds later, his handsome face popped up underneath a familiar red hat and a white jersey to the right side of the screen. Twenty-eight million hits?

She swallowed. A pro baseball player? No wonder he threw cash around like it was nothing. Oh, my. And all those girls.

The first link promised stats and a bio. She scrolled past it to his Twitter account and Wikipedia page. Then, the news.

"Pro baseball player suspended for alleged gambling." Her whisper came out raspy. The suspicion, proven. His career, over. Another lying cheat like Stephen.

She glanced across the field at his hunched, muscular figure. "You go, you silly beast." The cow deserved the win.

Kyle's shoulders heaved as he stomped back to the truck. He started it, the radio blaring one of Pa's annoying bluegrass bands. He'd tried to turn it earlier, but the knob stuck. With a jerk, he twisted it so tight it fell off in his hand.

He recalled another trip in the truck, years ago, probably listening to the same song. Pa had some trouble with a cow and couldn't get it to even take a step. He didn't lose his temper or swat at the beast. No, not Pa. Instead, he sang Ricky Skaggs. And when that didn't work, he turned to old folk songs and children's music.

Wrinkling his nose, Kyle rolled down the windows and backed the truck up next to the cow. The music blared, and she swatted her tail at the door.

"Whadda ya think, Gertie?" He grinned. "Does that sound enough like good ol' Pa?"

She poked her head in the window, chewing a hunk of grass and drooling on his sleeve. "So it is Gertie, is it?" Snickering, Kyle rubbed her head. "He's got you spoiled, don't he, girl?"

She let out a moo that sounded more like a whine, and whipped her head to the left, bumping the truck with her rear.

"Okay, fine." He reached out and stroked her ear. "The farmer in the dell, the farmer in the dell…"

The cow's ears perked, and Kyle grinned. He pulled forward a few feet, and she shuffled along beside the truck.

Fifteen long minutes later, he sped up a little, and she still followed. He grinned. Closest thing he'd had to a win in a long time.

He slowed to a crawl and took out his phone, opening the camera app. Glancing over his shoulder at her, he winked. "How 'bout a selfie, Gertie?"

She let out another whiny moo.

After snapping the picture, he posted it on Twitter. "There you go, fans. Something to talk about. Nothing wrong here. No guilt, no shame," he shot the cow one last look, "no baseball."

When he returned to the house, he eyed the billboard before heading inside. Melanie's shadow huddled behind the curtains. He'd checked on her several times, since his mind raced most of the night. Here they were, two people who'd lost everything and needed a new start. Maybe Pa had been right all these years. Helping others could help him heal himself.

And he'd start with a couple sandwiches.

Melanie peeled off the sweatshirt and tied it around her waist. Stephen wasn't coming. Dad wasn't coming. Mama never even tried. And apparently Kyle wasn't coming, either. She'd have to leave sooner or later. She couldn't stay forever. But what could she do?

Maybe she should give up. Do what a normal person would do, and let it go. But she couldn't. Not until she knew her next move.

She got up to stretch, resisting the urge to check the time on her phone, instead scanning the horizon for the People's Choice Bank sign. It stood above Harper's Minit Mart, a blur of blue LED lights. Sighing, she pressed the button and lit up her screen. Three thirty. And fifteen percent battery. Kyle had promised to recharge the portable charger, but that looked like another thing that wasn't happening.

A bird landed on her wedding dress, picking at the threads with its beak. She cast it a rueful smile. "You go on ahead."

To her left, a cloud of dust caught her eye. Kyle in that old farm truck, racing toward her.

She chewed her lower lip. On the one hand, he was as much of a cheater and liar as anyone. She'd read the articles. But on the other hand, she was starving.

When he got out of the truck, he lifted a wicker basket from the bed and looped it over his arm. This time, he climbed the tree without hesitation and scaled the ladder in less than a minute, a blend of cologne and cow hovering between them.

"Hey, Pun'kin."

She clenched her jaw.

"Bet you're hungry." He opened the basket and handed her a wrapped sandwich. "Ham on rye with mayo. Hope you like it."

She peeled back the wax paper and lifted the bread. "Spinach, cucumbers, and sprouts? My kind of sandwich."

"You seemed girly like that." He dodged her swat and grabbed his own sandwich. "I used to um… work for Subway. I get free subs whenever."

"Commercials, right?" Melanie looked over the bridge of her nose at him. His eyes widened. "Mr. Casey."

"Just call me Casey at the bat." A grin flashed across his face and then faded. "Well, not anymore."

Melanie shrugged. "It's your business. I won't pry." She picked a cucumber off her sandwich and chewed it slowly. "Besides," she swallowed, "I don't like baseball anyway."

They ate in silence for a few minutes, their hands brushing on occasion as they shared a bag of chips. After what felt like the hundredth time, she snatched a handful of chips and held them in her lap.

"What?" He reached over and grabbed one as she took a big bite of her sandwich.

Mayo dripped down her chin, and she wiped it with the bread. When she finished chewing, she faced him. "I want to make sure you don't have any intentions toward me. If you do, I'm not interested."

His face remained stoic. "Duly noted. But I'm not interested, either."

Heat flushed her cheeks. If he didn't care, then why was he feeding her?

He twisted the cap off a bottle of unsweetened tea and handed it to her. "It's hot up here. You sure you're not going to get dehydrated? I'd hate for you to die."

Her chest swelled. Of course, that was why he cared. She was a liability. "So good to know you have my best interests in mind."

Opening his own tea, he leaned back against the billboard. "Do you ever wish life had a replay button? Like a great moment you could live over and over again?"

"Yeah." She held a cool sip in her mouth until it warmed. "Like the last time Stephen looked at me with love in his eyes."

He waved his arm over the horizon. "All of my good moments have been on this farm, except winning a few games and playing in the major leagues. I've never had a good relationship. Every girl I've ever dated, we've fought from the start until I couldn't take it anymore."

She blew over the lip of the bottle, making it whistle. "I can see why. You're not the nicest guy I've ever met."

His eyes widened, and he pressed his lips tight. "What do you mean? Look at all this I've done for you."

"You won't stop calling me Pun'kin when I've asked you not to."

"That doesn't make me a bad guy."

"You cheated on baseball."

He opened his mouth, then covered it with his left hand. "Thought you weren't going to bring that up."

"I wasn't." She wadded her napkin in her fist. "But you're not trustworthy. It's on my mind. What's your endgame in helping me?"

"I don't know." He met her gaze directly. *Was* he telling the truth? And if he didn't know, what subconscious thought drove him to her?

As he held her stare, her pulse quickened. It was too forced. He wasn't telling the truth. And she'd seen his little cow selfie. So, what kind of publicity stunt was he trying to pull?

"I brought you something else." From the basket, he drew out a small battery-operated radio. He flipped a switch and extended the antenna. "Thought music might help."

Static crackled, and he twisted the tuning knob. A man with a deep voice resonated through the speakers. "Now hope does not disappoint, because the love of God has been poured out in our hearts by the Holy Spirit who was given to us."

She frowned at the radio.

The man continued. "When you feel you've lost hope, remember this. If no one else cares, God still cares." He paused, leaving a peaceful silence. "Thank you all for coming tonight. Don't forget everyone on our prayer list, especially that poor, hurting girl sitting up on that billboard. Melanie, if you can hear us, we're praying for you. If you'd like to come down and talk, our doors are open. Have a blessed week. We'll see you all Wednesday night at our regular time."

As the man's voice faded, the blend of a cappella singing streamed through the air.

Kyle turned the knob again, stopping on a music station. "Sorry. I didn't realize…"

"It's a gimmick." She massaged her forehead with hard strokes. "If God cares, then why does this hurt so much? Why does he let guys like Stephen do the things he did?"

"I don't know." Kyle set the radio on the deck and took a step toward the ladder.

"You're going?" She bit her lip. She hadn't meant to sound so eager. "I mean, I didn't—"

Kyle winked. "I know. It stinks to be alone when you have a broken heart. I can stay. It's not like I'm doing anything. Maybe I can at least help you pass the time."

Melanie gave him a shy grin as he dropped down and scooted next to her. "Thanks. I feel like I don't have anybody right now."

Slipping his hand over hers, Kyle faced her. "I know you don't trust me right now, or anyone else for that matter, but you have me. If nothing else, I promised your dad. I'll be here as long as you need me."

"Promise?" Her eyes moistened for the eight-hundredth time.

"Promise."

Chapter Six

"You can dance if you want to…" Melanie giggled, striking a vogue pose.

Kyle mimicked her. "Well, if you don't, you can't be my friend."

"We're getting ridiculous." Her giggles faded, and she took in several deep breaths. What had started as awkward small talk led to hours of conversation about life, love, and the pursuit of happiness. In spite of the circumstances, she'd almost had… dare she think it…? Fun. Still, she couldn't let herself trust him. How could she ever trust anyone?

Two beeps drew her attention to the parking lot. Again. "Look at those people all coming back. Well, not as many, but still…"

He glanced at his watch. "Yeah. I think they have a second service at six or something like that." Gripping her shoulder, he pulled her forward and pointed at the brick marquee. "See, right there. Evening worship, six p.m."

"What could they possibly have to talk about that hasn't already been said?" The right corner of her mouth twitched.

"Well, looks like they all have some kind of food." He pointed to a man carrying a crock pot. "I guess they eat. Hey, isn't that Wayne?"

Sure enough, Daddy pulled into a parking space and got out of the truck. Come to spy on her again, no doubt. Wait… Was he carrying food, too? She sat straighter. "He's going in. Can you believe that?"

Kyle yawned. "Wayne seems like a nice-enough guy."

"But he swore he'd never go to church. Took forever for me to convince him to let me get married in one instead of on a bluegrass stage. And this guy's talked him into waltzing right in. Twice in a day, for that matter." She shook her head. "It's weird."

"Well, their marquee says they broadcast every service. And look, it's a singing night. At least that's what the sign says. Let's listen in and see what's going on."

She sighed. "Daddy loves to sing, so that probably explains it."

He grabbed the radio and tuned it to the station where they'd heard the preaching that morning. Static and murmuring voices played over the air.

"So, why'd you do it?" No telling what kind of heinous monster she looked like, but Kyle didn't seem to mind. She ran her fingers through her tangled hair, separating it strand by strand. At least she washed the mess of makeup off and could look him in the eye. "Bet on the games, I mean."

"We weren't talking about this."

"I know. I'm curious. It doesn't seem anything like your personality."

Stretching his legs over the deck, he crossed them at the ankles and rested the toes of his sneakers against the bottom rail. "Game. There was only the one."

She held up her right hand. "I—"

"No, wait. I promise. No one else believes me, either, but I only bet on the one game." Reaching for the plastic bag he'd used to carry the sandwiches, he held her gaze steady. Not blinking. "I'm sure it was a setup. The guy was paid to bait me so they could catch me in the act. He tried too hard. Bugged me until I finally gave in."

Frowning, she searched his face. "Well, the paper said you—"

"Don't worry, Pun'kin." He gave her a sad smile. "I know where the blame falls. That guy may have cast the lure, but I didn't have to bite. In fact, I said no, but he kept asking. That never made the paper."

"Stop calling me Pun'kin."

Several minutes of silence passed. Melanie stared at the latecomers hustling into the church while Kyle inspected a callus on his left hand. She yawned and tapped her toes in her shoes. "So... how many times did he ask you?"

"I stopped counting at something like thirteen."

"Are you kidding me?" Thirteen. That wretched number, striking again.

"What?" He brushed her forehead, catching a strand of her disgusting, oily hair that had fallen into her eyes and tucking it behind her ear.

"Nothing. I hate that number."

"Thirteen?"

Her shoulders heaved. "That's the one."

"Why? Are you superstitious or something?"

"Long story." She clenched her jaw. A long story she wasn't telling.

"Do you hear that?" Kyle twisted the volume on the radio. "They're singing. I hear your dad."

She tilted her head, straining to hear the words. "Turn it up a little more."

"Trust and obey, for there's no other way to be happy..."

Sure enough, Daddy's rich voice overwhelmed the crowd. Tears pooled into her eyes. No way to be happy. Sounded about right. Although, the blending of their voices sent chills down her spine.

"You still don't trust me?" Kyle scooted sideways to face her.

"No." Why had he asked that?

His Adam's apple bobbed as he swallowed. "Well, you shouldn't. I'm a magnet for mistakes."

As the song faded and the next one began, a tear escaped and slid down her cheek. She and Stephen should have been on their honeymoon, maybe listening to the jazz singers on the cruise right about now.

"Like what kind of mistakes?"

"I haven't had a steady girlfriend my whole life. I always mess it up. Forget to show up for dates, leave girls waiting when I'm supposed to be there…a real class act."

"Oh." Melanie scratched the middle knuckle on her left hand, a nervous habit she'd picked up in grade school. Stephen had left her waiting as well. Was the universe trying to play some kind of cosmic joke on her? Tempt her from jumping out of one disastrous relationship right into another. "Why? Why would you do that?"

Kyle shifted his weight. He clearly didn't like talking about it. "I had my priorities mixed up, you know. Felt like being 'Kyle Casey, the man' was more important than being a class act." His shoulders slumped. "Those were Pa's words exactly. A few Christmases ago when I breezed in for about thirty minutes and then flew out to meet a bunch of my buddies in Vegas."

"Priorities." Melanie wrinkled her nose. "I don't even think I know what those are anymore."

"Yeah." Kyle nodded. "I think maybe it was a good thing this happened with me being suspended. I've had several weeks now to think about what those priorities are supposed to be. The more time I spend away from the hype and the public eye, the more I think I want to settle into a simple life. Maybe do some charity work or something. Remember that it's not all about me and how much my life stinks."

She cringed. He surely hadn't meant to point his finger at her, but the words still cut. She was being selfish. But selfish or not, she was seeing this whole thing out. When Stephen came and apologized, she'd come down.

Kyle stood, collected their trash, and set it in the basket by the ladder. "Guess I should be going. Probably need to check everything on the farm. I'll run out in a little while and get us something to eat."

"Yeah. About that. I never did thank you for the sandwich." She handed him a forgotten wrapper that had drifted beside her feet. "And for keeping me company. Trust you or not, I had a good time. And I do appreciate that."

Bad as she hated to admit it, she felt sorry to see him go.

Kyle backed his bright blue sports car into a parking spot and eyed the crowded restaurant. It had been a while since he'd stood in the middle of so many people. Most of them looked to be close to his age. Guys he'd gone to school with buying dinner for their wives and kids. Would they recognize him? Would they judge him? Maybe he should have driven Pa's beat-up truck instead.

He twisted the key and pulled it out of the ignition. Only one way to find out, he guessed. Unbuckle the seatbelt, slide out of the car, square his shoulders, and march inside like he'd never messed up.

When he passed through the double glass doors, recognition flickered on a dark-haired guy's face. The guy waved, knelt by his toddler son, and grinned. "Look Maxie. It's Kyle Casey. Remember how I told you there was a guy who'd struck out the other team's players twenty times in the same game? That's him."

Kyle rubbed his tongue over the back of his teeth. What was the guy's name?

The blonde next to them turned, shifted the baby she carried higher on her hip, and patted the guy on the shoulder. "Tyler, did you remember the formula?"

"Formula." He gave her a sheepish grin. "Right. Be right back, Elise."

Kyle stepped aside as Tyler hurried past him. Tyler Conner and Elise Marcum. Sweethearts since middle school. How could he have forgotten them?

Elise reached for Maxie's hand and offered Kyle a warm smile. "It's been a while, Casey."

"Yep." Kyle couldn't help but smile back. "Looks like time's been good to you guys. Two beautiful kids."

She chuckled and nodded to three teenage boys standing in line ahead of her, bent over an electronic device. "Five beautiful kids. But we finally got our girl." Nuzzling her chin against the baby's head, she cooed. "Don't we, Sylvie? Don't we?"

Kyle pressed his hands to his side. "Sylvie was your mom, right? I remember her."

"Yeah." Elise tugged Maxie closer. "She's been gone twelve years now. Can you believe that?"

Tyler raced back to her side, a brown and pink polka-dotted bag in tow. Three bottles poked out from pockets surrounding an inner pouch stuffed full of diapers and bibs. "Got it." He traded the bag for Maxie and faced Kyle. "So, how've you been, Casey? Aside from the obvious, I mean."

"Okay, I guess." Kyle tried to shrug, but it didn't feel natural anymore. "Managing this situation out on Pa's farm."

"Yeah." Elise giggled. "We've been watching."

"Watching?" Good grief. Kyle eyed the drink counter. Could he duck underneath it?

She snuggled the baby closer. "We go to that church. It's some 'situation' to find a scorned woman on your property. So, how's she doing?"

"Okay, I guess. Hurt and angry."

The line advanced, and her teenage sons leaned over the counter. As they gave their orders, Kyle drummed his fingers against his pants hem. Melanie was probably wondering what was taking so long. Although, she didn't seem like the kind of girl to throw a fit because she had to wait for something. In fact, she seemed more like the girl who sacrificed too much to make the relationship work.

When the entire Conner clan had their food, Tyler nodded as he carried a tray of drinks toward the lobby. "Good seeing you, Kyle. I manage the hardware store now. If you need anything, swing by and say hello."

"Yeah, good seeing you." Elise hugged him, bag, baby, and all.

"Thanks." Kyle cleared his throat as he stepped up to the counter.

"Who was that?" One of their boys directed the question with typical teen angst.

Tyler glanced over his shoulder. "A great guy that I always looked up to."

Kyle swallowed. Looked up to. As in the past. Until he'd pulled the ultimate idiot move. He dislodged his wallet from his pocket and stepped up to the counter, where a petite brunette wearing a peppy ponytail slapped a tray in front of him.

"For here, or to go?"

"To go."

"Name?"

Name? He frowned.

"So we can call you for your order, sir. Your name."

"Kyle." He fished out a twenty. "I'll take two of your three-piece grilled chicken meals, one barbecue and the other extreme heat. Red beans and rice for one of the sides, and um…" Did Melanie even like spicy food? He pressed his fingers against his lips. "I guess coleslaw."

"We'll have it right up." The brunette took his change and sent him to the drink counter, where Tyler fought with the napkin dispenser.

"Hey, man." Tyler gave the napkins a jerk and a healthy handful popped out. "Everybody makes mistakes. We lose our way and have to start fresh sometimes. All of us. You know that, right?"

Kyle grabbed a couple of the stray napkins that drifted to the floor. "Yeah. I know. Not everybody does them in the public eye."

"True." Tyler pointed out the window to the bright red skyline. "This town needs more heroes. Finding forgiveness might not be as hard as you think. I know all the ladies at church think it's awfully sweet that you're taking care of that girl."

"I'll remember that." Kyle held Melanie's cup under the ice dispenser and pulled down the handle. He filled it to the brim with unsweet tea, then got himself a soda.

As more and more people streamed into the restaurant, Kyle pressed himself against the baby chairs. He couldn't wait to get out of there and back to Melanie. Watching Tyler and Elise and their happiness almost smothered him. How could he ever hope to have that kind of happiness?

A balding man moved into his personal space and reached over him for a lid. "Well, well. If it isn't good old Gamblin' Casey. You know what *I* bet, son? I bet Pa Casey wishes you'd never been born to have brought the family so much shame."

Kyle's chest constricted. "I—"

"Don't bother apologizing." The older man bumped Kyle with his elbow as he moved past. "You brought a load of shame to this town. We were so proud of you. All that talent, wasted."

"I'm sorry, sir." Kyle scooted the two drinks back farther from the edge of the counter.

"Might as well move on out and start over somewhere else." The man filled his cup with diet soda and snapped the lid on. "We don't need any more no-good, gambling ne'er-do-wells in this town."

"Kyle?" The cashier called to him.

He snatched up the drinks and shoved his way to the counter. She passed him the bags, and he ducked out the nearest door, opposite from where he'd parked. As he walked around, little Maxie waved through the window. Sure, one couple who he'd been friends with might have given him a little encouragement, but the truth reared its ugly head. This town didn't want him. It didn't want his failure or his disappointments. He couldn't possibly make it up to them or to his family. So, why bother? He'd be better off to start over in a different town.

Minutes later, as he sped back to the farm with their food, the dismal grays spread over the skyline. Who was he kidding? Where could he go to find peace? When his story went viral, it spread to every last nook and cranny in the country. Who could forgive someone for doing something so un-American as to bet on baseball? Even if he went to another town, he'd face the same resistance.

The lights above the billboard danced like stars around Melanie's shadowed form, crumpled in a heap next to the ladder. She'd already cried herself to exhaustion several times. He'd convinced himself that she'd needed him to take care of her, but the truth was *he* needed to. Pa couldn't have known this would happen, even though he did probably feel like working on the farm would rebuild the character Kyle had shattered.

Unfortunately, Melanie would stop needing him soon, and she'd move on with her life. He ought to be relieved.

Chapter Seven

Melanie cocked her head side to side, her neck cracking and popping like rice cereal. Wasn't she too young for her joints to ache so badly?

Apparently not, because another quick twist of her neck set off another series of snap-crackle-pops as her cell vibrated on the deck. She nestled her phone between her ear and her left shoulder. "Hey, Daddy."

"Hey, Pun'kin. You know it's Monday morning, right? How you holdin' up? Ready to come down yet?"

She drummed her fingers against the warming steel, blinking out the bright sunlight. A yawn took over her entire being, and when it finished, she stifled another one. "Is Stephen ready to climb up here and apologize yet?"

Daddy's swallow lingered through the speakers. "About that…"

"Tell me." She grabbed the phone and pressed it against her other ear. "I'm a big girl."

"Who throws fits and climbs billboards."

"Daddy."

A long pause. "He took off for Jamaica without you."

"He did what?" Her blood boiled as she gripped the phone tighter.

"Yep." Daddy shot out a long blast of air. "He went on your honeymoon without you. So how long was it, thirteen days? You can't wait that long. Better come on down from there."

Thirteen days. Melanie ground her teeth. "I told you. I'm not coming down until he gets up here and apologizes."

"And then what?" Daddy's pitch rose. "Do you think things will automatically be better after that?"

"No, but I'll have closure."

"Closure." Daddy practically spat the word. "Well, I reckon I'll let you get back to your broodin' then. Call me if you get bored or hungry, and I'll take you home."

"I'm good. Kyle's been feeding me." She huffed. "Look, if you can't get Stephen up here, leave me alone."

Daddy cleared his throat. "In other news, I've got a surprise for you."

"I'm listening."

"Tomorrow night, they're having a big bluegrass shindig up here in this church parking lot. Barbecue, inflatables, and..." He made a trumpeting noise. "And yours truly is performing. At least you won't have to miss it. Unless you want to climb down and join us in person."

She couldn't stop her snicker. Daddy would find a way to perform in all this. "Yeah. I'll have the best seat in the house."

"I wish you'd come down."

"Love you, Daddy." She swiped to end the call and scooted back against the sign.

Stephen, on their honeymoon without her. Tears stung her eyes and burned into her very soul. How could she come down? Ever? Where would she go? What would starting over without Stephen even look like? Moving back home? Getting a job as a department store greeter since the bank probably wouldn't hire her back?

Well, she had a week and a half to mull it over. Surely something would come to her by then.

Kyle tightened the knot around the handle of Grandma's old picnic basket and hoisted the sub sandwiches up to the deck.

No response from Melanie. He climbed to the top and peeked over.

Her two bare feet poked out from the shelter he'd built for her.

Quietly as possible, he pulled himself up on the deck and sat cross-legged beside them. Not even the hint of movement. Was she asleep?

He leaned closer to where he could see the other side of her feet. Ouch. Bright pink from baking in the sun, surely to blister. Poor girl.

Her perfect toes curled. Should he wake her? At the very least, he needed to cover up those dainty feet. Nicer feet than he would have expected for an avid huntress like Wayne had described her.

Grinning, he retrieved the envelope from his pocket and poked a corner of it between two of her toes.

"Aaaggghhh." Something clunked behind the curtain and her feet disappeared. Seconds later, she emerged, rubbing her head.

"You were getting sunburned." He handed her the letter.

"What's this?" She held the envelope to the light.

"It's from the preacher of that church." He scooted toward her with the picnic basket. "I didn't read it."

He sat down and planted the basket between them, watching a sly grin span her rosy cheeks as she scanned the letter.

"What is it?" He leaned in.

"He says he'd like to thank me for the extra attention I've brought to the church. Apparently last night's crowd grew by thirty percent of what it usually is."

"No kidding." Kyle chuckled. "So maybe he doesn't want you to come down."

She scanned the rest of the page, folded it, and put it in her lap. "He was nice. Gave me his and his wife's phone numbers and said

if I still had battery left on my phone to call if I needed anything."
She snorted. "And, he gave me my second invite to some bluegrass
shindig happening in the church parking lot tonight."

"Yeah. I got one, too." Kyle grinned then frowned. "Who gave
you the second invite?"

She shrugged. "Daddy. He's performing." Her nose twisted into
a scrunch. "Ow. My feet hurt."

"I'll get you some aloe when I come back up tonight."

"For the concert, right?" She winked. "You gotta hear the ever-
talented Wayne Lee Turner strumming his magic on that banjo."

"Wait a minute." Kyle grabbed the sandwiches from the basket
and passed her one. "Do you mean *the* Wayne Lee Turner?" The
one Pa made him listen to every Christmas? How had he forgotten a
detail like that when Wayne had introduced himself?

"That's the one." She unwrapped her sub, picked off the
tomatoes, and tossed them over the edge of the deck. "Stephen
always used to joke with me. He liked to sing that country song
about her daddy's money and mama's good looks. I think maybe
since Daddy had a bit of notoriety, Stephen thought we were rich."

She tore a piece of bread off and popped it into her mouth.
"We do okay, but we're certainly not rich. Guess maybe that's why
Stephen cheated. He found out we couldn't pad his bank account.
Maybe he wanted an out."

"I have to ask." He grabbed a water bottle from the basket and
twisted its cap. "Do you?"

She reached for her own water. "Do I what?"

"Have more laughs than the comics. You know, like the song
says."

A lovely giggle erupted from her throat, and her eyes twinkled.
"You have no idea."

"Well, tell me something funny."

Holding her sandwich midair, she twisted her lips to the side. "Something funny." A deep frown twisted her soft, relaxed features. "Honestly, I don't remember the last time I laughed. I mean truly laughed. Stephen was always so serious."

"Then tell me what you were like before Stephen."

A tiny tear bubbled at the edge of her eyelid. "Well... um... okay, when I was little, Daddy used to bring me with him to all these odd jobs while Mama worked at the bank. Most of the time he worked on farms, and he'd let me play in the corn cribs."

Kyle scrunched his brows. "Wasn't he afraid you'd meet up with a rattlesnake?"

"He always said I was meaner than a rattlesnake. Even at age three." She gave him a spunky half-smile. "So anyway, we were on some farm and he left me playing in the corn crib with this older kid while he drove the tractor to do something. It may have even been *this* farm. I don't know."

Kyle shook his head. "Pa never had a corn crib that I remember. And any kids you played with on this farm would have been me or one of my brothers. I think I'd have remembered someone like you."

"Well, whoever it was, the clouds started pouring rain, and this kid decided we needed to go back to the house instead of waiting the storm out. He was afraid the crib would be destroyed." She snickered. "We hopped down to the ground and took two or three steps, then sunk into deep mud. And... I got stuck there."

"You got stuck?"

"Like the earth was sucking me in. Stuck. Daddy had to come back with the tractor and get me out. It was a flash flood, you know."

Kyle met her gaze directly. "Okay. Tell me a story where you're older than a toddler. What were you like in high school?"

She touched the back of her hand to her forehead, posing with extreme flair. "Most likely to engage in melodrama. There's even a picture to prove it in the yearbook."

"Let's see. You graduated in…" He tapped his fingers like he was counting.

"I'm twenty-six." A bitter laugh burst from her throat. "You know, like thirteen twice. My year of doom. At least it's almost over, and I'll turn twenty-seven soon."

"Which puts me at two years older than you. We would have been in high school together. Why don't I remember you?"

"Because Mama held me out an extra year. My birthday's in October. I would have been an annoying freshman when you were a senior."

"That's not soon—it's five months away."

"Four-and-a-half. Anyway, it's not a long time."

"Why didn't you know me?" He frowned. "I was one of the popular kids at school. I thought everyone knew me."

She flicked her eyes up under the lids and held them there for three whole seconds. How obnoxious. "I told you. I'm not a baseball fan. And I avoided the popular kids. They went around bullying everyone from what I remember. Were you one of the bullies?"

He scratched his chin. "Well, I guess we were away part of that time. You know, all I remember from the time I was very, very young is baseball drills. I took two gym classes as a senior for weightlifting and to practice pitching and batting. Ran to the field or cage immediately after school. Even in the off season."

"I spent all my time in the greenhouses. Remember Mr. Bettez, the Ag teacher? One time after school I was curious and he gave me a tour. He got me interested in all kinds of botany, and I enjoyed watching the plants grow. Of course, he also talked my ear off about how they regulated the temperature with a thermostat he built and designed. Of course, looking back on it, he was a huge Daddy fan. I'm sure he helped me so he could meet the great Wayne Lee Turner."

"Tell me another funny story." Kyle winked. "From high school."

"There was the time we all got locked back in the book room because Mrs. Frizz... whatever that woman's real name was. Mrs. Thompson or something like that. She walked off and left us, closed the door behind us, and then turned us all in for skipping. The principal and some teachers combed the school, and finally they thought to check the book room again. They had all these bottles of water stored for prom, so we had become thirsty and helped ourselves. And bored, so we started a game of something kind of a cross between Truth or Dare and Charades. When the principal opened the door, he found me standing with one foot on a stack of books, the other foot lifted behind me, my arm draped out in front of me, and water squirting from my mouth like a fountain."

"What did he do?"

She chuckled. "After I blasted him in the face with water, or before?"

"You blasted Nukas Lucas in the face with water?" Kyle palmed his face and peeked between his fingers. "How did you get away with that?"

"No, he wasn't principal then. It was Mr. Lloyd. The guy with the hairpiece that always set sideways."

"I guess I don't remember him. Tell me another one. Your dad said you were spunky and spontaneous. What did he mean by that?"

She yawned so long that two small tears streamed down her cheeks. "I know what you're doing. Getting me distracted and all. Hoping I'll remember who I used to be before Stephen. But Kyle, that girl is gone. Stephen never let me be spontaneous. It always got on his nerves."

"Why can't you bring her back? I mean, surely Stephen's out of your life now, since he's pulled such a stupid stunt. I can't imagine wanting to go back to someone like that."

As Melanie dissolved into tears, Kyle reached for her and pulled her close to him. She shook against his shoulders and dug her fingers deep into his arms.

The night he broke up with Lacey came crashing back to his memory. She'd clung to him this way. Cried more than he'd thought anyone could.

He drug his fingers through Melanie's hair, easing out the tangles and letting it fall to her neck. "This will all be okay. It won't hurt so much forever."

"I know." Melanie's lower lip quivered as she drew back from him. "I'm okay. It's hard to face the fact that the truth was in front of me all along. I changed everything I was for Stephen. Became a totally different person. If my life depended on me telling you a funny story during the time I dated him, I'd be hard pressed to find one. I guess I'm ashamed that I let him affect me that way and I didn't even realize it."

"We all sell out for a relationship at times." Kyle gritted his teeth. "Lesson learned, and now you can start over fresh." *With me.*

He grimaced. Where had that thought come from? And so natural. The last thing he needed was to fall for a fragile girl on the rebound.

She wiped her tears with her sleeves, a wicked grin spanning her cheeks. "Okay, Kyle Casey. You wanted funny. I have a joke for you."

Melanie stretched her arms out wide and counted silently to ten. Kyle had listened intently for fifteen minutes, and her sniffling had stopped. Now, the pause for dramatic effect… "And he died.'"

Kyle leaned closer. "What? You made me listen to all that nonsense about golf balls for this? Say it again. I dare you."

She let out several gasps of laughter. "And… he died."

"Why you…" Kyle mock-slapped at her leg and she caught his hand, lacing his fingers in her own.

Heat crept up the base of her neck and spread to her ears. She tried to release her grasp, but he squeezed tighter. "I like you, Melanie. I've enjoyed spending these past two days with you. But I have to go do farm stuff. I need to figure out what Pa wants me to do next."

Melanie gritted her teeth. Holding hands? No. Absolutely not. Butterflies rose in her stomach, and she filled her lungs with air to squelch them. No way would she let another handsome face lead her into a pointless relationship.

If his morals were so low that he'd bet on baseball, they were low enough to cheat on her, too.

She jerked her hand away and folded her arms.

"Sorry." His lips twitched into a frown. "I didn't mean—I'm not trying to be romantic."

"No, it's fine." She let her arms fall to her lap. "I'm still raw about the wedding is all."

"Well, Stephen was stupid. Sorry if I caught you off guard. You seem like a great girl, Melanie. After you were so upset, taking your hand felt... right. Like I needed to do something else to comfort you. I'm glad we're becoming friends. I don't have that many friends these days."

"Friends is fine, but no holding hands." She interlocked her fingers. "But I'm glad you're my friend, too. I'd be sitting up here miserable and starving if not for you. Maybe when this is all over we can do something normal together."

She regretted the words as soon as she'd said them. It was like her brain existed in an alternate universe or something. Mixed signals.

But Kyle didn't seem to mind. He moved to the ladder and disappeared under the deck. "See you later, Melanie."

"Bye, Kyle." Her heart thundered. Stupid involuntary reaction. But she had to face the truth. She didn't want him to go.

Chapter Eight

Tuesday evening. Four days down, and nine to go. Easy peasy.

Melanie flipped the page of the Christian fiction novel Kyle had brought her and shifted away from the direct glare of the lowering sun. The smoky, piquant aroma of barbecued meat curled around her nostrils, finding its way into her lungs. She could almost taste the ginormous vat of sauce sitting on the edge of the white tables.

"Testin'... one, two, three."

Daddy's thick country twang pierced the silence.

She sat straighter. Where had the time gone?

She'd gotten caught up in the story in spite of herself— she'd never seen herself reading anything like that. But Kyle had found an author who wrote about broken soldiers. There was a whole line of books on his deceased grandmother's shelf, and this was the first of them. Said he thought Melanie might like it because military men carry guns.

Military men carried guns. She laughed. When all this was over, she would teach that boy how to shoot and show him that former baseball players could carry guns, too.

She turned to the cover and traced her finger over the matte face of the hero. Ben. A strong man with muscular arms and broad shoulders who'd first reminded her of Stephen. As his attraction grew for Keeley, the female lead in the story, emotions swept over Melanie that she'd sworn she'd never allow her heart to feel again. Not soon, anyway.

But now, as she read more into chapter seventeen, images of Kyle filled her mind. Kind, at least on the surface. Thoughtful, and intensely handsome. Muscles that bulged out of his T-shirt, but a touch so gentle that he seemed to think she might break. Dangerous. She closed her eyes, seeing the news article announcing his fall from grace. Unlike the hero—he was dishonest, untrustworthy, unreliable. How many days would he help her until he got tired of it?

She frowned. He should get tired of it. Like the heroine, she was a spoiled brat. But Stephen had thirteen days, and she was going to see them through. Kyle or no Kyle.

Three notes from Daddy's banjo resonated from a microphone onstage across from the church parking lot. Two taller men walked up beside him, one carrying a washboard and the other a bright blue fiddle. They tuned the instruments then descended the stage and stood with their backs to the billboard.

Nature called. Melanie sighed, scrambling to the deck ladder with two baby wipes in her fist. Her shimmy down the ladder resembled a choreographed dance. Some of the branches had weakened under Kyle's steps, so she lunged for the rope and swung like Tarzan, pushing off a tree with the soles of her shoes.

When she landed, she raced along the river to the four close-spaced trees that had become something like an outhouse for her. As she squatted, a skunk meandered along the path she'd just come. It sniffed the ground, its proud white-striped tail waving behind it like a flag.

Great. That was all she needed. Kyle would stop helping her for sure if he had to climb back up to that stench. She held her breath. Twenty. Twenty-five. Thirty. Thirty-five.

The black-and-white beast caught a salamander in its mouth and pranced off opposite the way Melanie had come.

Her chest heaved as she stood and made her way back to the path. She ran, used the rope to pull herself up the tree, and leapt over to the ladder. When she reached the top, Daddy still stood with the two men facing the opposite direction. He'd squared his shoulders and tipped his chin high. No doubt, she wasn't on his mind at all. And it was just as well. Daddy deserved this moment.

When the man who owned the Bluegrass Barn shut it down, Daddy lost his venue. Other managers found him too old to star in a new show, and he quickly tired of gigs playing second fiddle to, as he put it, some "young, cocky whippersnapper."

This event seemed like it might be a big deal, too. Daddy had enough talent if he could get a little more exposure. People had forgotten why they loved him. Maybe this barbecue would give his music a second wind.

Melanie pressed her palm against her chest. She should be down there beside him. Supporting him.

But then again, he should have been beside her on Saturday. Supporting her. Not sending some stranger to talk her down.

Workers dragged white plastic tables from the church, both rectangles and circles, and they covered them all with tablecloths. They carried stainless-steel chaffers and three tall coolers from the back of a truck and lined them across three of the rectangular tables. Cars arrived in droves, and lines of people dragged blankets and lawn chairs to the big field behind the church.

Within minutes, children had overtaken the fenced-in playground, and the older ones tumbled and raced in the field with a football. Melanie's heart ached. Before Stephen, she'd shared many a night like this with Daddy, standing next to the stage in a long flowing skirt, clapping and singing along as the children danced beside her.

Thirteen months, and she hadn't been to a single show, even though Stephen claimed to be a huge fan. And Daddy, joining up with this preacher now? Performing a free concert for the community? Well, he knew exactly what he was doing. She crossed her arms over her chest. She still wasn't coming down.

Beside the back carport of the church, a man climbed a double-decker ladder and fiddled with an enormous floodlight. Mama had remarked about the light while they decorated for her reception.

"Such an eyesore," she'd said, and they'd debated for twenty minutes what its purpose might be.

"Guess now you know, Mama." Squinting, Melanie scanned the crowd for Mama's tight up-do. No sign of her. Not that there would be.

By dark, the crowd had tripled what her wedding had drawn. Rows of people in folding chairs faced the stage, holding white boxes in their laps. Her stomach growling, Melanie wrapped up in the blanket Kyle had brought her and sat cross-legged by the deck ladder.

A bulky, white-bearded man took the stage. "Ladies and Gentlemen…"

It reminded Melanie of the days Daddy spent watching wrestling. She half-expected the man to ask the crowd if they were ready to "rumple," like the goofy old announcer used to say.

Rustling beneath her culminated with a light ping as Kyle's rope looped around the deck rail. She secured it, leaned over the edge, and waved at him.

"Hey!" With a wide grin, he tied the rope to his basket and hoisted it up.

"Hey, yourself!" She reached for the basket, coming up shy. Intense smells drifted to her—savory spices and sweet aromas. "You brought barbecue. I could so kiss you right now."

Kyle wrinkled his nose, and she shrunk back to the billboard. Why had she said that? He'd think she was trying to flirt or something. Or… had he even heard her? Maybe he was concentrating on climbing the tree. He didn't answer, so she peeked over the edge again.

Wearing the same expression, he maneuvered the tree, making his way through the branches to the pole. He met her at the top with a white plastic bag containing four Styrofoam boxes. She could almost taste the sweet, smoky barbecue without even opening the box.

"Took you long enough." She grinned.

He shook his head. "That daddy of yours. He's a talker."

"Yeah. Why did you get so much food?" She took the bag from him and removed the top three boxes, catching a few spice grains on her pointer finger. "Are we expecting someone else?"

"Not exactly." His easy grin spread across his face. "Wayne sent you something and I thought you might like some pork fritters and dessert."

He climbed up beside her, grabbed the fourth box from the bag, and held it out to her.

When she opened it, she gasped. "Are you kidding me?" She lifted a folded red bandana skirt and set the box aside.

"He said you need to wear it over your jeans. People might see up your dress." Kyle covered his eyes and peeked through his fingers. "God forbid."

She snickered and stood. "He would say that."

As she slid the skirt over her hips, Kyle caught the hem of it. "My mom used to wear a dress like this, except it was blue."

She twirled then sat, and they dug into the meal—crispy pork fritters, chicken so tender it slid off the bone, Texas toast, creamy coleslaw, and spicy baked beans.

"I didn't get any corn." Kyle trilled air over his lips. "The line was so long, and—"

"I don't mind." Melanie patted his knee. "I appreciate the food. And everything you've done for me. When this is all over I'm going to have to return the favor."

Kyle muttered under his breath and shot her another grin. Did she imagine it, or did he mumble something about a kiss? Good grief. Shouldn't she be thinking about Stephen now?

When twilight fell, Daddy strummed the beginning to the group's first song, triggering an involuntary tap of her toes. The preacher manned the audio equipment while another man turned the spotlight directly on Daddy. He played his heart out, and the crowd got to their feet. She should be down there.

She finished her chocolate cake then sat on her hands while Kyle drummed his tennis shoes on the edge of the deck. Resting her head against the billboard, she sighed as the spotlight rolled across the crowd.

From the distance, she couldn't meet Daddy's eyes, but his face lifted toward her as he played. Truly in his element, he played to her heart. No question about that. But she still wasn't coming down.

When the song ended, Daddy took a small bow with the other three men onstage, and the bearded one pushed him forward. "Mr. Wayne Lee Turner, ladies and gentlemen."

The crowd roared and the spotlight turned to a light blue shade. It passed over them, illuminating circles of faces and waving hands. After a few wild gyrations, it settled directly on her.

"Oh, no." Goosebumps raced over her entire body. "Daddy, no. Please." She hid her face behind trembling hands.

Kyle scooted to the ladder and sat on the top rung.

"That there's a wide deck up there from what I can see." Daddy nodded toward her. "And the pretty brown-haired girl in front of the billboard—well, that's my daughter, Melanie. Stubborn as the day is long, that girl. Everyone say hi to Melanie."

A light breeze carried their shouts and hoots, and she cringed.

Beside her, Kyle clapped his hands. "Whoo Hoo! Helllllloooo, Miss Melanie."

"Shut up." She narrowed her gaze at him.

"I'd like to dedicate our next song to Melly." Daddy's left hand slid up the neck of the banjo. "Come on, Pun'kin. Stand up and clog it for us. In place is good enough. Don't want you to fall off the deck."

Kyle snorted.

"Stop it." She folded her arms across her chest as the crowd chanted her name.

79

"You'd better get on up, darlin'" Daddy strummed a couple lines. "We're not taking that spotlight off you until you dance for us. And we can do this every night if we need to until you get yourself down."

Even from the distance, she could see Daddy's grin. He'd do it. He played the first few notes of "Rocky Top," and she sighed and stood.

The deck barely gave her room to clog, and certainly not room to move like she usually did. But she'd show him. She clogged her heart out to the rhythm, holding on to the upper support of the billboard as she turned. When the song finished, she bowed, and the crowd hooted and hollered.

Well, there was something to be said for keeping her chin up.

When the spotlight returned to the stage, Kyle joined Melanie and clapped his hands to the first lines of Blue Ridge Mountain Blues. He leaned over and chuckled. "Once, I met a girl on a billboard sign. She was half huntress, and the other part..." He scratched his chin.

"The other part—what?" Melanie twisted her brown curls at the base of her neck then let them spill over her shoulders.

Angel. His mouth hung open, but he couldn't make the sound come out. Her natural beauty and rosy cheeks—if he'd drawn out what his soulmate might look like, he couldn't have described her better. Not that he wanted to get tied down to a woman, but Melanie fit his ideal.

"The other part what?" She slammed her fists against her hips. "Tell me."

"I haven't decided yet." He moved closer, grasping her upper arms and leaving about a foot between them. "Yep. I haven't decided yet." Resting his chin on her head, he closed the gap between them.

A pine needle poked out from her hair. He pulled it out. Then he brushed his fingers through her hair and curled it around his finger. He was right. Exactly like touching an angel. "Dance with me, Melanie."

She shivered. Was it the huskiness in his voice or the slight chill of the June night air. "We'd fall. You're going to get us both killed."

"You clogged and it worked out fine." He backed away from her, knelt, and brought up the rope. After tossing it over the upper billboard frame, he threaded it through three of his belt loops and handed her the other end. "Your turn."

She smiled, revealing her gorgeous dimples, her eyes twinkling like starlight. She took her end of the rope and fed it through her belt loops then they tied it securely to the rail.

"This is ridiculous." Laughing, she eased back into his arms.

"Sitting on a billboard sign for days on end to make a point isn't?" He tapped his pointer finger to the tip of her nose. "So, being as I bought your dinner, we're at a concert, and now we're dancing, could we consider this our first date?"

A frown flickered across her face and a tear sprung from the corner of her left eye. She pushed him away, her gaze trained on his face.

Stupid. Why had he said that? He always pushed things too quickly, and with her coming off an engagement, he'd made things worse for both of them.

But then, her lips curled up sideways. "Maybe."

He squeezed her arms. So this… the burst of energy and blood racing through his veins… the heart palpitations which were embarrassingly more like a woman's flutter than he'd like to admit… This was what Lacey had wanted him to feel.

And the rush—a vaguely familiar rush…

Over her shoulder a few miles away, the bright lights of baseball illuminated the skyline. He knew that rush. The rush of the game. Was it possible he could be growing to love something —no, someone—as much as the game? Could he move on with his life and not feel that void?

He studied the splay of freckles that crossed the bridge of her nose, then his gaze found its way to her eyes. "So, how is it for a first date, then?"

She rested her head against his shoulder. "Barbecue, giggles, dancing... best first date, ever."

Really? She'd seemed so distant moments earlier, but now she leaned toward him? "Is that so?" He tipped up her chin. "Well, Miss Melly, I think you promised to repay me with a kiss. Do you kiss on a first date?"

Surprise flickered across her face, and she gripped his arm tighter. "Only the good ones."

"Is this a good one?" With a deep breath, he inched closer, sweet barbecue sauce sticking to his lower lip as he met hers. He raised his arm and placed his hand on the back of her head... as the spotlight found them again.

The banjo stopped, and the other instruments faded. A hush spread over the crowd, and Melanie stumbled a couple steps backward. "I'm sorry. I shouldn't have—"

"Son?" Wayne's mic screeched. "What do you think you're doing with my daughter?"

Chapter Nine

When Kyle released her, Melanie landed square on her bottom. She freed herself from his makeshift restraint and faced the stage where Daddy waved a fisted hand over his head.

It was embarrassing, sure, but thank goodness for Daddy. She'd come so close to letting her guard all the way down. And there for the world to see.

Her phone chimed with Mama's ringtone. Fantastic. Mama was in the crowd. Yep. There she stood, leaning up against the stage with a hand on her left hip. Why had she come? Mama had stopped going to Daddy's performances a long time ago. She hated barbecues. Had Daddy talked her into letting him orchestrate this whole thing so he could humiliate her and try to get her down?

No way Melanie could answer right now. She could hear the chiding. "Melanie, are you crazy? Out of the frying pan into another fire? Have you already forgotten Stephen? Have you forgotten the public embarrassment you've already wrought on our family? You have no money, no car, no job… Girl, what are you going to do with your life?"

Melanie ducked her head as the spotlight shifted. Mama would be right, too. How wrong was it to be flirting and dancing with another guy when she'd just ended an engagement? And to almost kiss him? If only the billboard lights would go out, then she could bury her face and have a good cry.

Kyle scooted away from her and started down the ladder.

"Where are you going?" Pulling herself upright, she gritted her teeth. "Leaving me up here to suffer all this by myself?"

83

He sat on the top rung and leaned back against the deck. "There are news crews down there, Melanie. We'll be all over the gossip sites in the morning. I don't need this kind of publicity. Not after—"

"Not after you made a public mistake?" She pointed to the crowd, where a sea of heads had turned their direction. "Kyle, sometimes you have to face the music before you can move on with your life."

"I have to face the music?" He burst into bitter laughter. "Like the jilted bride who climbs up a pole and refuses to come down?"

She bit her lip. Why had she even said that? "I didn't mean… Look, I meant that it might help people to realize how sorry you were if you didn't completely hide from the public."

He lifted himself back up to the deck and stretched his feet out beside the ladder. "I've tweeted since it happened. It earned me more grief."

"But you haven't apologized. Have you?" She scrunched her nose. How had she let him smooth-talk her so easily? He was a cheater. Like Stephen. No remorse. "Well, other than that awful PR statement they forced you to make."

His lips twitched. "You watched that?"

"I was curious." She crossed her arms. "And speaking of apologies, tonight was a mistake. I led you on, and I'm sorry."

Kyle's chest heaved and his eyes darkened. "It was a mistake. You're right to not trust me. I kiss every girl on the first date. It would have been a special kiss for you and a trivial one for me."

"Well, then." Why did her stupid lip have to quiver? "Guess we dodged that bullet. Maybe you should climb down and go back to your cows. Leave me alone."

"I didn't mean to hurt you." He tapped his fingers on the deck. "I got caught up in the moment. That's all. You're a beautiful woman, Melanie. Strong-willed, and desirable. Exactly the type I go for." His chin dipped. "Maybe you're right. I need to stay away from you.

Which is why you need to get down from this billboard and get off my property. Well, Pa's property."

He thought she was desirable? No, stop. She couldn't let him distract her from her purpose. "Oh, no you don't." She pressed her fists into her elbows. "I'm not leaving until Stephen comes back and says he's sorry."

"What if he never comes back? Are you planning to stay up here forever?"

"Thirteen days."

"Thirteen days. That's ridiculous."

"Don't mock me." Her eyes narrowed to slits. "Kyle Casey, I want you to go away. Right now. Get down from this billboard and leave me alone."

"Fine."

"Fine."

He lowered himself to the ladder, stopping when his head poked above the deck. "Mel, I am sorry."

"Don't call me Mel."

"But I am sorry."

She scooted toward her PVC shelter and slid behind the curtain. "Whatever."

Banjo music blared across the courtyard. Not Daddy's. Melanie peeked out the curtain to the stage. A short, scrawny man had taken over for him. And Daddy's truck had left its parking spot. There it was, spinning the gravel along the driveway to Kyle's house. Great.

A few minutes later, Daddy's shout bellowed at the base of the sign post. She crawled out of the curtain and climbed partway down the ladder.

"Melanie Dawn, get yourself down here this instant." Daddy hobbled closer, wincing.

"Are you hurt?" She frowned. Selfish Melly strikes again. He'd probably twisted his ankle or something in his rush to get here.

85

"I'm fine. But you need to come on home."

She shook her head and gripped the rung tighter. "What did you think, you'd shame me into it? That having all those people staring and laughing at me would lessen my resolve?"

Daddy braced himself against a tree. "You're twenty-six years old. Well past the age to be throwing fits like this. And then, to be up there smooching on another fella right after what happened... well, you're not being very consistent. That's for sure."

"I'm hurting!" She hurled the words at him with a fury that melted when he dragged his fist across his right eye. Was he crying?

"That was my fault, Wayne." Kyle stepped out of the shadows. "I got caught up in the moment and lost my senses. Knew she was vulnerable, too. I shouldn't have gotten so close."

"I oughta get my shotgun and teach you a lesson."

"I deserve that." Kyle ducked his head. "I'm sorry, Wayne. You trusted me to take care of her and I—"

"Don't need anyone to take care of me!" Rage bubbled in her chest. "I am a grown woman. I'm not some brittle child." She climbed up a rung. "We only danced for a couple minutes. It's not like we had an overnight tryst."

"It looked bad." Daddy's cell rang, and he fished it out of his pocket. "That mama of yours has been driving me crazy all day, and now it's amplified tenfold."

Melanie crinkled her nose. Mama would. "What does she think about you shaming me in front of a crowd?"

Daddy chuckled. "She gripes about everything I do. You know that."

"And you do what you want anyway." Melanie blew him a kiss. "Which is why I'm climbing back up and waiting on Stephen. After tonight, there's no way I can back down."

Kyle trudged down the path to Pa's truck, Wayne following a few feet behind him. When he reached the driver's-side door, he patted his pocket. Shoot. Forgot the key fob.

"Somethin' wrong?" Wayne came up beside him and slapped his shoulder.

"Dropped my keys in that bag with the food." He rubbed his left eye with his palm. "Guess I'll have to go back up and get them."

"Before you do, let's have us a talk." Wayne moved to the open tailgate and pulled himself up. "What were you thinking, trying to romance my daughter?"

Kyle kicked at a tuft of grass then walked around the truck to join him. "I don't know, Wayne. But you're right. I have no business trying to romance anyone's daughter. I've made so many mistakes lately. I'd hate for her to be another one. Especially with her coming off a broken heart. She's amazing, though. Funny, quirky, and beautiful. How could I not be enticed by that?"

Wayne leaned closer, his strong spearmint gum stinging Kyle's nostrils. "Let me tell you a secret, son. I'm convinced that girl never loved Stephen. She was so bent on doing everything by thirteens. She had to marry him, you know. He was her thirteenth boyfriend. Melanie and that crazy number thirteen."

"She's told me a little about that. So why did you let her almost marry him?"

"Girl's got to make her own mistakes." Wayne grinned. "But who do you think let the cat out of the bag that he'd had an affair?"

"Are you serious?" Kyle jerked to face him. "How long did you know about it? Why didn't you tell her?"

"She'd have never believed me." Wayne combed his salt-and-pepper hair with his fingers. "And I only knew a couple days. I never thought he'd go through with the wedding. Expected him to back out of it the whole time. So, when it got closer, I hired a private investigator to look into his affairs."

"And you caught him cheating."

"He spent the weekend with another girl in a cabin." A snarl crept over Wayne's face. "I slipped the pictures in an envelope and put them on one of her bridesmaid's seats. Figured it might come better from one of them."

"Maybe." Kyle picked a gravel loose from his bed liner and tossed it to the ground. "But what if she hadn't told Melanie? Would you have stopped the wedding?"

Wayne shrugged, his broad shoulders rising so high they framed his face. "I'd have probably sucker-punched him before ever walking her down the aisle. Much to the chagrin of her dear mama, of course."

Kyle swung his legs under the tailgate. He deserved a sucker-punch, too. It was easy to villainize this Stephen guy, but if Lacey hadn't caught him cheating, would he have gone through with marrying her? Would he have kept cheating?

"So, out with it, Kyle. Save me the money of hiring an investigator for you. What are your intentions with my daughter, and what nasty skeletons are hiding in your past?" Wayne chortled. "Well, most of yours are public, I gather. Tell me why you decided to bet on baseball."

"I don't have any intentions, Wayne. I've always been more of a spur-of-the-moment kind of guy. That's my problem." Kyle hopped off the tailgate and moved to a large tree stump. He ripped off a piece of grass and tore it into thin shreds. "I've enjoyed talking and laughing with her. It felt great to get to know someone who didn't treat me like a pro baseball player. And tonight, the music and the atmosphere... dancing with her felt right."

"So you haven't been trying to talk her into climbing down?"

Kyle scuffed his shoe over a large root. "I guess I was trying to give her something to climb down to. Distract her from her pain and make her want to face life again."

"And the baseball? Your affair?"

The knot in Kyle's stomach twisted. Might as well tell him the whole story. "The girl's name was Lacey Robbins. She was a spitfire like Melanie. And obsessed with me." He swallowed. "We dated for a little over a year, and she talked me into an engagement."

"What's that have to do with baseball?" Wayne held his foot out in front of him and flexed it, wincing. "Why'd it make you gamble?"

"One night after a game, we went club-hopping with some of the fans, celebrating Roderick Flynn's winning home run. I drank too much and cheated on her with a team groupie, and she caught me."

"Yep. I read all about it."

Kyle raised his hand to his head and dragged his fingers through his hair. If Wayne knew, then why'd he ask? "Well, I felt awful, but no amount of apologies would fix it. She broke up with me."

"As she should have."

"Her brother was my best friend from college. A teammate who loved baseball and gambling. He acted like nothing had happened between me and Lacey and kept taking me out with him to clubs." Kyle puffed out a long, unsteady breath. "And then he started in on me. Wanted me to throw a game. I refused, of course."

Wayne shook his head. "Let me guess. He kept after you with the betting and turned you in."

"Pretty much." Kyle ripped apart a second blade of grass and started on the third. "Don't know if you follow baseball, but remember when Kevin Snedeker had that bad shoulder injury? We all knew we'd lose the game. Daylen, her brother, caught me at a low moment, and talked me into placing the bet. Guess he had someone waiting to snap my picture and ruin my life the way I ruined his sister's. I didn't even realize he was upset over it."

He buried his face in his hands and closed his eyes. How had he been so stupid? Though he'd had a few drinks and recreational drugs at parties, he'd avoided falling in the pits of alcoholism and addiction that had plagued many of his teammates. But women? Always a weakness.

Wayne's hand gripped his shoulder. "Chin up, Son. Pa wouldn't want you sitting around feeling sorry for yourself. He wants you to get your life back together, right? Don't you think that's why he's brought you here?"

"I'm sure it is. I'm sorry, Wayne. I'd feel terrible if I hurt Melanie in any way. She's such a sweet girl."

"You're not the only one who's made a mistake or two with women." Wayne cleared his throat. "Now, Melanie doesn't know this, but her mama and I have hit a few rocky patches along in our marriage. Twice, I strayed, and Louisa's forgiven me."

"You cheated?" Kyle lifted his gaze.

"I gave in to temptation when my songs climbed the bluegrass charts and got some attention from fans. But I've been faithful for the last twenty-two years. It was a mindset change. A matter of deciding that I'd be true to her no matter what and sticking to it." Wayne nodded to his truck. "Get in, and I'll drive you back to the house. Think I remember where your Pa hid his spare house key. You can get the truck keys tomorrow when she cools off."

"I didn't want to cheat." Kyle stood and paced, his hands shoved in his pockets. He meandered to the side of the truck and opened the passenger door. "And I've stopped drinking. Although, I've wanted to lose myself in a bottle of whiskey every day since it happened."

When they pulled up to the house, Wayne lifted a brick at the edge of the flowerbed and came out with a small metal key chain. "Here you go, Kylie. You can be a better man. Remember where you came from." A wry grin spanned his cheeks. "When we boys get to thinkin' we're bigger than our britches, we get ourselves into trouble. It's like the old preacher said this morning. We have to be humble. Lesser by choice. Stop worrying about falling off your own pedestal and work on lifting someone else's up."

"I'll stay away from Melanie from now on." Kyle let himself into the house and held the door open a crack. "Well, I'll get the truck keys tomorrow, and then stay out of her way."

Wayne stared at him for a long moment. "At least for now. I'll be here at six in the morning, and we'll take care of that hay."

"Sounds good. See you." Kyle fastened the chain and pushed the door closed, exhaling in relief. And gratitude for the unexpected fatherly support. He scratched his goatee. If he didn't know better, he'd say Wayne might not be all that opposed to the relationship.

Chapter Ten

A car horn jolted Melanie from her fitful sleep. She lifted the bottom of her shower-curtain canopy and scowled. All those people, and so early in the morning. What were they doing?

Three men lugged plastic lawn chairs into the church parking lot. They set them out and one man returned to his truck for a cooler. Were they watching… her?

She powered up her phone and checked the notifications. Mistake. Apparently, everyone in America loved reading about Kyle's mysterious billboard girlfriend, almost as much as they'd loved gossiping about his fall from baseball grace. Somehow, they'd found her Twitter username and Facebook page. Why had she not made it private? So many comments. None of them flattering.

No sense in reading them. They probably all said the same thing. She was an idiot. An idiot for throwing her fit, an idiot for letting it last for four days now, and an idiot for letting some other guy charm her when she'd been played a fool.

She deleted thirty-seven messages from her "other" folder without reading them. Holding her finger poised above the screen, a name caught her eye. A pretty redhead.

Lacey. Hadn't she seen or heard that name before?

Her heart pounding, she clicked on the message.

Dear Melanie,

You don't know me, but I used to date Kyle Casey. I thought we'd get married, but he broke my heart the same way your fiancé broke yours. Promised me everything and cheated on me. Watch yourself.

If you know what's good for you, you'll stay far away from Kyle.
If I could, I'd drive down to Milton and sit up there with you. Best
wishes, and I hope your pain eases soon.

Lacey Robbins.

Her jaw clenched. Another reminder. He was a rotten cheater like
Stephen. Thank goodness Daddy caught them before she'd let things
go any farther.

After five straight hours in the early morning sun, Kyle popped into
Pa's house for a shower. He dug out the old clippers and trimmed
his hair short, then shaved off his goatee. Facial hair and farm sweat
didn't mix.

And, it wasn't bad. A long morning, but not bad. Perfect bales of
hay dotted the field, and he'd finally learned how to drive the tractor
in a straight line. Wayne had even told him he did a good job.

His stomach growled. Melanie must be starving. And probably
furious he didn't bring her anything for breakfast. He tore through
the cupboards and scrounged up a couple of peanut-butter
sandwiches. Then, he shook his head. She'd be a lot hungrier than
that.

Twenty minutes later, he'd grilled chicken and vegetables and
packed it all up in a cooler. He grabbed a couple sodas and some of
the miniature Hershey bars from Pa's candy jar. When he walked out
to the truck, he smacked the top of his head. He'd forgotten it was
still parked back at the billboard.

He could walk. But it was a long walk in the hot sun. He kicked
up a piece of gravel and flinched as it struck the tractor. Oh, wait!
The tractor. Slower, but still. It beat walking. He'd come back for it
later when the sun started going down.

As he cruised at turtle speed across the field, the cows' ears
perked. They marched in a line toward the tractor.

"No. Go back, you stupid beasts." He adjusted the speed to the higher setting, labeled "rabbit" and pressed down hard on the pedal. "Can't this thing go any faster?"

The cows closed their distance. Who knew they could even move at that speed?

He glanced over his shoulder. "I'm not feeding you right now!"

Food. He blasted air from his cheeks like an explosion. He'd forgotten the cooler with the food.

Making a wide arc, he turned the tractor back toward the barn lot and parked it. He raced back into the house as the phone rang.

A number popped up on the caller ID. Some random area code he'd never seen before. Probably a telejerk, but what if it was something important? He tapped the counter then snatched the phone from its cradle. "Hello?"

"Kylie." Pa's raspy voice carried a hint of excitement.

"Pa. It's about time you called." Kyle laughed. "I've had a battle and a half with your cattle."

"What's this I hear about you kissing some girl up on that church billboard?"

"I didn't kiss her." Kyle palmed his forehead. "And how did you hear about it?"

"Arlene saw it on the Facebook. It was trendy in her news page." Pa let out a wheezy cough. "Think I'm going to have to get me one of those Facebooks."

"You're going to have to lay off those cigars, Pa." Kyle shook his head. Some things never changed. But some things apparently did. *The Facebook. Trendy.* "Hey, there's not a spare key to your truck, is there?"

"In the kitchen drawer. But Kylie, the reason I called is because of the church. Paul told me they've had people sitting in the yard all night long trying to get a glimpse of you two. It's going to make it hard for them to have services tonight. I want you to go over there and talk to them. Make them leave. And get the girl down."

"Melanie. She's not 'the girl,' Pa." The junk drawer jammed and he tugged it loose from its track. "So, about the stuff you wanted me to do on the farm—"

"Wayne Lee's girl." Pa laughed. "You'd do well to land a Turner. But you need to get yourself together first."

"I'm trying." Kyle glanced at the keys and shoved the drawer back into its compartment. "So, anyway, you left me a note to fix the fence. But I haven't found the place where it needs—"

Click. That was Pa. When the conversation was over, it was over.

Kyle grabbed the cooler and headed out to the tractor. As he drove across the field, the cows turned up their noses. Had to love them.

When he reached the billboard, he tossed up the rope. Ten seconds later, it flew back to the ground.

"Hey!" He shaded his eyes and looked up the ladder. "Melanie!"

No answer.

He threw the rope again, managing to loop it over the rail. It slipped off and landed at his feet. Was she not there? "Melanie Dawn Turner, you answer me."

"What?" Her crisp voice came from behind him.

Pivoting, his face twisted in surprise. "What are you doing?"

"Look at you with your baby face and buzz cut. Suits you." She held up a dead squirrel. "I'm catching my lunch."

"You're going to eat *that*?" His stomach lurched. "How are you going to cook it?"

Grinning, she pointed to the deck. "I saved that aluminum foil from the barbecue and fashioned myself a sun oven."

"A sun oven."

"Yep." She brushed past him and slung the squirrel over her shoulder, its tail knotted in a sling she'd made from one of the bandanas he'd brought her. In mere seconds, she scaled the pine and hopped over to the ladder. "Our chemistry teacher had us make one

95

back in high school. We grilled hot dogs using the reflected rays. I don't see any reason I can't clean and grill a squirrel."

"Other than it's gross." He held out the bag. "I brought you food. Made grilled chicken and veggies, and even brought you some chocolate and an Ale-8."

"I don't want anything from you, Kyle." She took a deep breath. "Well, maybe I do want the chicken. And the chocolate. But that's it."

"Can I bring it up?"

"Suit yourself."

When they both reached the deck, his breath caught. Her soft brown hair glistened and wispy strands blew about her face. So pretty, and so dangerous. He needed to leave her alone, or he'd hurt her like he did Lacey. And those eyes… they must have darkened thirty shades.

"We have company." She gestured to the church parking lot below. "So I went for a swim. Washed my hair. It felt great."

"How did you get down without…?" He stifled a snicker as she flattened her body, crawling across the deck to her curtain. She'd lined the rail with the bandanas, giving herself a perfect cover. In a few seconds, she emerged from the curtain, stretching her arms. Shouts rang from the parking lot, and he cackled. "Oh, you're a sneaky one."

"Well, that tree perfectly blocks the ladder." She scooped up her shoes, propped in a cross on a Styrofoam box so they stuck above the rail. "And if a bunch of idiots want to stare at a pair of empty sneakers all day, that's fine by me." Her lips dipped into a frown. "If you come up here, they'll all talk about you."

"I'll stay here on the ladder." He winked. "They'll think you're talking to yourself."

She scooted close to the ladder and took her portion of the meal. The crowd across the lot stirred, and he looped the bag handle over his wrist.

"You know what, think I'll leave you alone, like you asked. But I will bring you supper tonight."

She tipped up her chin. "That's okay. I got my squirrel."

"Whatever floats your boat."

He climbed down and hiked to the gate. Pa's spare set had at least fifteen keys. Surely one would open it.

The eighth key finally turned in the lock. He got in and circled to the back of the building, hopping the fence so he'd be approaching them from behind.

A sixty-something white-haired man stood at the side door, his arms folded. A middle-aged redheaded woman tapped her foot next to him. Squaring his shoulders, Kyle approached them.

"Are you the preacher?" He flashed the man a quick smile.

"Yes, sir." The man extended his hand. "Paul Mitchell."

"Like the hair guy?"

Paul chuckled as the redhead went back into the church. "Sadly, no. Unfortunately, I'm losing mine. What can I do for you?"

Kyle swallowed. "Well, you see, that's Pa's farm next door, and I'm real sorry, but—"

"Kyle Casey." Paul swept him into a hug. "Your pa said you might drop by. Have to say, I didn't recognize you without the facial hair. And, that buzz cut. It's a good look for you."

"I guess so." Kyle patted Paul's back then pulled away. "Anyway, about this crowd. I take full responsibility, and I can ask them to leave if you—"

"Nonsense." Paul pointed to the stage, still up from the barbecue. "I'm getting ready to preach me a sermon. It's not very often I have a whole crowd of potential sitting in my parking lot."

"You're going to preach to these people?" Kyle pointed to a bald man with a cooler popping the top on a beer. "They don't seem like your type."

"Might as well. Isn't that my job? What I was called to do?"

"I guess so."

Paul nodded to the billboard. "Wayne Lee's stubborn daughter might be the best thing to ever happen to this church. We've gotten so much free publicity. Had two baptisms this morning. A couple who listened to all my sermons on the webpage and decided to obey the gospel. vWayne Lee himself has attended two services. Such a blessing. And such a pleasure to hear him sing last night. I let him have my place, and the crowd loved it."

"But Pa said you were…" Kyle scratched his chin. "Oh, wait. I bet this was his ploy to get me over here talking to you."

Paul pulled a mic from his suit coat pocket and plugged it into an extension cord. "Maybe so. But I'm glad you stopped by. Your pa's been coming to this church for six years now. Became a Christian within weeks of attending. Turned his life over to God and found happiness he didn't think possible. And a wife."

"Pa, a Christian?" Kyle snorted. "He used to hassle Mom and Dad all the time for their missionary work. Regardless, he lied to me. Told me I was coming home for his funeral."

Paul's shoulders shook, and he laughed from deep in his belly. "I don't think he lied on purpose. Your poor ol' pa kept accidentally calling it a funeral. Couldn't bring himself to say wedding, maybe. It about drove Sharon crazy."

"So you don't want me to ask all these people to leave, then?" Kyle started back toward the gate.

"No."

"Well, I guess I'll see you around."

Paul placed a light hand on Kyle's wrist. "You know, even if the Commissioner of Baseball won't forgive you, God will."

Kyle jerked his hand away. "I don't need forgiveness."

"We all need forgiveness, Kyle. For all our sins. And we all deserve a chance at peace. Don't you want that, Kyle? Peace? And love?"

Love. Kyle's jaw twitched. Maybe he did want love. Maybe God was giving him a second chance—at love and everything.

"You know, Paul, I do want peace and love. And I want that for Melanie. Do you think I'm wrong for helping her? Or for hoping we might find our way together? All those people have said so many things on social media. Am I crazy for standing by her?"

Paul shielded his eyes from the blazing sun and squinted toward the billboard. "There's never any reason to apologize for kindness, Kyle. The more good you can do for others in this life, the better off you'll be. Is it too soon to jump into a relationship with her? I'd say yes. I wouldn't even think about trying until you've both healed. Crazy for helping her? Not at all. You're learning compassion. Make it more about your service than what she can emotionally return to you."

Kyle glanced at the marquee in front of the church, where letters of different sizes covered the sign. *Let us not grow weary of doing good... Galatians 6:9 Join us this Sunday morning and learn about Christian service.*

Christian service. How many times had Mom and Dad said the same thing? How many times had they chided him about the good he could do with his money instead of hoarding it? Maybe he should listen for once and hear what Brother Mitchell had to say.

Chapter Eleven

Melanie shrunk, covering her ears as the microphone squeaked. Worse than nails on a chalkboard. Brother Mitchell. The man who she and Stephen had conned through six sessions of marital counseling that they were ready. The preacher who'd almost pronounced them man and wife. The aspiring Bluegrass musician who'd charmed Daddy. He now stood in front of Kyle and faced the crowd. Next thing she knew, Kyle would probably be singing her a love song, and she'd have to sneak off to the woods again.

"I'd like to thank you all for coming out this afternoon for our Wednesday afternoon service. When the police stopped by this afternoon, I told them not to bother you. I was glad for the audience." Brother Mitchell jumped off the stage and moved closer to where they all sat in their lawn chairs.

Several of the men scrambled to shove containers in their coolers.

"Oh, no rush." Brother Mitchell held up his right hand. "Let's start things off right. How about a round of Amazing Grace?"

His rich tenor boomed across the lot and drifted up to where she sat, sending chills down her spine. "I once was lost, but now I'm found…"

Did she imagine it? Two burly guys at the edge of the crowd joined in.

While he sang the rest of the song, she pressed her back against the sign. When was the last time she'd ever done anything with that kind of passion? Had she ever?

"If you guys have the time, I'd like to tell you a story." Brother Mitchell paced in front of the crowd. His authoritative voice could have carried to the billboard without a microphone. "Have you ever been broken?"

Broken. The word struck her heart. Was she ever.

"I mean, like really broken. Low as you can possibly be. No money, no food, no hope?"

A woman in the front raised her hand. About six people near her started toward the cars.

"Well, I've been broken." Brother Mitchell clears his throat. "Before I became a preacher, I was a blackjack dealer in Vegas."

The six people stopped mid-step.

"Abandoned my family. Shot up cocaine every night. Can you believe that?" He cleared his throat. "Lost my job, because Vegas prefers their blackjack dealers to be clear-headed. We can take more of your money that way."

Kyle sat down on the stage, and Melanie scowled at him. Heartbreaker, maybe. She was the broken one.

"You name the sin, I've done it. Women, check. Lies, check. Gluttony…" He patted his stomach. "Check. And murder…"

The whole crowd leaned toward him.

"We'll call it murder by neglect. There was a beautiful girl who worked at the casino. Sarah. She made me laugh like no one ever had before. I wanted to marry her. And the night I was fired, I was supposed to meet her at the staff entrance. But I chose to get wasted and lay in the street."

Brother Mitchell's voice quivered. "They found her the next morning. Half-dressed in an alley. Bruised, beaten... no telling how long she waited for me."

He straightened. "Maybe as long as God's been waiting for you."

A light breeze carried his words to Melanie, and she shook her head. God didn't have anything for her.

Except maybe Kyle.

She shook away the thought.

"For years, I tortured myself." Brother Mitchell wrapped the mic cord in his hand. "Wondered if I'd shown up to meet her, if I'd have encountered the same troublemakers she did. Blamed myself for her murder, because I couldn't be the man she needed me to be. Wondered why I got to be the one to live. And, wondered why a God who supposedly loved us all could let something like that happen.

"But it's sin that's the problem. Where do things like murder, hatred, and brokenness come from? Not a loving God. No. They come from a devil, who weasels his way into our hearts and convinces us that we have no hope." He knelt before the woman who'd raised her hand. "A woman found me in the street, lying in a pool of my own vomit. She asked to pray for me."

Tears strained his voice, and Melanie's eyes burned. Why was she letting this guy get to her?

"I told her…" He held up a finger. "I told her I wasn't in the mood to talk to God."

"She said she didn't mean talk to God. She wanted to talk to Jesus. My mediator. My intercessor. The one who would appeal to God on my behalf and petition for me. She asked if I knew him."

Brother Mitchell stood. "And I didn't know him. I knew Baby Jesus, and Easter Jesus. But not the Jesus of Luke 4:18. The Jesus who came to this earth with a purpose. The Jesus, who after being tempted for forty days and not sinning, quoted from the book of Isaiah, saying, 'The spirit of the Lord is upon me because he has anointed me to preach the good news to the poor. He has sent me to heal the brokenhearted. To free the captives, and restore sight to the blind…'"

Melanie blinked. She scooted into the curtain and wrapped herself in the blanket Kyle had brought for her. Why couldn't this guy shut up? It would be worth climbing down from the billboard if she could get away from him.

"I didn't know the Jesus of Matthew 9, who alone has the authority and power on earth to forgive sins. You see, I thought it was up to man to forgive my sin. But man didn't forgive, and man didn't forget. Jesus offered me forgiveness before I ever even asked. He died on the cross that I might live, knowing one day I'd be born, and I'd need Him.

"Sin, my friends, is an oppression. One that we must overcome. If the world is against us, then we need a victory." Brother Mitchell blasted air into the mic. "Faith is that victory. The victory that overcomes the world. Come, visit with me. Let me tell you more about Jesus. Let me help show you how He can heal your brokenness. How you can be free from your pain and addictions."

Free from pain. Melanie gritted her teeth. That wasn't happening anytime soon.

"A wonderful savior is Jesus, my Lord. A wonderful savior to me…" Brother Mitchell's tenor grated her nerves. As he sang about hiding his soul in the cleft of a rock, she dug into the cleft of her chin with her fingernail. Strangely comforting words.

"He covers me there with His hand."

If only those words were true.

Something rustled in the trees below. She peeked out the curtain. Kyle still sat onstage, staring toward Brother Mitchell. So, who was climbing up to the billboard? Was it Daddy? Stephen?

The ladder clanged. She cowered in her blanket as black sneakered feet plodded across the deck. Maybe Stephen?

"Come on, Christian. Bring the camera on up. Think I see her." A deep male voice accompanied the hand that swept away the curtain.

She looked up into piercing blue eyes framed by a chiseled tan and feathered blond hair. Stark white teeth punctuated his cheesy smile. Bart Handley, annoying community reporter from Milton's six o'clock evening news.

Kyle narrowed his eyes at the two men standing on the billboard. He leapt to his feet and dashed to the gate. How stupid he'd been to leave it open.

He raced through and paused long enough to secure the lock. Minutes later, he'd scaled the tree and started up the ladder. His heart raced. Would the deck even hold the weight of them all?

"Like I said, I want to talk to you, Ms. Turner. Ask you some questions." The polished male voice held a flicker of annoyance. "When are you planning to come down? Are you involved with Kyle Casey?"

Kyle forced his fist to unclench as he reached for the next rung. "Leave her alone. And get off my Pa's property before I have you arrested."

"Mr. Casey?" Through the deck slats, the reporter's sneakers stalked across to the ladder.

"In the flesh." Kyle moved to the bottom rung. "If you want an interview, come on down. I'll talk to you." He lowered himself and dropped to the grass. "Leave Melanie alone."

"No." Melanie swatted her arm at the cameraman. "I'll talk to you. Don't bother Kyle."

"I said, leave her alone." Kyle drew out his phone. "Calling the police right now."

"We're coming. We're coming." The cameraman jerked away from Melanie, coming dangerously close to the edge of the deck.

Within a couple minutes, Bart Handley stood next to him, his cameraman fiddling with the lighting. "We can still interview you, right?"

Kyle paced beside the pine he'd scaled so many times. What was he thinking? This guy would shred him.

Everyone judged him. The baseball commissioner, Pa, Melanie, Lacey… he'd been a decent guy most of his life. All he'd done was make a few mistakes. Everybody made mistakes, right?

"But there's a bigger story I'd like to get. You haven't apologized yet, have you?" Bart smirked. "And there's a long list of girls who've aired their grievances against you through social media."

You haven't apologized yet. To hear the reporter echo Melanie's words struck a painful chord. Kyle sat on a root and tore a couple leaves from a vine.

As he shredded them, Bart's laugh grated his spine. "Better hope you're invincible."

"What?" He tossed the leaves aside.

"Poison ivy." Bart pointed to the base of the tree that attached to his root. "You're sitting in a big patch of it."

"Oh." While Bart and his cameraman laughed, Kyle jumped up and ran to the riverbank. He washed his hands off with the water as they hurried to catch up.

"I was kidding, Kyle." Bart panted behind him. "Thought maybe we needed something to ease all this tension."

When he turned, their faces had twisted into guffaws. And he laughed, too. He reached out his hand to the cameraman. "I remember you from school. Christian, right?"

"That's me." Christian frowned at Bart. "You sure that wasn't poison ivy?"

"It wasn't." Bart drug his arm over his sweaty forehead and wiped it on his pants. "You can shake his hand."

Kyle skipped a rock across the water. "Thanks for coming down. Melanie needs to heal right now. She doesn't need to be bothered."

"I can respect that." Bart dug through a pile of stones and selected a smooth pebble. He tried to skip it, but it sunk to the river bed. "I appreciate you being willing to do an interview."

"Yeah, man. I followed your career the whole time." Christian reached into his wallet. "Even got one of your baseball cards." He flipped through plastic sleeves and held it up. "What happened to you? Why did you do it?"

"Wait." Bart pointed to a couple boulders beneath a small break in the canopy of trees. The sun shone down on them like a spotlight. "Can we do this live? Maybe set you up over there?"

"Sure." Kyle bit back a retort. He needed to do this. He needed to tell his story. To show his true regret.

After Christian finished adjusting the camera, he counted down from five.

Bart sat straighter, holding the microphone close to his lips. "Thanks for joining us for tonight's 'In Your Community' segment. We're at the farm of Pa Casey, grandfather of Kyle Casey, who's been in the news a lot lately. His most recent attention has involved a woman who's climbed up a billboard on his property and refused to come down. Kyle, what can you tell us about this woman? Are you romantically involved?"

"We're not." Kyle caught his lower lip between his teeth. "As I'm sure you've heard from the others you've interviewed, Miss Turner received some bad news about her fiancée moments before the wedding, and she's been distraught ever since."

"You were dancing, right?" Bart shoved the mic in his face.

Kyle nodded. "We did dance one time. I thought I might cheer her up and make her want to come down. Mr. Turner had asked me to help him. I know it looks bad, but that's the truth. There's nothing romantic going on between us."

"Is it true that you've been bringing her meals and clothes and such?"

"It is. I promised Mr. Turner that I wouldn't let any harm come to his daughter." Kyle pointed toward the billboard. "Poor girl is heartbroken, that's all. If people would give her some space, I think she'd come on down."

"So, what brings you back to Milton, Kyle?" Bart nudged the mic closer.

"Can I …" Kyle drummed his fingers on the rock. "May I?" He reached for the mic.

"Go ahead. Tell us why you came back home after all these years." Bart passed it over.

Swallowing, Kyle closed his eyes. Now or never. "I lost my roots. Slipped up and made a few mistakes." His chest heaved. "Made a lot of mistakes. I spent all this time trying to convince everyone in the world of baseball that I only slipped up once. And as for the betting, yes. I only did it once. But I made so many more mistakes than that. I got bigger than my britches, I guess, as Pa would have said. Got caught up in the party life and having fun. So, I've come back to Milton to find myself again. Spend some time on the farm sweating it out. And learning to do more for other people than satisfying myself. Service, as Paul Mitchell would say."

Bart reached for the mic, and Kyle shook his head. "I remembered what Pa told me when I was a boy about helping others and always putting people before yourself. He wasn't all that religious when we were young, but Mom and Dad were, you know. They could talk about the life to anyone, but Pa lived it. Before he even started going to church, he lived like he ought to."

"That's great, Kyle, but—"

"I guess what I'm trying to say is that tonight, when Paul Mitchell stood before a crowd of beer-toting strangers and bared his soul, he exposed mine, too. I remembered why Mom and Dad tried to teach me to be selfless. And, more than anything, I want to say I'm sorry. I'm so sorry to everyone involved. Lacey Robbins, I'm sorry for breaking your heart. And Daylen Robbins, I'm sorry for hurting your sister and being a rotten friend."

Bart caught the handle of the mic, but Kyle pulled it away. "Mom and Dad, I'm sorry for being a jerk of a kid. Commissioner Stevens, Joe C, and all the team… and the fans, I'm sorry for betting on baseball. I'm sorry for not taking the opportunity seriously and counting it as a blessing."

Kyle looked directly into the camera. *Please, let people see the sincerity in my eyes. Let them believe I want to change, and I can change. And let me do it. Let me change.*

Bart lunged again, this time snatching the mic. "Well, folks, that's not our typical community segment, but there you have it. A heartfelt apology from Milton's own fallen hero." He held the mic between his neck and chin and clapped his hands. "Kyle Casey, former pro player turned farmer. And that's what's going on tonight in your community."

Christian shut down the camera as Bart stood and brushed moss from his khakis.

"What kind of sorry segment is that?" Kyle stood over Bart, suddenly proud of the way his muscles bulged out of his T-shirt. "What were you trying to pull? A video gossip column? Shaming people on television? How can you call stuff like that news? What were you going to do? Badger me until I gave you every sordid detail? And when it started coming out freely, you wanted the credit?"

Bart ducked and dove to the side. "No harm, no foul man. My station manager lets me do it. Keeps us all in the know about political stuff and county troubles. Sometimes we do positive segments."

"Yeah. Like once a year." Christian snorted. "But on a positive note, WMTV only has about twelve viewers, and six of those are related to Bart."

Bart gave him a playful swing. "We have more viewers than that."

Kyle crossed his arms. "Well, you can use the footage if you want to, but why not try to make it something for good? A segment about helping others. I bet that would be way more popular." He gave Bart a curt nod. "Now, we're going to walk to that gate, and I want you to get off my property. Leave Melanie alone."

When Christian and Bart passed through, Kyle hesitated. Helping others. Maybe that *was* the key to getting his life back together. It did feel good to help Melanie.

Brother Mitchell stood at the edge of the stage wrapping the cord around the mic. The crowd had thinned, other than a handful of men who surrounded him. Kyle darted across the lot and crossed over to them. If anyone could show him how to help others, he'd bet Brother Mitchell was the guy.

Chapter Twelve

Thursday afternoon, Kyle found his way to a Milton High School baseball game with Brother Mitchell, who insisted that Kyle call him Paul. He propped his elbows on his knees, resting his chin on clenched fists. Three men on base. Two strikes and two balls. And a seventeen-year-old boy who knew that the game rested on his shoulders.

If he hit it out of the park, the four runs would put them over the top. Three runs would tie. One run would be enough, though. He could send it past the second baseman and they'd all be safe. "Slow and steady, kid. You're no Barry Bonds."

Paul leaned over and grinned. "It's in your blood, I can see. You know, just because you aren't pro anymore doesn't mean you can't serve through baseball."

Kyle reached between his feet into his bag of peanuts. He cracked a shell and tossed it into the wind. "What do you mean?"

Paul nodded to the boy at the mound. "Take my grandson, Chip there. He's a great kid. Not a bad pitcher. But I guarantee you he's going to blow this one, and they'll lose the game."

"What makes you say that?" Kyle popped the peanuts into his mouth and washed them down with his Dr. Pepper. "I sure wouldn't place my confidence in the batter. Look at his stance. Shifting his weight like that, the uncertain twitch in his lips…"

"Chip is going to walk him. You watch. He'll have perfect form until the last second and hesitate. Then, he'll throw the ball too hard and walk the whole team."

Sure enough, within the next five minutes, the other team had the four runs they needed, and the pitcher's shoulders slumped so much he could hardly wind up for the next at bat.

Paul shook his head. "Poor kid. He's going to be so hard on himself. Maybe you could talk to him after the game? We could go get ice cream or something. Don't you need to get food to take to Melanie? I could buy this time."

"I guess I could." Kyle winced. Other than hitting up the drive-thru and a couple stores, he'd tried to stay invisible as much as possible, especially after Wayne had called him out on the billboard. Of course, if anyone watched Bart Handley's clip of his awful attempt at an apology, that would change.

"It would mean a lot to him, Kyle. And to me."

Were those tears in Paul's eyes? The preacher had spent the entire afternoon trying hard to convince him he deserved a second chance. And he obviously believed his grandson deserved a second chance as well.

"You know what, I haven't been to the Dairy Queen here in about ten years. I'd love a banana split." Kyle grinned. "And I'd be glad to buy one for Chip, too."

At the Dairy Queen, Kyle held court in the middle of about thirty high school boys sporting colors of the winning and losing teams. Their parents formed an outer shell, along with several restaurant patrons who decided to stay and listen.

"Talk to them," Paul had said. "Tell them your story."

Kyle stood and backed up against a table. "Well, first, I want to say thanks. I've always heard that you can't go home again. That you'll be terribly received. But you guys have been great. Parents, players, coaches…" He gripped the edge of the table and took a deep breath. "Tough game tonight. You guys played your hearts out. It could have been anyone's game. Well coached, great sportsmanship." He laughed. "Chip, you lost your cool, man. Got nervous, that's all. But you lost to a great team. I tried to buy your ice cream tonight, and I couldn't talk Dawson's coach out of picking up your tab. How often does the coach of an opposite team do something like that?"

Applause filled the restaurant.

"But I don't want to talk to you about that tonight. I want to talk about mistakes. Mistakes, and why I made them. Why you don't have to."

Paul gave him an encouraging nod, and he grinned. But the boys seemed... disappointed. If he stuck around Milton, there'd be plenty of time to teach these boys those lessons.

"But first, let me tell you what it feels like the first time you step on the field of Yankee Stadium. How the air grabs your first pitch and carries it with a hint of music."

The players leaned forward in their seats, and Kyle raised his hands as though swinging a bat. Speaking of firsts, for the first time in months, he felt great.

Melanie rubbed her dry eyes and yawned. Guess Kyle wasn't coming tonight. Her stomach growled. Maybe she'd have to eat a squirrel after all. Although, she'd have to wait until tomorrow to cook it. Maybe he'd come late.

For now, she needed sleep. Sitting on the billboard day in and day out had already worn down her stamina. Could she manage it for eight more days? On the one hand, she was tired. Surely no one would judge her any less if she came down. But on the other hand, if she didn't see it through for the thirteen days, she'd be a quitter.

She couldn't win. She couldn't quit.

She curled up in her blanket and cried soft tears. How dare Stephen put her in this predicament? And how dare Kyle use her for... whatever purpose he had decided to use her for. What was his endgame, anyway? A conquest? To make himself look better so society would forgive him?

His face swirled in her mind as she drifted off to a fitful sleep. After what felt like seconds, something tickled her feet.

"Wake up, Pun'kin." Kyle's voice had a singsong quality. "Brought you some food."

She sat up quickly, striking her head on the PVC pipe. With a jerk, she threw open the curtain open and met his gaze, spewing fire from her own.

"I'm sorry, Mel. Didn't mean to let it get so late."

Sure, he didn't.

He handed her a paper box. "It's roasted barbecue chicken with baked beans and corn. That okay?"

The flames diminished as she searched his earnest face. Faker. "It's fine. Thanks."

"The most incredible thing happened tonight." He went back to the ladder and grabbed two drinks from the basket. "I went to a baseball game."

She laughed then covered her mouth. No way. She was not letting this be easy for him. "That's incredible?"

"It was a high school game. The preacher took me to watch his grandsons play."

"The preacher." Melanie wrinkled her nose. "What happened?"

"Well, the team his son and son-in-law coaches lost, and he asked me to go out for ice cream with them. I ended up talking to all the boys on both teams. And then, the parents." He grinned. "Several have asked me if I'd be interested in giving some private lessons. I arranged two for next week."

"That's great, I guess." She frowned. Didn't they know he wasn't trustworthy?

He sat down next to her and took a long sip through his straw. "Melanie, I am so sorry for hurting you. I knew you were vulnerable, and I should have kept my distance. But I do enjoy your company, and I'd like to be your friend if that's okay. At least until your thirteen days are up, and then you can move on with your life and hate me if that's what you want."

"Lacey messaged me." She bit her lip. Why had she blurted that? Now he'd want to talk about it, and with everything that happened in her relationship with Stephen, it was too painful.

"Lacey." Kyle scratched his head. "I—"

"All this time, Kyle. I've sat here and poured my soul out to the enemy." She slammed her fists on the deck, knocking over her soda. "How long would it have been? How long until you carried me off into the sunset and dumped me on the ground to pick up the pieces while you ran off with some other girl? We can't be friends. We can't be anything. I can't risk it."

"I can't make any excuses for Lacey. I was a louse. Horrible."

"Pathetic." Melanie righted the cup. "And yes. No excuse for it."

"I deserve any terrible name you want to call me."

"Bottom-dwelling low life. Pusillanimous worm." Melanie sighed. Calling him names didn't do any good. She sat on her hands and swayed a fraction of a degree side to side. Why couldn't he be some gross, sloppy guy? Those deep brown eyes, reflecting a strange sense of hurt, melted her soul.

They'd known each other less than a week. Why would he be so hurt at her words? Her breath evened, and she rested her hands in her lap at the edge of her plate. "Believe me, I've sat up here and thought them all. Called you names and called Stephen names, and honestly…"

She pinched a bite of the roasted chicken between her fingers, loosening the crusty skin. Grounds of pepper slid beneath her fingernails, and she licked her lips before shoving a bite of it in her mouth. As she chewed, fresh tears brimmed on her eyelids. "I want him to come up here and explain it to me. To tell me why I wasn't enough. Or what I did wrong."

Kyle scooted sideways so he faced her. He reached out his right hand then let it fall to the side. "Lacey didn't do anything wrong. She was a sweet, earnest girl. She treated me like a prince, better than I deserved. And I'm sure that's the case for you as well."

The muscles in her face flinched.

"The flaw was in me. I was the problem. I didn't give her a fair shake at love." He reached again, and she jerked away.

"You are the problem. You deserve it if she hates you."

"I've already put more effort into helping you than I've ever put into my relationship with her. Or with anyone."

"What did you do to her?" She swirled her beans around with a plastic fork. "Why did you hurt her? How could you?"

"I got caught up in the crowd." He folded his hands in his lap. "Went out with the guys after the games. Ignored and dismissed her."

"And you cheated."

"One night after a game, I was upset from the loss. I had way too much to drink. Girls were always hanging around our buses and hotels. Somehow, a couple of them made their way into my room, and that was all she wrote. It wasn't an intentional affair. But I didn't intend not to, either." He inched closer. "I'm not that man anymore, Mel. You have to trust me. I haven't had a drink since that night I gambled on the game."

Melanie plunged the fork in her baked beans so hard it made a hole in the bottom of the Styrofoam bowl. As the sugary sauce dripped into the chicken box, she snatched her napkin, folded it, and set it underneath the bowl. "Well, it's like this mess I've made. When you let out all the trust, you can't get it back in."

"True." Kyle brushed a lock of hair out of her face.

Melanie ducked her head to the side. "Stephen did worse than that. He went away with this girl for a whole weekend. Claimed it was a business trip and met her there. Purposed. Deliberate."

"I'm sorry, Mel." Kyle hooked her arm at the elbow. "All I know to tell you is that some people are rotten. They do bad things. They only care about themselves. And I've been that person. I've made all kinds of mistakes. You're right to not trust me."

He released her arm and clasped his hands in front of his chin. "But I want to be a better person. For whatever reason, Pa's trusted me with his farm. I'm completely inept, but he's trusted me. Given me a chance. And I'm going to make it good. I wish you could do the same."

"Give you a chance?"

Kyle swallowed. "Go out with me. Leave this billboard and let me take you out to dinner. No big thing. A little date."

"I'm not ready to date anyone." She tore another piece of chicken loose. "You are a likeable guy, Kyle. A real charmer. But I'm done with charmers."

"I'm not asking for a long-term commitment." He fiddled with the button on his polo shirt, loosening the collar. "I want us to get back to a point where we can sit and talk again. Be friends. Help each other heal."

"Heal. I don't know where to start with healing. Tricia Billings is model pretty. Stephen was more attracted to her than me. I mean, why wouldn't he be? I'm such a tomboy. Everybody says so. My mama, all my friends..." Melanie picked up the chicken leg and bit into it. She chewed and forced the bite down her throat, then put the leg down. "Man, I hate these freckles."

"I like your freckles." Kyle leaned closer. "Maybe she distracted him."

"No. Stephen chose to be distracted by her."

Kyle swallowed. "She might be model pretty, but you're angel pretty." He laughed. "Billboard pretty."

Heat warmed Melanie's cheeks. "I wasn't fishing for compliments."

"I'm glad to give one." Kyle took another sip of soda. "Truth is, you're whirlwind pretty. That's why I was so tempted to kiss you. You have this natural beauty. The way your eyes dance when you smile. The way your mouth sets in that determined grit. And the way your blush covers your freckles, but it doesn't hide them completely."

Melanie felt herself blushing now. She wiped her mouth with her napkin to hide her face. Could he just quit with the compliments already? If she wasn't careful, she'd forget she wasn't supposed to like him. "I tried to force things to be good with Stephen." She picked up her drink and took a long swallow. "I see that now. Made him feel trapped, I'm sure. Demanded so many things."

Kyle nodded. "Lacey did that. She thought she could change me by insisting it happen. But I had to decide on my own. And I wasn't willing to do that. Truth is, I never saw her in the first place. Never saw our relationship for what it could be. I'm sure that's part of Stephen's problem, too."

"Thanks, by the way." Melanie lifted the corn, holding it in front of her mouth to hide her grin. "For convincing that loser reporter to leave me alone."

"It was nothing." He popped the cap off his drink and turned up the cup. As he crunched the ice, his eyes widened. "Look, Mel."

In the church parking lot, Daddy sat in a lawn chair beside his truck next to the preacher. They'd bent their heads together, looking at a book.

"What's he doing?" She wrinkled her nose. "Is that a Bible?"

"Paul's real nice." Kyle took her empty box and carried it back to the basket. "I'm thinking about going to his website and listening to some of his sermons. We could do that together if you're interested."

"Church has never been my thing." She shook her head. "Or Daddy's. But apparently he's interested now. Well, that, or he has to do something to kill the time until I decide to come down."

"Why don't you, then?" Kyle cupped her chin. "Come down. If nothing else, I'll take you out to Dairy Queen tomorrow night and buy you a banana split."

She blinked back tears. "I can't. I have to see this through. Thirteen days."

Chapter Thirteen

Friday morning, the air grew hot and sticky. Melanie checked the weather on her cell, and fresh tears stung her eyes. Thunderstorms were coming. Well, they were nothing compared to the storms in her heart.

Staying on the billboard would put her in grave danger. Stephen would probably love for her to be struck by lightning, though.

The cell vibrated in her hands, and her heart sunk. Mama. She tapped the screen.

"Melanie Dawn, get yourself down from that billboard right now."

"Hi, Mama." Melanie wiped sweat from her forehead with a wadded napkin.

"I'm not joking. It's supposed to storm all day. You've made your point. And I told your daddy I'd keep my nose out of it, but I'm not going to watch you sit up there and make a fool of yourself any longer. First throwing your fit over Stephen, then up there kissing that boy—"

"I didn't kiss him. We were dancing. People dance at a concert, Mama. You've never complained about me doing it before."

"Well…" Mama clucked her tongue. "Either way, I demand you get off that sign and come home. Right now. Get down before the storms come."

"Not happening." Melanie tapped the screen to end the call. If Mama'd cared so much, she would have made everyone leave instead of going on with the reception. As far as Melanie was concerned, Mama could climb on up here and get her if she wanted her to come down so bad.

Her cell rang again, and Melanie switched it to silent. She needed to charge it again. Hopefully Kyle would bring the charger back when he brought her supper.

She picked up the new book Kyle had brought her and lost herself for the next couple of hours. When she looked up, the sky had darkened. Looming black clouds swirled in the distance. Didn't matter. She wasn't coming down.

She gathered all her stuff into a plastic tub Kyle had given her and fixed it to the rail of the deck with the rope. Then, she scooted inside the PVC shelter and wrapped her arms around her knees.

"Pun'kin!"

Daddy's muted shout brought new tears. She blew air out her pursed lips and stepped onto the deck.

"Melanie!" Kyle called to her from the tree. "Get down from there. There's tornado warnings and everything with this storm. Wait it out with us in the cellar. If you want to be stubborn and climb back up after it passes, that's fine, but right now, you need to get down."

Feet clanked against the ladder, and seconds later, his head popped over the deck. "Please, Mel. Come down. At the very least, wait out the storm with us."

Daddy waved from the pine. "Pun'kin!" He leapt toward the ladder, missing it, and plummeted to the ground as the clouds opened up above them.

"Daddy!" Melanie rushed to the ladder, barely giving Kyle time to climb down before shimmying to the bottom herself. As rain poured over her, blending with her tears, she fumbled in her pocket for her phone. "Is he alert?"

Daddy blinked and groaned, water puddling on his chest. His leg lay twisted in an awkward angle underneath him, and she reached for it.

"No, wait." Kyle caught her hand. "We can't move him. Need to call 911. He could have other injuries since he's fallen so far."

She made the call, somehow managing to give the operator the address to the church. Kyle took off to unlock the gate, and she knelt beside Daddy. "I'm so sorry. My stubbornness has caused you so many troubles over the years."

Lightning flashed above them, and she winced. "We need to get you out of this storm."

"I... I'm... oh." Daddy twisted his head to the side, his face scrunched in pain. "Leg's... broken, I'm... pretty sure."

The rain fell in sheets, stirring up loose twigs and leaves. A branch scratched her cheek, and her blood dripped down to the ground, swirling in a pool of muddy rain.

A few minutes later, the EMTs rushed in and checked his vitals. They splinted his leg and picked him up under his arms.

Thunder boomed overhead, and Daddy held up his hand. "No, I'll walk out. I'll be fine."

With Kyle's help, he stood, leaning on the two EMTs as he walked. They made a few steps, and Kyle turned back to Melanie. "You coming?"

She caught her rain-soaked hair in her hand and squeezed it. She should go. But Daddy would be fine, and Mama would be furious. She couldn't be around that right now.

Daddy faced her, his eyes pained.

She held her breath.

"You're not, are you?" Kyle's eyes narrowed, barely visible under the rain dripping from his forehead. "You're going to climb back up that stupid pole and wallow." He shoved his phone in his pocket. "That's it."

He lunged for her, scooping her in his strong arms. Pressing his wet cheek against her shoulder, he gripped tighter. "I'm taking you with us."

She squirmed, kicking, and trying to wriggle free from his grasp. How dare he? "Put me down. Right now."

Daddy dipped his chin and shook his head. "Let her stay, Kyle. Let her be her own sorry self." He winced, and the EMTs carried him toward the gate.

Several bolts of lightning danced around them. The wind rose to a fury that matched her broken heart. Kyle held her for several minutes as she sobbed against him, the rain falling so hard it burned her face.

"I hate you!" She screamed into the wind, the words lost to its roar.

"What?" He scowled as he lowered her to the ground.

"I hate you." The words hung on her lips, and she beat her clenched fists against his chest. "I hate you, I hate you, I hate you!"

"Oh, you do not." He caught her wrists in one hand, holding them over her head, and swept her close to him. "I'm not apologizing for this one!"

She strained to hear his shout. "What?"

"I'm not sorry." He shouted again in her ear, then planted a light kiss on her cheek.

She wiggled and tugged at her wrists, but he held them tight.

"Still not sorry." He whispered into the other ear and kissed the tip of her nose.

Jerking her arms, she stumbled when he released her then landed on her bottom in a muddy puddle. He held out his hand, and she shoved hers both in her pockets, scooting back against an old tree stump.

He knelt beside her, cupping her face in his hands. "Not sorry at all!"

The rain broke, and his shout carried through the woods. He planted his lips on hers, taking away her breath as she tasted the sweetness of a piece of hard candy. She twisted and writhed, but he persisted, until she yielded to the kiss. Strong, passionate, and deep.

He pulled away too quickly, releasing her face and leaving a void. As he stood and pivoted, she caught the hem of his pants.

"Leave me alone!" She wiped away the rain and tears with the back of her muddy hand.

He knelt beside her again, tucking his hands under her arms and lifting her to her feet. Leaning close to her ear, he warmed her neck with his breath. "Fine. But I bet you won't be up there thinking about how horribly Stephen wronged you all night."

"Jerk!" She stomped in the puddle beside him, sending mud splashing onto his jeans. "It doesn't count! That kiss doesn't count!"

His brow arched. "Why not?"

"Thirteen." She stalked back to the tree, her shout dropping to a whisper. "Thirteen."

Kyle started Wayne's truck and ripped down the mud-soaked gravel road to the driveway. He turned onto the main road and sped to the hospital, pulling in beside a grayish-blonde woman who could have been Melanie's sister.

She slammed the door to her older-model Lexus, and her purse slipped off her shoulder. As it tumbled to the pavement, Kyle dove for it, catching it in his right hand before it landed in a puddle.

"Here you go, ma'am." He handed it back to her, and she smiled.

"Bless your heart, dear. I appreciate it." A flicker of worry creased her brow, then she straightened. "My husband's in there with a broken leg. He had knee surgery several months ago, and now this." She made a tsk-tsk noise. "Don't know what I'm going to do with him. Or our crazy daughter."

Kyle brushed his wet forehead with muddy fingers, stifling his grin. Yep. This must be Melanie's mom. "Mrs. Turner, right?"

"Yes. How did you…?" Her lips twisted into a snarl as she appraised him. "Never mind. You're that Casey boy."

He nodded. "Guilty as charged, ma'am. I tried to talk your husband out of climbing that tree, but—"

"He wouldn't listen. Nobody in this family will listen. Not even me, I guess." She sighed, her thin frame constricting to almost paper thickness as the air whooshed from her lungs. "How's Melanie?"

What? She wasn't going to throw some diatribe about why he shouldn't have cheated on baseball or why he needed to stay away from her daughter? He fell into step beside her. "She's okay. Brokenhearted and stubborn as the day is long, but I think she's starting to calm down."

"I told Wayne we needed to get the fire department to go up and get her, but he won't let them. Says she needs to work through all this on her own. And I guess that's true, but I hate her being out there so vulnerable." Her heels clacked as she crossed through the sliding glass doors into the hospital foyer. "Vulnerable is not the best word to describe Melanie. She's resourceful and a master at a slingshot.

Although she always was vulnerable when it came to Stephen. I don't know why."

Kyle followed her down several long hallways to the ER lobby. "Stephen seems like a creep."

"He was impressed with Wayne's notoriety. That was all." She shrugged. "And all in for the wedding because he thought we were filthy rich."

Odds were this woman knew all about him. So, why was she being so nice? Especially when Melanie seemed so irritated by her. He shoved his hands in his pockets while she went up to the front desk. When she finished with the receptionist, she turned and waved him in. "Come on. Wayne will want to see you."

He headed down the long hall to the last room on the right, a waiting area with snack and drink machines.

"Guess I should introduce myself. Name's Louisa. Was a Harper before I became a Turner." She sat in a paisley chair and crossed her ankles as her heels slipped off her feet. "Your mom and I were friends in high school. We spent every afternoon together at the Dairy Queen after school. Well, it was the Burger Queen back then."

"No kidding. You know my mom." Kyle grinned. "I never even thought about me and Melanie having parents the same age."

"We're still good friends, just not in person." Louisa faced him. "Talk to her on the phone twice a week. We have for years, although we missed a few when Wayne took me and Melanie on tour."

Interesting. Kyle scraped his fingernail over something sticky on the arm of the chair. "So I guess you know my whole story."

"I do." Louisa leaned closer to his chair. "All of it. Your mom and I had several long conversations about you and Melanie. You need to call her, Kyle. Let her know you're okay."

He shrugged. "She'd badger me about getting back in church. That's all she wants to talk about anymore."

Louisa sighed. "Yeah. She brings that up with me all the time, too. But I've been adamant that church and I don't get along, and she's let it go. Kyle, she misses her sons. All of them."

"Wayne went to church the other day."

"He did." Louisa shook her head. "He likes that fiddle-playing preacher. Imagine that, some guy in a bluegrass band can get my bear of a husband in a pew."

"Why did you guys stop going?" Kyle took out his wallet. "I think I'm going to buy a drink. You want something?"

"No." She tucked her bare foot underneath her. "I got tired of people judging us and wanting to debate all the time. We'd miss a Sunday or two because Wayne was out performing, and they'd throw a fit. Wouldn't let me teach Bible class because of it."

"I quit going because I got tired of the rules. I couldn't keep them all, so why try to keep any of them?" He flattened a dollar against the machine. "You don't seem terribly worried about Wayne. I think I'm more nervous."

She laughed. "If you had any idea how many times I've been in this emergency room with that man. But honestly, the nurse told me I could go on back with him. I wanted to talk to you."

Weird. He fed his dollar into the reader and pressed the button for a water. "Oh."

"Call your mom, Kyle." She handed him her phone. "Here. In case you don't have their new number."

"I've got it." He popped the cap on the bottle and took a long swig. "I'll call her."

"Good." Louisa stood and grabbed the collar of his shirt in a vice grip. "And don't go pulling any of that smooth talk on my daughter. I love your mother like a sister, but I could take you down in a heartbeat, muscles or no muscles." She twisted the neck tighter. "And, with her blessing."

"Yes, ma'am." When she released him, he ducked his chin.

A gray-haired nurse poked her head in the room. "Mrs. Turner?"

Louisa disappeared for about five minutes then came back with a grim face.

"I'm going back with Wayne now, but they said only me for the moment. It'll probably be three or four hours before they set his leg. You might as well go home and get some sleep. I'll tell him you were here."

"What about Melanie?"

Louisa tossed her hands up. "Let the stubborn girl do whatever she's going to do. How many more days can this insanity go on? The less attention she gets, the more she's likely to let it go. I say leave her there to suffer it alone. She'll eventually get bored or hungry and come down."

On the TV screen above Louisa's head, the radar showed the remnants of the storm creeping into the next county. His heart rate slowed. She'd be fine tonight.

He brought the water bottle to his lips, pressing the plastic against them. Oh, that kiss. She'd be fine, alright, but boy, she'd be stewing.

Chapter Fourteen

Saturday morning. Almost a week since the wedding, and finally one of her friends bothered to make contact.

Melanie narrowed her gaze over the edge of the billboard where Lizzie gripped a low, thick branch. She had no desire to talk to her. Although, the sight of her hair-and-nail bestie trying to place her dainty little foot somewhere on the trunk of the tree was more than worth it.

"Lizzie, what are ya doin'?"

The buxom brunette hoisted herself a few feet higher then jumped from the tree to the ladder. "I'm comin' up to talk some sense into ya, girlfriend."

"Hey, Melanie. Sorry, I couldn't stop her." Kyle shimmied up after her.

"You didn't have to tell her how to climb." Melanie slammed her book closed and shoved it in the plastic tub. She turned to Lizzie. "Talk all you want. I'm not listening."

"How'd you know I told her how to climb?" Kyle slipped off the backpack he'd worn up and tossed it to her. "I brought more sunscreen. Thought you might be running low."

"Lizzie's never climbed a tree in her life. She couldn't have made it up without you. Not so easily, anyway."

"Sorry." He stepped over them both and looked over the PVC pipes suspending her shower curtains. "I thought you might want to see your friend."

Melanie sighed. "It's fine." She twisted her hair into a loose bun and sat in the lotus position. "I mean, we're not friends anymore, but she can waste her time sitting up here if she wants."

Lizzie bounded up the rungs and skipped across the deck. "Don't ya think it's 'bout time to give up this racket?"

"Breathe in, breathe out." Melanie filled her lungs to capacity and emptied them slowly.

"I'm awful sorry, Melly. I shouldn't a told ya."

"In, and ouuuut." Melanie pursed her lips.

Kyle chuckled. "Ayowwwt." His angel suddenly picked up a deeper country twang. Did all her hometown friends have that effect on her? He dodged Lizzie's glare and leapt to the ladder. "Here's your lunch, Melly."

Lizzie folded her arms and slammed them against the chest. "You have no right ta be callin' her that."

"Thayyyyat?" He winked. "Would you a be passin' her this chick-un san'wich?"

Lizzie swatted at him.

He sidestepped her. "Mel, call me if you need anything."

"Bye, Kyle. Thanks." Melanie snatched the sandwich bag and turned her back to him and Lizzie.

With a sly grin, he climbed back down to the truck.

She knew what he was thinking. That kiss must be bothering her something fierce. She couldn't even meet his gaze. Because it was.

All night long, she had tasted his lips. When she closed her eyes to sleep, his image became even clearer in her mind. She saw herself clutching his plaid shirt with her fists and drinking in the scent of his sporty cologne. Once, she woke tangled in her blanket, thinking she was in his arms. It wasn't fair. Stephen had never got her in such a predicament. This was purely physical.

Tearing off little pieces of the bread and chicken, she savored the sandwich. He hadn't brought her anything this morning, and if not for stupid Lizzie, she'd have demanded to know why.

"Can't ya talk to me?" Lizzie's whine could grate anyone's nerves.

"You knew, Lizzie. You couldn't be bothered with tellin' me, though, could ya?" Ugh. Stephen always made fun of her for sounding so country when she was around Lizzie. She couldn't stop herself.

Lizzie sniffled. "I knew it'd plum destroy ya. But ya like this baseball guy, dontcha? I can tell."

"Kyle has been very supportive, which is more than I can say for any of my other friends." Melanie huffed. "You haven't even called or texted since that first day."

"Wayne told me not to bother ya. He said let ya stew."

"Since when do you listen to anything my dad says?" Melanie took out the fresh tube of sunscreen Kyle brought her and squirted some into her hand. She rubbed the tops of her ears and her nose then spread it over the rest of her exposed skin.

"Ya know Wayne had them pictures taken of Stephen with Tricia. He slipped 'em in my chair so I'd find 'em and tell you."

"Daddy knew?" Bile rose in Melanie's throat. Maybe she didn't feel sorry for not going to the hospital after all. "He knew and didn't tell me."

"Maybe he didn't know how ta. But I'm glad he did it before ya married 'im." Lizzie squeezed her hand as tears streamed down Melanie's face.

"I loved Stephen. How could he have been so cruel?"

"I dunno, Melly. Some guys are creeps."

"Yeah."

They sat in silence for about an hour, sharing quiet tears until Lizzie finally stood. "I am sorry, Melly. And I hope you'll be my friend again when this is all over."

Melanie swallowed, a world of emotion sticking in her throat. "You're still my friend. I was hurt, that's all. Thanks for comin', Lizzie. I needed to see you."

She pivoted and stood, and they exchanged a fierce hug.

"Wish you'd come down." Lizzie squeezed her shoulders. "I miss ya."

"I miss you, too." Melanie shook her head. "But I have to do this."

When Lizzie disappeared into the trees, Melanie crawled back into her PVC shelter and wrapped herself in the blanket. She finished her sandwich with the added flavor of salty tears. Shame on Kyle and his stupid kiss. He'd known exactly what he was doing… at first, at least. He'd wanted to fire her up. To make her mad enough for… for what? Not to get her to come down. Surely he knew she'd be mad and stay up there. Unless… was he trying to help her make it thirteen days? Had he listened, and he honestly cared that she would?

It was ridiculous. Borderline crazy. But Kyle had never questioned that.

She wadded her sandwich wrapper and stuffed it back in the bag. A folded blue paper at the base of it caught her eye. A letter?

After retrieving it, she unfolded the paper, her heart pounding. From Kyle?

Dear Melanie,

I'm sure you're wondering why I kissed you. Part of me wonders myself. But the truth is, if you were going to be stubborn and climb back up that billboard, I didn't want you to be thinking about the jerk that dismissed you. I wanted you to be thinking about the jerk who's been trying to take care of you. And trying to change.

A tear dripped from her eyes and stained the paper. The words blurred, and she folded back the top of the page.

I wanted you to sit up there and think about the future. Make new plans. Dream about new kisses. Conjure up new adventures. Don't wallow in the past and what didn't get to happen. I've made that mistake too many times.

"Okay, 'Dear Abby.'" She wrinkled her nose. What did a washed-up, former pro baseball player know about a simple country girl's dreams?

I met your mom last night. She was kind. And a little scary.

Melanie laughed. Good way to describe Mama.

She loves you so much her breath hitched when she said your name.

He'd skipped a few lines, leaving dots on the page as though he was trying to think of what to say.

I've never had anyone love me like that in my life other than Pa. Dad always criticized my every move and Mom always treated me like somebody needing fixing. But I'd like to find that kind of love.

With you.

A gasp bubbled in her throat, and Melanie swallowed it. She brought her fingers to her lips as fresh tears spilled. The sad thing was, she could see herself with Kyle. The hint of stubble growing on the chin he'd shaved. Those dark eyes that sat atop his half-smile that peered right into her soul. How could she ever see him the same after that kiss?

Fiercer by far than any Stephen had ever planted on her. Intense with a passion she'd never felt before. Pure lust, Mama would have said. But chemistry, too?

She crawled behind her curtain and curled up on her mat, closing her eyes as though that would shut out his face. Shame on him to be so right. Maybe... maybe she should come down. Go on a date with him like he'd wanted. Give him a chance.

Would he still want her after her thirteen days were up?

"**S**ir, you can't go in there." The nurse's chirpy voice carried into the hospital room. "Didn't you hear Mrs. Turner?"

Kyle bolted upright as a preppy, tall guy in khakis and a golf hat burst into the room, loosening the button on his navy polo shirt.

"Wayne. You okay?"

Wayne lifted his head from the pillow and blinked groggy eyes. He jerked up and raised his fist. "Get out of here, Stephen. I don't ever want to see your lousy face again."

Kyle leapt to his feet, dashed to Wayne's side, and folded his arms across his chest. Good thing he'd worn the shirt Lacey had always called his "muscle-man" tee. "If Mr. Turner says get out, you have to leave."

The nurse dashed in behind him. "I tried to stop him."

Kyle snarled. "We heard."

Stephen gave a dismissive wave and moved to Wayne's other side. "You have to put a stop to this, Wayne. Get her down from there. People are driving me crazy. They're calling day and night, posting on Twitter, berating me with videos… I had to leave Jamaica early." He pointed to the TV. "I even got a call for an interview from that loser mountain station you like to call news."

Kyle smirked. This guy was the jerk that stole her heart? This whiny punk?

"What are you laughing at?" Stephen narrowed his gaze. "Oh, wait. I know you. You're that baseball player. How's suspension going for you?"

"Not bad. I've been getting to know this great girl." Kyle walked around to Stephen's side of the bed. "Mr. Turner is resting. I'm going to count to three and you're going to be out of this roo—"

"Or what?" Stephen sneered.

"We'll have to call hospital security." The nurse backed out the door. "I'm going to do that right now."

"We don't need security." Kyle nodded to the window. "Let's take this conversation to the parking lot. Like I said, Mr. Turner is resting."

"Fine." Stephen stalked out, and Kyle trailed him. They marched down the steps and out the side door, finding a smoking area with several patio tables.

Stephen looked ready for a fight, so Kyle sat down at a table, dodging a pile of bird droppings. "I guess you want my permission to go talk to her."

Stephen frowned. "Why would I need your permission?"

Kyle shook his head. The nerve of this guy. "She's on my property. You'd have to trespass to get there. And trust me, if you stomp in like this, I'm calling the police the minute you cross the fence line. You are not going up there to treat Melanie that way."

Stephen snorted and leaned against an opposing table. "I'm not climbing up some stupid billboard. If she wants to talk to me, she can come down here and talk. I'm already mad I had to cut the trip short."

"Your honeymoon?"

Stephen arched his brow. "Excuse me?"

"Wasn't it your honeymoon?" Kyle traced the grooves in the wrought iron table with his fingers, willing them to not curl into a fist.

"Whatever. I took one of the bridesmaids, but don't tell Melanie that. She thinks all those friends of hers are innocent." Stephen shook his head. "I figure you of all people should understand having a woman or two on the side."

Kyle grimaced. What could he say to that? "Look. She's already been up there since last Saturday. So exactly a week, right? She's planning to stay up there six more days, and then—"

"Stupid number thirteen. That girl plans everything around a number. She's insane, man. I've known it since I met her."

"Then why did you propose?"

"She wanted me to." Stephen faced the parking lot. "So, what's wrong with Wayne, anyway?"

"Broken leg. And they had to do surgery this morning to reset his knee." Kyle drew in a deep breath. Why was he telling Stephen all this? He deserved to know nothing more about this family.

"Climbing up to get her, no doubt."

Kyle cleared his throat. "Well, you could have prevented that if you'd talked to her when this first happened instead of running off on a trip with some other girl."

Stephen pulled off his hat and wadded it. "What I do or don't do is my business. A better question might be what you were doing trying to kiss her days later."

A man on a motorcycle whizzed by, its roar enough of a distraction that Kyle unclenched his fist. "Don't you have at least a hint of remorse? It's apparent you've dated this girl for—"

"Exactly thirteen months."

"Exactly thirteen months, with no intention of ever falling in love with her." Saliva had gathered in Kyle's cheek, and he spit it toward Stephen's feet. "Her mom says you thought they had a bunch of money."

"He is Wayne Lee Turner." Stephen laughed. "Not-as-famous-as-he-thinks-he-is Wayne Lee Turner."

Kyle stood and took three paces closer. "You know what? None of that is relevant now. Way I see it, you have two choices. Either agree to a kind apology, and I'll let you come talk to her, or get out of dodge. I can, and will, take you down if I have to."

Stephen held up his palms between them. "Wait. Are you... threatening me?" He patted his pocket, where the outline of his phone showed. "I can destroy you in minutes."

Kyle shrugged. "I've already been destroyed, man. There's nothing you can do to me worse than I've already done to myself. But I can't let you destroy Mel any further."

"Mel." A guttural sound came from Stephen's throat. "So, that's how it is, then."

"That's how it is." Kyle brushed past him, strolling toward the parking lot.

When Stephen's fist made contact with his face, Kyle clenched his teeth. As Stephen's ring tore into his skin, he grabbed Stephen's wrist, twisted it hard, and wrapped it up behind his back.

"Stop!" Stephen wriggled like a toddler under Kyle's grip.

"Move and I'll break your arm." Kyle growled, yanking further and shoving Stephen up against a car. "Let me tell you how this is going to be. One, you're going to let Melanie play out this little game of hers as long as she wishes. Thirteen days or two more days. It's her call. Two, you're going to march back into that hospital, ask the receptionist for a pen and paper, and write her a letter. Give her the apology she deserves."

Stephen grunted painfully.

"And, three, you're going to stay out of her life forever. Now, let's head to the reception desk and see if that woman can get the paper. Then you're getting lost for good."

As Stephen hustled inside, Kyle wiped away the blood under his eye with his palm. No way was this loser hurting her again.

Chapter Fifteen

"**Y**ou've got to be kidding me." Melanie snatched the letter from Kyle's hands, wadded it into a ball, and tossed it over the edge of the billboard.

Kyle grinned, drawing another folded page. "I thought you might do that. I made a few copies. There's more in the truck if I need to get them."

"I do not want some force-fed, written apology." She reached for the note, grunting as Kyle held it over her head.

"Well, I don't want some pretty-boy loser bouncing on my property and treating you like trash." Kyle caught her wrists in his other hand, wrapped the arm with the letter around her waist, and tugged her closer. "Besides. I thought you might need more time to ponder my kiss before you saw him. You know, make sure you really care about what Stephen has to say."

"Agh!" She stomped her foot on the deck. "I hate you."

He laughed. "At least you're thinking about me." Releasing her and the note, he stepped aside as the paper fluttered to the deck floor.

She plopped down and unfolded it in her lap. "I still can't believe he punched you." Her lips twisted into a snarl. "I want to punch you."

He knelt beside her and offered his cheek. "Go right ahead, my dear."

"I'm not your dear."

"Can we be serious for a minute?" He brushed a hair from her eyes.

Why did he have to go and touch her? Her tongue scraped over her lips involuntarily, and she clamped her hand over them.

"Do you want me to leave so you can read it?"

Her lips quivered. "No." She traced her fingers over Stephen's words.

My dearest Melanie,

"Seriously?" She flung her fist against her thigh. "How dare he call me his dearest anything?"

I apologize for hurting you. Please forgive me. Um, no thanks.

Kyle inched closer, and Melanie's frown deepened. "He says he cheated on me the entire time we were together. That he used me and never planned to marry me, but since I insisted..." Hot tears stung her eyes. "I never insisted anything, Kyle. I told him it had been almost thirteen months. We needed to break up or move it to the next level."

"Sorry, Mel."

She sniffled. "Everybody thought I was pregnant because we planned the wedding so fast. I've always been known for my rash decisions and rebellious behavior."

Kyle snickered. "And here I thought you were so innocent." His face sobered. "So, now that you've seen his letter, what did you think about mine?"

She shrugged. "Pretty words from a beautiful man."

"You think I'm beautiful?" He planted an arm on her shoulder as she covered her mouth again.

Had she said that out loud?

His eyes twinkled. No escaping it now, she supposed. "You are nice looking, but it doesn't mean anything unless you have a trustworthy heart. Which you don't. You've already proven that."

When his shoulders slumped, a pang struck her heart. Why had she been so mean? Kyle wasn't Stephen. And even though he'd been a jerk to that other girl, he'd been kind to her. Still didn't mean she wanted to date him, but he didn't deserve her venom. "I'm sorry, Kyle. I…"

"It's fine." He stood and walked to the ladder. "Have a good afternoon, Mel. I'll come by in a few hours with your supper."

After an afternoon of reading and napping, the ropes shifted at the end of the deck. Melanie crawled over to the basket, finding a Wendy's bag, a soda, and a note saying to have a good night. She grabbed them and peeked over the edge as the rope slacked and the basket dropped down to the base of the ladder. Kyle's head poked out from between the tree branches, facing the ground. He disappeared into the woods, and she bit her lower lip. Guess he wasn't coming back up.

Fine by her.

Sunday morning, Kyle sent Melanie breakfast in her basket and stole through the gate to the church lot. He checked both directions for traffic then darted across the lot to the front entrance. He was late, so probably no one saw him, but they'd all be turning around to stare at him when he walked into the church. People always did that.

He hadn't been since his eighteenth birthday, when he marched out of his house and moved into the dorm to play college baseball. Mom and Dad more or less disowned him, other than the occasional Christmas dinner, although they enjoyed making jokes about the prodigal son at his expense.

He didn't even know why he was going, other than it would be a lot easier to call Mom if he'd made an attempt. And since he'd promised Louisa…

When he reached the double-oak doors, a man in a bright red sports coat reached out and grasped his hand. "Welcome, son. We're glad you could make it."

"Thanks." He accepted the crisp white brochure the man shoved into his hands and crossed the threshold into the lobby. A marbled aqua tile covered the floor, and three little blonde girls raced across it in flip-flops.

"Millie!" A haggard younger woman with a brown ponytail chased after them. "Kylie, Lindsey! No running!"

Kylie. He thought she meant him at first. He chuckled, dodging the third, shortest girl, and fell into the line of people streaming into the auditorium. But wasn't he late?

He checked his watch. Three minutes after eleven. Guess they were all late.

The lights in the auditorium blinked twice, then came back on dimmer. Chatter died to a lull and a twenty-something man with a shaved head strolled up to the mic and adjusted his Peanuts tie.

Kyle slid into the third pew from the back, in front of an elderly lady in an enormous hat. He nodded to her then faced the screen.

"I'd like to welcome you all to services at the Milton Church of Christ. We've got a lot of visitors today, so members, please turn to the new friends sitting next to you and extend them a friendly greeting." Charlie Brown Tie Man arranged papers while everyone in the pews shook hands with the people to the right and left of them.

Since no one else was close by, he shook the hand of the man in front of him and turned back to the elderly lady. "Good morning, ma'am."

"Good morning." She clutched his fingers in a death grip. "Marilyn Sullivan."

"Kyle." He grinned his charming smile that wooed all the girls and tried to wriggle free. "Nice to meet you, Ms. Sullivan."

"Kyle who?" She shifted her hat as the man up front waved for the crowd to sit.

"Casey. Pa's grandson."

Her face stiffened. She knew all about him, no doubt.

"As far as announcements today, Paul's leaving in three weeks for his trip to Guyana, and he needs someone to take over the Monday night home studies while he's gone."

A man in the audience raised his hand. "I can do that."

"Great." Charlie Brown Tie Man wrote something on his paper. "Now for prayer requests. Liza Roberts and Kathleen Cooksey are both recovering from their surgeries. And Bennett Myles is having those heart tests on Wednesday. Anyone else?"

The preacher stood, walking up from his side pew. "Wayne Lee Turner had a bad fall on the neighboring property. Guess most of you have probably heard about that. They ended up doing a surgery for his broken leg and fixed something they'd messed up in his knee replacement surgery. And, keep praying for Wayne's daughter. As you're all aware, she's going through a rough time."

Ms. Sullivan leaned forward, sinking her plastic nails into Kyle's shoulder. "They need to go up there and drag her down if you ask me. I don't know why you keep feeding her."

Kyle stifled his groan as half the room turned to face her. If she'd meant to whisper, it certainly hadn't come out that way.

As the announcements droned on, Kyle snatched a visitor card and golf pencil from the songbook rack and wrote his name across the top line.

"Let's pray."

The crowd collectively bowed their heads, but Ms. Sullivan boxed Kyle's ear.

"Agh!" Kyle squinted and scooted away from her as heads whipped up all over the room. Shoulders shook and eyes widened.

Ms. Sullivan plopped her folded arms over the back of the pew. "Hey Casey boy, aren't you feeling sorry for everything you've done? You going to repent today?"

The swirls in the carpet melded into an imaginary black hole. Kyle slumped his shoulders. If only he could dive in.

The announcer cleared his throat and everyone snapped to attention. Heads bowed once more.

"I'll be praying for you." Ms. Sullivan rasped in her not-a-whisper.

When Paul took his place at the podium, he held up a hardcover book. "Now some of you folks might think this is a mere songbook, but remember that many of the hymns are inspired by Bible verses or biblical thoughts. I'm starting a new series of lessons tonight exploring the deeper contextual meanings that can be drawn from certain songs."

Kyle shifted in the pew, crossing his left foot over his right. The sermon sounded interesting. Nothing like the old-school sermons Dad used to preach about how everybody and their brother was in danger of hell if they didn't change their wicked ways, like getting tattoos on their ankles or coloring their hair. No wonder Pa liked this church. Didn't seem like Paul planned to beat the Bible into anyone.

"I had Roy lead 'My Jesus, I Love Thee' this morning, and you all sang it beautifully. Such a poetic song, that one. If I'm not mistaken, it was written in the late 1860s or early 1870s. It's one of those public domain songs and translations exist in several other languages." Paul stepped away from the pew, adjusting his lapel mic. "Now think with me for a minute about that first stanza. Here. Let me read it to you."

He held up the songbook. "'My Jesus, I love thee'… Remember how I told you that love was a verb? It's an action, and a choice? Think of this first line in that way. My Jesus, I love thee. I choose to love thee. I choose to…"

Kyle sat straighter and snatched another visitor's card from the pew. He turned it over to the blank side and scrawled furiously.

"Okay, now, listen to those words as me speaking them. Me, Paul, I choose to love you, Jesus. I choose to do the actions that demonstrate to others how much I love you. To…"

Kyle's pulse raced. That was it. His whole problem in a nutshell. He didn't love Lacey because he didn't do loving things for her. But, if what Paul said was right, he could choose to love Melanie. Maybe it would be the happiness they'd both hoped to find.

By the time Paul finished preaching, Kyle had written six cards' worth of notes. And he knew exactly what to say to Melanie.

"**H**ear me out."

Melanie peeked through the curtain crack. Kyle could stand out there all day if he wanted. She wasn't coming out.

"It all came together for me today, Mel. Paul's sermon, the singing… I finally realized what I should have learned a long time ago."

"That you're an idiot?" She clamped her hand over her mouth. What was she thinking? She wasn't speaking to him.

"Fair enough." He sat on the deck, two feet from the opening of the curtain. "He talked about love today. Not hell, not how wrong we all were for doing bad stuff. Just love. And I think for the first time, I understand that word. Love."

Love. Melanie balled her fists and pressed her knuckles together. No way he'd ever understand love. How could anyone?

"I mean, you would have had to be there." Kyle scooted a wrapped sandwich close to the curtain. "They sang this song. 'My Jesus, I Love Thee.' Have you ever heard it?"

"No." She furrowed her brow. "Why would I have heard it?"

"Well, that's right. You haven't been to church. Anyway… he sang this song and talked about love being an action. Something we choose to do. And then, he rewrote the lyrics from other angles, like…"

Shaking her head, she opened the curtain a couple inches. He sure was bumbling this. Was he nervous? He'd done gone and lost his mind.

He grinned at her. "Listen to this. I wrote it for you like he did it." He whipped a stack of 3x5 cards from his shirt pocket. "Melanie, I choose to love you. I choose to only behave toward you in a way that demonstrates love."

She snorted. "You can't possibly love me."

"I'm not saying I do." He frowned. "Would you please listen? I know I don't feel that deep love for you that you're looking for. But do you agree that love is an action? Do you believe that I can choose to do loving actions toward you and commit to that?"

"I don't believe you can commit to anything." Pursing her lips, she flicked her gaze skyward. "Fine. Tell me the rest of it."

"I know that you are mine."

"This is ridiculous, Kyle."

He handed her the card. "Fine. Read it."

She held it up in front of her. *I know that you are mine. My gift from God. What I don't know is what kind of gift. Are you a friend? A future spouse? Or someone God has placed in my path to help steer me back in the right direction? Either way, I know you are mine. Mine to take care of over the next few days. Mine to encourage. Mine to treat with dignity and respect when others are making you feel small.*

Tears welled in her eyes. "I don't know what to say to this."

"Then let me finish." He held out the next card.

For thee, all the folly of my past life, I resign. I resign the alcohol and the parties. I resign the nights with the boys staying out all hours while someone waits at home. I resign the selfishness and immaturity.

She tossed the card over the deck rail. "You're so in love with me you plagiarized a hymn."

"I—"

"No. You don't get to talk now." She shoved the curtain all the way open and grabbed the buttons on his shirt. Clenching them in her fist, she yanked him closer. "I am so tired of words, Kyle. Tired of

Daddy's words. Tired of Stephen's words. Tired of Mama's words. And I don't need your words. Especially when they weren't your own."

"Melanie, I'm sor—"

"You gambled on baseball, you cheated on your girlfriend, and now, you're trying to win me over with some sorry attempt at stealing lyrics and—"

He cupped her face with both hands, mashing her lips in a kiss so she couldn't speak.

She jerked away and smacked him square in the jaw. "Did you miss out on reality? I don't want to kiss you, Kyle. I don't want you to choose to love me. It doesn't work like that. You fall in love. You don't choose."

His face contorted like a wounded pup. "But—"

"But nothing." She snatched the curtain and closed it between them, her heart thundering at Mach speed.

Tingles pulsed her body, and dizziness swarmed her mind. Here he was trying to make a sweet gesture, and she was spitting acid. How could she be so cruel? And especially after he'd been so kind. But at the same time, how could he be so stupid? No, she didn't want to date or kiss him, but she didn't want to crush him, either.

The deck creaked as his footsteps clanged to the ladder. With three steadying breaths, she flung the curtain open again and crawled out after him. "Wait."

He paused mid-step.

"I'm sorry, Kyle. I didn't mean—"

"You meant exactly what you said." He planted a foot on the ladder. "It's fine. I'll bring you food for the next few days and then you can move on with your wallowing and self-pity. I'll put it in the basket and—"

"Kyle! The tractor!" Melanie rushed to his side and pointed to the field where a cow butted the Massey Ferguson from the rear.

"Oh, no." Kyle palmed his face. "It's rolling. I must have rgotten the parking brake."

"Is she... the cow...?" Melanie half-gasped/half-snickered. he's pushing it toward the pond, Kyle."

"I... um... It's Gertie. Got to go." He hustled down the ladder id disappeared into the trees.

The cow gave one last butt, and the tractor rolled down the bank, front wheels sinking in deep mud.

Melanie shook her head. How would city boy Kyle ever manage at one?

Chapter Sixteen

Kyle groaned as he rubbed his aching back. Forget quicksand. Mud had to be far worse. He pressed his legs to the left. If he could reach the tractor, he could at least lean against it and maybe take some of the weight off.

Stretching his arm, he lunged and caught hold of the bumper. With some effort, he managed to pull himself another inch through the muck.

At least he'd worn his hat. The impending sunburn would blister his neck, ears, and arms, but his scalp was safe.

Rocks scattered at the muddy edge of the pond, some rolling down the bank and lodging beside the tractor.

"Kyle?"

Melanie. She came down to help him.

He leaned backward, catching her curious gaze from the opposite side of the tractor. Waist-high mud or no mud, he wanted to embrace her. She'd lied up there on the billboard. She'd wanted the kiss as much as he did. He'd garnered that much the other night in her passionate response. But she'd been right. He was an idiot. To use that song was a stupid idea. Completely unoriginal. An epic fail. Still, why was she here? "See you left your billboard."

"Yeah. She grinned. "I figured you had no idea how to hook the truck up to the tractor, and certainly no idea how to get it out of the mud."

He pulled his cap off and shoved his hand over his head. "Nope. I googled it and found the parts I needed to use, but I still have no idea."

"Are you... stuck?" She giggled. "I ought to tweet a picture of this one. Kyle Casey, former pro-baseball star, stuck in waist-high mud. I hope you're not too attached to your shoes."

"Stop laughing." The veins in his wrists bulged as he lunged forward again. "And I wore Pa's old muck boots. So, no big deal."

She raced around to his side of the tractor. "Oh, Kyle. Bless your heart." Her snickers erupted into full-blown cackles, and he covered his face with his hands.

"Okay... well..." She pressed her palm against her chest and snickered again. "Don't um... panic. Right. Don't panic. It'll make you sink lower. Or so they say. I have no idea if that's true or not. I've never been stuck in waist-high mud."

"Figured that one out." He grunted and strained. If he could pick up his feet...

"Hmm... let me check the truck."

"I found some hitching stuff Pa had in a drawer of the toolbox. Not sure how to use it, but I grabbed whatever looked useful. It's laying over there on the ground."

Three minutes later, she returned with a shovel. "Your pa's like my daddy. He always keeps a shovel behind the seat of his truck. And, you're lucky he's got that ladder mounted on the back."

She tossed the shovel. It landed three feet in front of him, and he dug out a trench around his left leg. The mud filled it back in before he could even finish. "Agh!" He slapped the shovel against the bank. "It's not working."

"Wait a minute and let me get this ladder out to you." She loosened the clamps holding the ladder and dragged it over to the bank. When she laid it across, it came right to his waist. "Now. Hold still and I'll grab the chain."

"There were two chains." Kyle caught the last rung of the ladder and tried to pull himself forward.

She hooked one of the chains to the end of the ladder and attached it to the tow hitch on the truck. Then, she attached a second chain to the shovel and tossed it to him. "I want you to use this to loosen one of your legs. Try to wedge it down to your knee and see if you can work one leg out at a time. It'll be awkward and uncomfortable for you, but that's the best way. Then, try to work the other leg and stretch yourself across the ladder. If you can, pull yourself up."

It took some serious wrangling and wriggling, but finally he sat next to her on the bank, the entire bottom half of his body caked in mud. He'd even managed to dig out the old boots.

"You want to tell me how you managed to pull that off?" Her hair hung in sweaty clumps around her face, and she twisted it into a knot.

"You tied your hair."

"Yup." She waggled her finger. "Stop trying to change the subject. How did you end up stuck in the mud?"

Up the hill, the cow gave a low, throaty moo, and Kyle scrunched his nose at her. "Ask Gertie."

"Gertie?"

"That stupid cow has been out to get me since the first day I arrived in Milton. You wouldn't believe the stunts she's pulled." He scuffed his pants against the grass, dislodging a thick chunk of mud. "I mean, who knew cows had developed brains, let alone demonic tendencies."

"I told you she was pushing the tractor." Melanie giggled again. She couldn't stop herself, apparently. And although it hurt his pride a little, Kyle couldn't help but enjoy seeing a twinkle in her eyes instead of sadness.

"I think she looks like a fine cow." She waved. "Gertie, you're a fine cow, aren't you, girl?"

Another low moo.

"She's something, anyway." Kyle stuck his tongue out at Gertie. "As for the mud, I was trying to get that front wheel unstuck. I didn't realize the pond would try to swallow me."

"Well, for future reference, it's tough to get anything out of thick mud."

"Thank you, Ms. Teacher." He winked. "So, you came down to help me. Were you watching?"

"Just because I didn't want you to get yourself killed. Then who'd bring my supper?" She stood. "In fact, we need to get this tractor out so I can go back to my post."

"Tell me what to do."

She unchained the ladder and he mounted it back on the truck while she hooked the chain to the tractor's tow hitch. "Did you get anything that looks like a cable?"

He pointed to the truck bed. "Pa had a wall in his shop labeled 'hitches' and I grabbed everything I saw. The two chains, some hooks and stuff…"

"Oh, good. You've got a come along."

"A come along?" He snickered. "As in, come along with me?" He secured the ladder to the rack. "So, why isn't it called a come hither?"

"You're killing me, Kyle. You can walk into any tractor supply store and ask for a come along, and the clerk would immediately know what you needed." She swatted his shoulder. "Pass me that piece with the cable and hooks, and I'll show you what it does."

A huge tree stood to the right of the pond, and she carried the come along on its side. "Okay. If you wrap this around the tree and crank it," she used the ratchet to tighten the cable, "it will help us set the tractor upright. Then, we should be able to pull it out with the truck."

He picked up one of the hooks. "So fasten this to—"

"I'll do that." She snatched it from his hands. "You're stronger than me. You crank the ratchet. Your job is simple. Keep it tight."

"Keep it tight. Gotcha."

"I don't know for sure how much weight it will pull." She frowned. "There is a slight danger that the tractor will be too heavy and the chain or cable can break and snap back. Watch it."

As she stepped over the deep grooves that had formed where the tractor rolled, Kyle faced Gertie. "You'd better stay away from Pa's truck."

Gertie flicked a fly at him with her tail.

Melanie linked the hook over a metal piece on the back of the tractor. "Now, crank it. Tighten it good, and it should close that angle between the rear wheel and the ground. I'm going to hook this chain up, and then when it's straight, I'll get in the truck and pull."

Twenty minutes later, Melanie sat in the truck, revving the engine while Gertie nudged Kyle on the shoulder. He nudged back. "She's going to get it out, Gertie. You'll see."

The wheels of Pa's truck spun, digging into the soft ground. Would she get the truck stuck, too?

Gertie butted her head against him, and Kyle stumbled forward.

"Tighten the winch!" Melanie called from the truck.

"I'm trying, if I could get this aggravating cow out of the way!" Dodging Gertie, Kyle cranked the ratchet as tight as it would go, and Melanie backed up. She revved the engine again, lurching forward and tugging the tractor about four inches.

He grinned. "Progress."

"Tighten it!"

As he cranked, Gertie butted him again.

"Would you stop it, you stupid beast?" He bumped the cow with his hip.

"She might be more cooperative if you stop calling her stupid." Melanie backed up once more then gave Kyle a thumbs-up out the window frame. "One, two…" She leaned against the steering wheel. "Three!"

This time, she dragged the tractor almost to the top of the bank. "Tighten! Hurry!"

When the tractor rolled over the bank on solid ground, she hopped out of the truck. "We did it!"

"You did it!" Kyle ran to her, picked her up, and spun her around. "We did it!"

Her face glowed, a more genuine smile than he'd ever seen from her. She clung tight to his arms, their faces mere inches apart, and he held her that way for as long as he could. Man, he'd love to kiss those full, upturned lips again. But she'd probably slap him or something. And he'd deserve it. Squelching the fire building deep within him, he set her down.

"You didn't have to help, you know."

"I know." She touched his shoulder, almost tentatively. "I didn't mean to be so hateful, Kyle. I do kind of get what you're saying. We could choose to be in a relationship and choose to be kind to each other. I could see us going down a path that might lead to love if we both committed to it."

He jolted. "You can?"

"Well, yeah, I'd be lying if I didn't say I was attracted to you. But that doesn't mean we will take the right path and end up together. What if you choose to hurt me instead of love me? What if I choose to hurt you?"

"I don't have any intention of doing that."

"You don't now, but intentions change. Listen, drive the tractor back to the house, and I'll follow you in the truck." She moved to the tree and unhooked the cable. "I want to make sure it's still running okay, and you won't end up stranded next time you drive it."

"Aww, look at you being all protective." He loosened the chain from the tractor then carried it to the truck bed. "Thanks for getting me out."

She shrugged, though one side of her mouth offered a hint of a smile. "Can't let anything happen to my meal ticket. Girl's gotta eat. Besides, I probably owed you a favor or two."

"You did." He ruffled her hair, and she mock-swung at him. "Although after that kiss, I wouldn't blame you if you held out."

"I was over it until you had to go bring it up again."

"Admit it. It was a good kiss. An incredible kiss."

She held up her fist, loosening it as though she was holding a mic. "Kyle Casey can do more than play baseball, people. And forget the fact that he can't maneuver in the mud. The boy can kiss. There. You happy?"

"Ecstatic."

Back at the house, he pulled the tractor through the driveway into the barn lot and strolled back over to the truck. She'd scooted to the passenger side.

"I'm going in to change real quick." He opened the door and reached for her hand. "Why don't you come in for a while? Let me cook us something, and we can sit down at the table to eat for a change."

Her eyes darkened. "I can't, Kyle. Will you please drive me back?"

"Forget Stephen. Forget why you're up there. Let me prove to you that I meant exactly what I said. Please, let me prove to you that I *can* choose to love you." He moved in front of her. "You can use Pa's bathroom and take a real shower while I cook. And then…"

"I can't."

He brushed his hands over his jeans sending a cascade of mud tumbling to the floor of the truck. "Let me change, and I'll—"

"Please? Take me back." As she batted those green eyes, small tears pooled in the corners.

"Stay." He interlocked his fingers in both her hands and tugged her to face him.

"No."

"Melanie, I'm begging you. Stay. Let me—"

"I said no, Kyle. No."

He backed away and pivoted toward the house. "Fine. I'll go make you a sandwich then. You're more stubborn than Gertie."

"I don't need a sandwich."

"I'm making you a sandwich." He stormed to the house, threw open the screen door, and fiddled with the old lock. What would it take to make her see that he was sincere? How could he convince her that he could change? That she'd completely worked her way under his skin, and he could barely draw a breath without thinking of holding her in his arms or laughing with her?

He raced to the kitchen and snatched the multigrain wheat bread he'd bought the night before. After laying out four pieces on a paper towel, he slapped ham and cheese on them and added a bit of mayonnaise. He grabbed a can of Dr Pepper, some chips, and a handful of miniature chocolate bars then tucked the sandwiches in a plastic bag. Less than three minutes. Had to be some kind of record.

Clumps of dried mud crunched beneath his feet as he hurried back to the truck. When he stepped onto the porch, he met Melanie's determined gaze from behind the steering wheel. What was she doing now?

As the screen door slammed behind him, the engine revved once more. Pa's truck jerked into reverse, sending dust dancing over the gravels, and shot forward again. Gripping the sandwiches, Kyle raced across the field after her. That girl was going to be the death of him.

So, why did he feel like he'd been brought back to life?

Chapter Seventeen

Melanie's cell blared early Monday morning, and she bolted upright. She'd dreamed all night of Kyle's dark brown eyes, earnest and pleading as he uttered that single word, over and over. *Stay*. But how could she stay?

He'd chased her in the truck across the whole farm and practically thrown the bag of food at her. Then, he'd driven back to the farmhouse, leaving her to climb up alone.

She fumbled through the small plastic tub that held all her billboard belongings and fished out the phone. Great. Mama. She'd have to call her back, or the phone would ring all day. Well, maybe not all day. It only had twelve percent battery.

Groaning, she tapped the screen. "Hey, Mama."

"How dare you sit up there waiting on that boy like a fool when your dad's in the hospital?"

"Good to hear from you, too, Mama." But why hadn't she called before now? Daddy had been in the hospital for a while. "Kyle told me Daddy was fine."

"He's having another small procedure today. You should be here."

"Why? So I can sit in the waiting room and listen to you gripe me out all day? No thanks." Melanie drummed her fingers against the deck. "What do you want, Mama?"

"While we're in Lexington, I'm heading out to pick up a few things Daddy needs. Going to buy you some new sheets for the bedroom. What color do you want?"

"What?"

Mama cleared her throat. "Sheets. For when you move back in to your old bedroom. The others are worn thin."

Melanie slammed the back of her head against the billboard sign. She'd given no thought to what might happen next after she came down from the billboard. After all, she'd already let her apartment go, and she'd not be moving in to Stephen's place as planned. Still, Mama would make her life miserable. "I'm not moving back home, if that's what you're insinuating."

"You have to." Mama let out a heavy huff. "You have no job. No apartment, no money, no nothing. You don't even have a car anymore."

She sighed. "How many times are you going to bring that up?" Although, Mama was right on that account. Why had she let Stephen talk her into selling the car? They offered thirteen hundred dollars and she'd thought it was a sign. "I'll get a job next week. And I can stay with Lizzie until I have the money for a car and apartment. She lives downtown by all the banks. Surely one of them needs a teller."

"If they'll take you. Besides, we didn't send you to college to be a bank teller your whole life."

Thirteen semesters to finish her management degree and master's in public administration. Commuting from home, of course, so in Mama's eyes she'd never left the nest. But the jobs hadn't poured in like she'd been promised, and up until last week, she still worked the same job she'd had since high school. Yet another example of how the wretched number had failed her. "Mama, I will look for something next week. In Public Administration or Management. I promise. Something professional."

"I don't know who'd hire you. Not after you've made your public display of stubbornness."

Melanie rubbed her right temple. "Mama—"

"You know you've been all over the news and Facebook."

"Yeah. And I've seen all the people sitting at the church. I'm a real celebrity now."

Mama whistled as she sucked in her breath. "Rumor has it some guys from CNN were at Reuben's Barbecue last night. That boy is a bigger deal than you bargained for, Melanie. Your face will be all over the national news, and who's going to hire you then?"

Melanie blinked back fresh tears. CNN? Would they bother her? Would they bother Kyle?

"Although, it might garner your father a little welcome attention." Mama laughed. "You know how he feels about free publicity."

Did he want the publicity? He seemed bothered by it. The CNN reporters would climb up like those others did. But Kyle had forced the local guys off his property. She'd hate for the big guns to bother him when he was working so hard to get his life back together. Especially when she'd crushed him. "I don't have much battery. I need to let you go."

"What color sheets?"

"I'm not moving back home." Melanie tapped the phone against her temple three times.

"What color?"

"Navy. Get navy. It's pointless, but get navy."

The phone screen went blank, and Melanie tossed the cell back into the tub. How could she go back home? She was in her twenties, for crying out loud. Half the other girls her age were already toting around two or three kids. And the ones who weren't were those self-professed singles mavens. Too professional or classy to be bothered with anything more than casual dating. And there were the girls like Lizzie, of course, who flitted from guy to guy because they couldn't hold them in their clutches. Melanie didn't fit with any of them. She was supposed to be married. To Stephen. And he was supposed to be a decent husband who'd take care of her.

A tiny voice nagged in the back of her mind. When had Stephen ever taken care of her? It was always, "Get me a drink, babe," and "Fix me something to eat." Here was Kyle offering to cook something for her. If they were married, she could envision them spending time together in the kitchen. With Stephen, she'd have signed on to a life of servitude. Why had she not seen it before?

She remembered a discussion in one of her high school social studies classes, one of those rare courses that ended up filled with girls and only a couple boys. The teacher had presented a lesson on Renaissance customs, and the conversation derailed into one about marriage and how women should be treated. This, of course, turned into a series of questions about what the girls should look for in a future spouse, and the teacher had given them a copy of the list she'd made before meeting her husband.

What was that woman's name? Mrs. Tenny.

Melanie sifted through the plastic tub for a notebook and pen. At the top of a blank page, she wrote in flowing text. "What I Want in a Man."

Ugh. It felt like being back in the third grade. Or desperate. She scratched out the words and placed the tip of the pen below them. "Okay. What I Want Out of Life."

What did she want out of life?

"Happiness. Contentment. Security." The ink dulled on the page as she tapped the base of the pen against her forehead. It was a good start. "Someone to make me laugh. Like Daddy."

Kyle made her laugh. In fact, when she didn't feel like killing him, practically all they'd done had been laugh. With Stephen, even when things were "good," she'd cried far more than experiencing any kind of merriment.

She ripped the page from the notebook and wadded it into a ball. This was futile. What did she want out of life? Who knew? But she had four more days to figure it out.

Kyle stretched his arms up and bent them behind his head. As his shoulder muscles tightened, he winced. That mud escapade did a number on his back.

"You okay?" Coach Dave Mitchell came up beside him and sat on the half-wall separating the dugout from the field.

"Yeah. I had a little bit of an um... accident yesterday on the farm."

"Dad told me." Dave's shoulders shook, and he gave a goofy, laugh-stifling grin. "We appreciate you coming out to help the team."

Micah Overbee, one of Paul's grandsons, swaggered up wearing a deep frown. "See? I don't throw it fast enough, and it always drops too low."

Kyle held out his hand. "Let me see the ball." He placed his fingers across the seam. "Try holding it this way and gripping it with your fingertips. You're not getting a good snap."

Micah gripped an imaginary ball. "So, like this?"

"Yeah." Kyle acted like he was going to throw it. "Remember to keep your fingers behind the ball when you release it. If you get them in front of the ball, they'll absorb some of the energy. The point is you want as much kinetic energy as possible to be transferred to the ball."

"Behind the ball." Micah simulated a throw. "Guess it'll take practice."

"Yeah." Kyle scooted a pile of dried mud from the pitcher's mound with the sole of his shoe. "It looks to me like you're over-throwing it. You're trying too hard and straining your arm. Then, that release... you're bending your fingers funny. Some of the energy of the throw is going into your fingers rather than into the ball." He nudged Micah's shoulder. "And... are you skimping on your conditioning?"

Another player came up behind them. "He only skimps on days that end in Y."

"Shut up, Jacob." Micah mock-punched the kid.

"You can't possibly hope to throw it fast if you don't bulk up." Kyle glanced at Chip, Paul Mitchell's other grandson. He and Micah could be twins with their soft brown hair and ruddy cheeks. Amazing that the boys came from different parents. Although, to not be blood related, the two coaches favored each other. Made sense that their sons would. And they both had great, easygoing personalities like Paul did. Easygoing didn't always cut it when coaching, though. Maybe they were a little too easy on the boys. "Do you guys perform long toss drills?"

Chip shrugged. "We do, but I can only get about ninety feet. I want to throw farther, but I can't."

"Longer is faster. If you condition like you should, maximum effort, and you have good form, you'll be able to throw longer because you have good velocity. But then again, you don't want to overdo it. If you fatigue the arm, you'll lose strength and put yourself at risk for injury."

Coach Overbee blew his whistle. "Hydrate, boys." He walked over to Kyle. "I appreciate you coming out. It was a big inspiration for the team after they've had to deal with such a horrible loss."

"No problem. I'm glad to, and besides, I owe your father-in-law a couple favors." Kyle met his handshake with a brutish squeeze. "Anytime."

"Some of the parents were wondering…" Coach Overbee hooked his thumbs in his pockets. "They wanted me and Dave to start a clinic where they could get private lessons. For specific skills, you know. I know some of them have already approached you about this. Would you maybe be interested in running the clinic? Like managing the whole operation, I mean. There's a trust fund this old man set up when he passed to establish it. They'd pay you by the hour."

Kyle couldn't stop his grin. A clinic, working with teen boys would be awesome. He wouldn't need the money. Except… his grin faded. It would be awesome until they remembered who he was. "Would they want me? A washed-up jock? After everything that's happened, I—"

"Milton's a place all about second chances, Kyle. You know, there's that old warehouse down on Seventh Street they converted into a bowling alley. The back half of the place is reasonable, and the rent is cheap. It would be a perfect space for an indoor cage, and it backs right up to Hiler Park. We could split everything in thirds if you didn't want to do it by yourself. Me, you, and Dave. Something to think about."

"You should do it! Help my boys out." Paul slapped Kyle's shoulder while Chip and Micah nodded from behind him.

"Yeah!" Chip pretended to pull off a fast pitch, and Jacob shoved him to the side. They fell to the ground in laughter. "You could make a difference for our team."

"I could." Kyle's chest heaved. "I don't know how long I'll be staying in Milton, though. Pa asked me to take care of the farm while he's out of town. I'm not sure what my next move will be after that."

The smiles left the boys' faces, and Kyle scratched the stubble on his chin. Staying wouldn't be terrible, he supposed. Especially if he and Melanie… if they what? To be honest, he didn't know that much about her. Did she live in Milton with Wayne, or had she come home for the wedding? What kind of work did she do? Would she be okay with living in the city, or would she want to stay in the country?

"You with us, man? Think you zoned out for a while." Micah waved his hand in front of Kyle's face. "You were probably thinking about that chick, weren't you?"

"Yeah, tell us about the billboard girl." Chip brushed the dust from his pants. "You dating her or what?"

Had the kid read his mind? Kyle folded the bill then set his new cap back on his head. "She's a spitfire. That's for sure."

"But are you guys dating?"

"She wouldn't have me if I tried, and I don't need to be trying." Kyle grinned. "You young guys need to listen up to this advice. There are three kinds of women you need to stay away from: women who want your money, women who have an agenda, and women who are on the warpath. It can't end well."

"But you're not staying away from her." Micah snorted. "We all see you going up there every day."

"I can't abandon her." Kyle met Paul's knowing stare. "She's staying on my property. I have to make sure she's safe."

"That guy's my third cousin." Jacob took a swig from his water bottle. "You know, her fiancé? He used to brag about all the stuff he did behind her back at our family dinners. Said he was after her father's money and he'd use it to buy a timeshare in Pigeon Forge so he could rent it out and make money."

Kyle shook his head. What kind of moron would brag about stuff like that? "She says her dad doesn't have that much money. Why would Stephen think he did?"

"Rumor has it that Wayne Lee has some hidden treasure somewhere. Money stashed back from his gambling days." Jacob kicked at a tuft of grass. "Guess you two would get along. Anyway, it wasn't a ton of money, but enough to leave Stephen sitting pretty."

Guess they'd get along. Kyle shook off his irritation and stepped in front of Jacob. "What was Stephen planning to do? Off the guy?"

"Nah. I dunno. Probably get her dad to give the money to Melanie and leave her. Mom said that's what he did with his last wife, too. As soon as she deposited all that money in their joint account, Stephen closed it and left town."

"Crazy." Kyle knit his brow tighter. Did Melanie know Stephen had been married before? She hadn't mentioned it.

"Yeah." Jacob walked over to a metal bench and stuffed his water bottle into a sports bag. "Some people are, I guess. Like the ones who climb up billboards. Anyway, I heard him tell Dad he's going to let her throw her fit a couple more days then try to get her back."

Kyle flinched. Over his dead body. Stephen wasn't getting close to her on his watch. "Thanks for telling me that, Jacob. I'd better go, though. Have to take care of some things on the farm."

"Yeah. Like the girl. I hope you win her."

Like the girl. On the way back, Kyle stopped by Matilda's, a new little burger joint, to pick up something for dinner. He needed to find Stephen. Make it clear that he wasn't welcome on the property. As he passed the money to the drive-thru cashier, he leaned in closer. "Hey, kid. If I was trying to find some local lowlife, where would I look?"

The kid blinked. "Lowlife?"

"You know. Those guys who are in their mid-twenties and early thirties, but still live at home. No job, they rip and run, that sort of thing."

"Oh. You'd go to O'Baba's for sure. Downtown bar, attracts a bunch of real winners. But I wouldn't go picking a fight with any of them. Although I think you could take them."

Kyle chuckled. Too late for not picking a fight. He already had. And, he had every intention of winning—the fight and the girl.

Chapter Eighteen

Melanie patted her full belly and grinned. When she came down from the billboard, she'd have to eat salad for an entire month. "I'm so stuffed."

Kyle passed her the box of fried mushrooms. "I know. I have to stop feeding us junk. But that Matilda's place had so many good choices. Pa's got a nice garden. I picked some green beans the other day and broke them. I'll fix you some tomorrow night."

"Sounds good." Melanie winced at her wistfulness. She looked forward to every moment with Kyle. But at this point, was she leading him on? "How's Gertie?"

He laughed. "That cow has a vendetta against me. I'm telling you. This morning, she rammed the passenger door of the truck. I think she was trying to flip the thing over."

"You're going to have to work a little harder at winning her heart, Kyle." Melanie brought her fists up together over her chest. "Try bringing her some treats. I've heard that cows like apples and cucumbers."

"I'll have to try that." He scooted around to face her. "I want you to explain this thirteen fixation."

Where had that come from? He'd laugh at her. "It's stupid."

"Try me."

She bit her lip. "Okay, so on my thirteenth birthday, we were at Virginia Beach with all my cousins. Walking the boardwalk and this woman was riding a bike with a sign saying she read palms. Of course, we all had to do it. She told me it was my birthday, and thirteen was my number. Said it would bring me great fortune and true love."

"And?"

"I started living by that. I checked my watch religiously. Tried hard to remember what happened in the thirteenth minute of every hour and the thirteenth hour of every day." Her cheeks warmed. "I know. It sounds ridiculous now, but you wouldn't believe how many good things happened that corresponded to those times. I believed in it wholeheartedly."

Kyle pressed his lips tight. At least he was trying not to laugh. "So you started planning to do things at those times."

"Yeah." She sighed. "If I had to make a decision, I'd do it on the thirteenth minute of the thirteenth hour of the thirteenth day of the month. Like June thirteenth, one thirteen in the afternoon."

"What a coincidence." Kyle brushed his fingers over her hand. "Today's the thirteenth day of June. I'm here with you, not Stephen. Maybe that's a sign *we* should be together. You like me."

"Seriously?" She flicked her gaze skyward, where white puffy clouds hung overhead. Such a beautiful afternoon. "Anyway, Stephen was the thirteenth guy who'd asked me out. My first real relationship, because all the others ended after a few weeks. It had to be…"

"But it wasn't." Kyle scooted back against the billboard sign and draped an arm around her shoulders. "Besides. You didn't set your wedding to the thirteenth hour of the thirteenth day. What if thirteen isn't your number? Could it have been something that woman made up because it was your thirteenth birthday?"

"Maybe. I couldn't set the wedding date for the thirteenth. Stephen had already booked the trip. And the preacher wasn't available until two o'clock." Melanie leaned her head against his chest. "I think in my heart I knew the fortune teller's prediction was fake. But I wanted it to be real. I wanted it to work out."

Kyle shifted his weight so he faced her and tipped up her chin. "Do you think you tried to force it too hard? Especially your relationship. Like can you name all the things you loved about Stephen? Can you name even one?"

"Do you want the truth?" She raked her fingers through her hair, grasping it at the back of her skull. "All the things I thought I loved are now things I can't stand. I was thinking about it last night. How he tried to bully you at the hospital. I used to brag to Daddy about how tough he was."

Kyle laughed. "Well, I got the upper hand in that one, didn't I? Almost broke his arm and got you that letter. But, I don't like how he thinks he can waltz back into your life and sweep you off your feet again."

"You should know that Stephen never gives up. No matter the cost." She shuddered. "He has this way of getting exactly what he wants from everyone."

"Well, he's not getting to you." Kyle flexed his muscle. "I won't let that happen."

"Good to know." She tucked her arm under his and snuck her fingers through his. "I'm sorry I flipped out on you about the song. I'm scared, Kyle. I don't know what to feel anymore. I had my whole life planned, and now it's all uncharted waters."

"Me, too. But I think that's the beauty of it. I can literally do anything. Go anywhere. A completely new start." He glanced at his watch. "Hey. You've only got four more days to go, right? Maybe we can launch our new lives together after that."

Her breath caught as she met those earnest brown eyes. Did he mean together like a couple? Was he still holding on to that idea? Was she? She was, after all, holding on to his hand.

After a minute-long stare, he rubbed her left arm and stood. "I'd better go, Mel. I've got something I need to do in town."

"In town? This late?" She gave him a sideways frown. Was he going to one of the bars? He'd talked about how proud he was to not be drinking anymore. "Kyle, please. Don't go. Stay."

He knelt beside her, his determined face softening as he squeezed her fingers.

"Stay." Her voice shook with the word. She forced a grin and pointed to the skyline. "I don't think you want to miss this sunset."

He dropped to the deck and scooted close to her, easing his arm around her shoulders as she tucked her head under his chin. "You're right. I don't. I don't want to miss any great moments with you."

As their breath fell into sync, she closed her eyes. Maybe she'd been wrong to push him away. Maybe this could be the start to their forever.

After a long, hard gaze at the billboard, where Melanie seemed to be staring after him, Kyle set off to the dark side of Milton. He dodged a monstrous fly as he reached for the grime-covered steel handle to the frosted glass door. The acrid smell hit him like a brick—years' worth of stale smoke crossed with a blend of cheap cologne. How had he ever stood places like this?

A strobe light pulsed overhead, and beside it, a crooked picture frame boasted a cheeky blond man clinging to the shoulders of an old has-been actor in Vegas.

Rainbow lights darted around the room like bees, illuminating the occasional exploratory throat surgery by some sleazy tongue.

Kyle's breath hitched. What was he doing here? If not for Melanie…

He'd taken enough food at lunchtime to hold her until later tonight. After he climbed down, he heard a sound in the woods and circled around on high alert before heading back to his truck. That's when he discovered the private spot in the woods where she'd set up a makeshift vanity. The small mirror he'd brought her hung suspended from a low branch of a walnut tree, and she'd turned a row of three stumps into a display of the beauty products she'd sent him after on day three.

Footprints and disturbed leaves revealed the path she'd taken between the stumps and the creek. Melanie was like a nymph—completely at home in the woods. Her almost otherworldly presence crept under his skin and deep into his heart. He wanted to love her and cherish her more than he'd ever wanted anything in his life. More than he'd even wanted baseball.

That thought sobered him. Hopefully he could finish with Stephen early enough to make her the special dinner he'd planned after leaving her last night.

Last night. She'd clung to him like plastic wrap, her grip on his arm so tight he could almost still feel it. She'd nuzzled against him and breathed contented sighs. Had she changed her mind about giving him a chance?

When he'd finally pulled away from her, even as she slept, she'd held tight as he pried himself from her fingers and carried her into her shelter. Leaving her side had packed a different kind of punch.

Speaking of packing a punch…

Clusters of beer-guzzling drunks occupied every corner, surrounded by scantily-clad girls who were likely underage. Kyle knew the type. They'd sell their soul for a fragment of positive attention.

A small group parted like someone had cracked open an Easter egg, half of them swaying in a drunken boogie to the dance floor and the other half sauntering to the pool table. And in the middle sat the big yolk. Or, the big joke. That slimy snake Stephen, as Melanie called him, draped all over a tank-topped twig who couldn't have been a day over eighteen. He snapped a quick picture with his cell.

Kyle closed the gap between them, his mouth watering as he passed the bar. He shook off the taste of beer as the smell overwhelmed his senses. He wasn't that guy anymore.

When he reached Stephen's table, Tank-Girl gasped. "Oh, Stephen, look! It's that baseball guy. I recognize him from TV, don't you? How cool is that?"

Kyle would have groaned and burrowed from the recognition, but how could he not smirk at Stephen's scowl?

"We need to talk." Kyle pointed to the side exit.

Stephen snorted, prying himself free from Tank-Girl and pointing to the chair beside him. "You want to talk, sit."

Kyle plopped in the chair and scooted closer to Stephen than necessary. "Outside might save you some shame."

Though he held his face stoic, a rush of air filled Stephen's lungs. Kyle grinned. He was already getting to the creep.

"Well, go ahead." Stephen drained his beer stein and slammed it on the table. "Trixie, go get me and my good buddy Kyle here a drink."

"No, thanks." Kyle's jaw twitched. Stephen must know more about him than he'd let on.

"So, one beer then?" Trixie's gaze flitted between them.

"Two." Stephen grinned like a cat who'd caught a huge mouse.

Fine. She could bring two, but Kyle wouldn't drink it. He didn't plan to stay that long anyway. As Trixie be-bopped off, he grabbed Stephen by the collar. "Rumor has it you're planning to try to win Melanie back. Well, if you know what's good for you, you'll stay away from her. For good." He shoved Stephen back against his chair. "And I dare you to set even a toe on my property."

When Kyle released him, Stephen raised his fists. "You came in here to threaten me? In my turf? I should sic all my buddies on you, Casey. Show you what a real fight looks like."

Kyle stood and pushed his chair into the table. "Let me put it this way. If I find you trespassing, I'm going to assume you've accepted my invitation to pummel you into the muddy ground. If you bring friends, you'll all end up in jail. I have no qualms about taking you down one by one."

The right side of his lips turned upward. Imagine Stephen trying to wiggle free from waist-high mud. He pivoted and nudged his way toward the exit.

Three stick-figure girls in short leather skirts and fringe tops caught him by the door. "Hello, sugar!" The tallest one, a redhead, planted a red-lipped kiss on his left cheek, and the brunette next to her puckered to his right one. The third girl knelt in front of him and wrapped her arms around his leg.

"What are you doing?" He met the lens of Stephen's cell phone camera as he jerked away.

"Maybe we should step outside after all." Stephen snapped several more pictures while Kyle tried to pry himself free from their grasp. He pocketed the phone and shoved Kyle into the heavy steel door. Red light from the exit sign reflected into Stephen's eyes. This guy could be the devil himself.

Kyle stumbled over lip-locked bodies into the dark narrow alley separating the bar from a decades-old bank. Stephen bumbled after him, lunging and knocking him into the brick wall cheek-first. Blood trickled from above his right eye. This was enough.

He twisted Stephen's arms and crossed them over his chest, catching his wrists and pinning him as he picked him up off the ground. Stephen kicked the air with his preppy brown loafers. Where were those friends now?

"I don't think you want to fight me." Kyle lowered Stephen and tossed him aside. "Let me say it once again. Leave Melanie alone. She doesn't want you back. You're wasting your time."

Rubbing his arms, Stephen sneered. "You're falling for her, aren't you? Who knew tough guy playboy Kyle Casey could fall for a daddy's girl country bumpkin."

Fists at his side, Kyle spat at Stephen's feet. "She's so much more than that. How can you not see it?"

Stephen laughed from his gut. "I knew it. You do care about her. She's so much more. Ha. She's so much more than one of your little ball groupies, isn't she?" He stepped forward and waggled his finger in Kyle's face. "Well, think about this. If she returned your feelings, then why's she still sitting up there waiting for me?"

Chapter Nineteen

What a long, boring Wednesday. Melanie finished off the last of the sandwiches Kyle had brought that morning and tossed the wadded wrapper into the trash bag she'd hung over the side of the billboard. Good thing she'd saved it. Was he never planning to bring her supper?

And, would he care to explain the bruises and cuts on his face? He'd fought with someone. Was it Stephen?

She moved to the right of the billboard and peeked over the back of it toward the farmhouse. His sports car sat in the drive, and lights shone from several windows. He'd popped up with more water and promised to cook for her after he finished up some things on the farm. Wonder how it was going.

After a good hour of stomach rumbles and fidgeting, she pulled out her cell and tapped his number. No answer. Ten minutes and thirteen tries later, she slammed the phone against her thigh. Eight percent life before the phone would die. Well, maybe she should try one more time. Even if he didn't want to talk, she needed to get him to recharge her pocket battery.

"Kyle Casey. Leave your number."

His voicemail beeped and her shoulders slumped. "Hey. It's Melanie. If you didn't get the last bazillion messages I left, then here's one more. My phone's dying, I'm starving, and I'm starting to worry."

Someone beeped in on the call. Oh, it was him. She tapped the screen. "Hey. Everything okay?"

"It's fine. I'm almost finished cooking." He laughed. "I had to search for everything. Poor old Pa has all the dishes out of sorts. You wouldn't believe these cabinets."

"Oh. Well, I was worried because it was late. And my phone's dying."

A pot clanged in the background, and Kyle gasped. "Hold on a sec… Okay, so I was thinking. I want you to come down and have dinner with me. In the farmhouse. Stay for a while and play some cards or something. Hang out. Maybe leave the billboard entirely."

A pit formed in Melanie's stomach. Leave the billboard? But she'd come so far. "Can't you bring it?"

"Why are you doing this?" His sharp tone jolted her. "What are you still trying to prove to that loser?"

"Kyle? I thought you were supporting me. I thought you understood."

Air blasted the speakers. "I don't understand, Mel. I don't understand why you can flirt with me and act all grateful for what I do for you but persist in hanging on to this dream that you guys are going to have a peaceful resolution. I know it's too soon for a relationship or anything, but I like you. I thought we might have something budding. I realize now that you're using me to bide your time until you can go crawling back to him."

"But I—" She fingered the handkerchief shirt which lay folded at the bottom of her crate. "I like you, too, but I said I was going to stay up here thirteen days, and I'm going to follow through."

"Do you?" Vitriol dripped from Kyle words. How had he gotten so angry with her so fast? "If you like me, why can't you forget Stephen? Forget the billboard and the wedding, and let's start over. Come and eat with me. At my—well, at Pa's house."

Her tears spilled over. "I can't, Kyle. I need to finish this. I don't want Stephen back. Why do you even think that? This isn't about him anymore. It's about not backing down and finishing what I started."

"That makes no sense." Kyle's growl blasted through the speakers. "Why can't you come down and move on with your life?"

Her phone had to choose that very instant to die. She sniffed, blinked her burning eyes, and pounded her head against the billboard. She couldn't quit now. Why couldn't he understand?

His words hung in the air between her billboard and the farmhouse. What was it about? Pride? Embarrassment? At some point, it stopped being about Stephen, that was for sure.

She stretched out across the deck and propped her chin on her fists, looking out over the farm. Was it her imagination, or was the cow staring, too? And was he planning to leave her here to starve?

After a half hour, the lights went down in the farmhouse, and a shadowy figure made its way to Pa's truck.

Melanie's pulse raced as the truck sped across the farm toward her. Even angry, Kyle was coming. He was coming!

When the rope struck the ladder and the basket eased close to the top, she peered over the edge of the deck where the moonlight struck his face at the perfect angle. His hard-pressed lips softened for a moment, then tightened again.

Without a word, he climbed up and offered her a plate of lukewarm steak and mushrooms. Melted butter leaked over the side of a loaded baked potato and dripped from the top of a plump yeast roll.

He sat cross-legged beside her, grabbed his own plate, and handed her a knife and fork.

"Thanks." She held her breath.

Not even a grunt. He took out his cell and tapped the screen, setting a romantic jazz song to play.

Between the soft pulse of the music and the squeaks of their forks and knives against the plates, her soft sniffles faded into the background. Salty tears dripped from her cheeks into the plate and rolled over her lips.

Kyle emptied his plate and set it in the basket. He crossed his hands in his lap and leaned his head back against the sign.

"This was fantastic." Melanie swallowed. "I appreciate it."

He muttered something that sounded like "Thanks."

She arched her neck back toward the billboard and closed her eyes. "I'm sorry, Kyle. I know you wanted to make this special for me."

Silence.

Unsteady fingers moved across Melanie's forehead and through her hair. She opened her eyes to find Kyle sitting on his knees, his hand a mere inch from her cheek.

He lurched back and moved closer to the ladder. "I'm sorry. There were leaves."

"Leaves. Right." She blinked away more tears. "Kyle, what if we just met? Not the billboard, not the baseball... What if we happened upon each other at a restaurant or something? Randomly crossed paths?"

His jaw flinched. "Given my track record, I'd have flirted a little."

"And?"

"I would have promised to call and forgot you existed." He turned his gaze toward the deck. "What about you?"

Melanie picked the leaf fragments from her hair, dropped them over the side of the billboard, and watched them flutter to the ground. She pulled her hair back and with a few deft twists, she fashioned a loose braid. Grimacing, she grabbed ponytail holder and wrapped it around the ends. She flipped the braid over her shoulder and shrugged. "I'd have pretended to ignore you. Told myself that Stephen was worth remaining pure for. You'd have never gotten my phone number."

"So, what does that mean? In our normal worlds, we'd have never made it."

"And in a few days, we go back to our normal worlds, right?"

He nodded to the farm. "I don't. Not until Pa comes back, at least. And definitely not back to baseball. I don't even know what my normal is anymore."

She lifted her hand to her forehead, shielding her eyes from the billboard lights. Across town, the bank sign flickered between the temperature and time. "I guess I don't, either. I didn't give my two-weeks' notice at the bank, so I doubt they'll be in the mood to give me my job back."

Kyle's cheeks stretched into a wide grin. "I could maybe use a farmhand. I have no idea how to do anything, in case you haven't noticed, and you seem to be an expert with the outdoors."

"A farmhand." Memories of her middle school and teenage years working with Daddy on various farms came flooding back. "I suppose I have a little experience." She laughed. "The great Wayne Lee Turner wasn't always so famous. He dragged me to every odd-end job he worked until he was discovered. I learned how to do a lot of things that you might find helpful."

Kyle pushed aside a thick cluster of branches at the back-right edge of the billboard sign and pointed. "I was looking through the farm records last night. There are two double-wide trailers in that front corner closest to town with their own entrance. I don't think anyone's lived in them for the past seven or eight years, at least by what Pa's noted. They might need to be cleaned up some, but it would be a place you could live rent-free until you get on your feet."

A trailer on the farm. Complete isolation until she got her life back together. Maybe it could work. "Okay."

He grabbed both her hands and squeezed. "And maybe when Pa comes home, I could move into the one next door to it. We could start from scratch. You know, see where things lead."

Melanie grimaced. He was persistent, if nothing else. She shook her head. "Kyle, I appreciate everything you've done for me. And, all your effort in taking care of me. But I can't think about dating right now. I can't. Not coming off such a huge disappointment. And I'm afraid if I stayed on the property, it would make things awkward for both of us."

He jumped up with a scowl. "I wish you'd change your mind. Come down. Give me a chance." He swung his legs over the ladder and descended halfway. "Give us a chance."

Melanie hoisted the basket down to him. "I'm sorry, Kyle. I can't."

"Why can't you?" He gripped the handles with white knuckles. "I think at this point you're only staying to prove a point. And I don't know what your point is anymore. Do you even know? Melanie Dawn Turner, taking stubborn to new heights. Stubborn and selfish. All you can see right now is your pain. Forget about the whole world of people down here who care about you. Wayne, Louisa—"

"It's not your business." She raised her palm, blocking his face.

He pointed his finger at her. "You're on *my* farm. It *is* my business."

She flicked his finger away. "I'm on your *Pa's* farm. Have you already forgotten why you're here? Why I can't trust you? I didn't climb up here to draw your attention. I climbed up here to be alone. To think. All you've done is confuse my emotions."

His face twisted into a pained expression, and he leapt over to the tree. The silence between them seemed to grow into a thick fog, pushing him farther away than even space allowed. Mission accomplished. She was making her thirteen days, no matter what Kyle or anyone thought.

"Guess I'll see you tomorrow, then."

She winced at the dejection in his voice, but could not stop the ice from covering her own. "Don't bother. Leave me alone. I need some space. I don't even need food."

"I'm not letting you starve, Mel. That's ridiculous. You could get dehydrated or anything."

Her voice quivered. "I said I need space. Here I am trying to heal and all you want is to push me into a relationship. Make plans for a future together. Will you please respect that I'm not ready for that, and I want to be left alone?"

"But I promised your dad."

"Unpromise him. I'm a big girl. I'm so tired of people condescending and treating me like a child."

"Maybe if you quit throwing a public fit and come down—"

"Whose side are you on?" She disappeared over the top of the deck then poked her head over again. "Agh! Please, go away and leave me alone. I'll come down when I'm good and ready."

His shoulders slumped as he walked back to the truck, and she loosened her collar. The strangling, oppressive guilt spread through her body, burning deeper than even her pain.

Maybe Mama was right. Maybe she did have an attitude problem. Still, she wanted to be left alone. At least for now...

Kyle sat at Pa's kitchen table polishing his phone with a microfiber cloth. He scrolled through his contact list to the M's and tapped the line he'd avoided for months. Mom.

Chewing his lip, he hovered his finger over the screen. It was late, but she'd still be up. She'd be glad to hear from him. She'd likely been more worried than angry. But what would they talk about?

He stood the phone up on its base, and rolled it on its side a full 360 degrees. When he made the last turn, the phone slipped, and he accidentally tapped the call icon. Great. It was ringing. Fate, he guessed. No going back now.

With tight-pressed lips, he turned on the speaker and held his breath. Maybe it would go to voicemail. Then he wouldn't have to answer, but she'd see that he called.

Nope, the phone was ringing. To answer or not to answer. He rested the phone face down on the table as the ringing persisted.

Louisa's words came to mind. Mom missed him. He propped his elbow on the table and took a deep breath. Fine. He'd talk to her.

As he tapped the screen to answer, the ringing stopped. Okay, so he'd call her back. Now or never.

"Kyle?"

Panic filled Mom's voice, and guilt washed over him. "I'm here."

"Kyle? Is it you? Are you okay?"

"Yeah." He chewed the skin from his lower lip. "I'm doing great, Mom. I'm working some things out on Pa's farm."

Her yawn must have lasted twenty seconds. "So I heard."

And… silence. He tapped his toes in his shoes and darted his gaze around the kitchen. "Um, I was wondering how things were going with you and Dad. I miss you."

"Good. They're good." She whistled through the speakers. "Hey, Denny. It's Kyle. Wake up."

"Sorry it's so late." Kyle glanced at Pa's old grandfather clock, which had stopped working about the same time Grandma passed away. So many memories in this house. Sitting around the table with Mom and Dad, laughing and playing cards.

"No, it's fine. I was hoping you'd call. Wanted to call you, but I figured you wouldn't answer."

"Mom, I'm sorry. Truly sorry for everything."

In the pause that followed, Kyle's entire world flashed before him. The days of his youth where she scrubbed his uniform pants to keep them white. The meals and snacks she'd cooked for all his friends. And the nights she stayed up waiting for him to make it safely home. She'd always been a servant to him. More than mother to a child.

And to Dad as well. How many nights had she rubbed his shoulders and back by the fire, trying to ease the pain out of Dad's muscles? Pain from the injury that took Dad out of the game and likely drove him to push Kyle so hard to play.

"I forgave you a long time ago." Mom's voice was tender. Not sharp like he'd expected. "I'm glad things are working out for you at Pa's. Louisa said you were doing a real good job."

How would she know that? And was he? Sure, no animals had died, but Gertie still had some sort of vendetta against him. "I'm trying."

"You staying in Milton?"

"Thinking about it." Kyle swallowed hard. "Don't have anywhere else to go."

"Your dad and I are thinking about coming home." She cleared her throat. "He's ready to retire, and I told him we need to be there for you."

"So you're not mad?"

"I've been through all the emotions, son. All of them. Anger, fury, denial, shame..." She sniffled. "Sorrow."

Shame and sorrow washed over him, too. His selfish actions had hurt so many people. Deeply. "When?"

"He has three more weeks until his summer classes finish. But I'm thinking about coming down early. Maybe as soon as Sunday. Do you need me?"

"I..." Kyle's eyes moistened and burned. Were these tears? His entire heart melted out onto his sleeve. He'd pushed her away for so long. But now, all he wanted was to fall into the arms of the mother who'd done so much for him over the years. She'd made things so easy. Why hadn't he picked up the phone to call before now? He drew in a deep breath. "I do, Mom. I need you. More than you could ever know."

Chapter Twenty

Wednesday night passed without incident, but for Melanie, it might as well have been an earthquake, tornado, and volcanic eruption wrapped up in one. Kyle hadn't spoken a word to her, and he'd sent enough food up in the basket to last long enough that he wouldn't have to return. That's what she said she'd wanted. To be alone and process her feelings for Stephen. To fight her way through the anger and work toward healing and forgetting.

Problem was, she couldn't keep her mind off Kyle for even a second.

Oh, to laugh with him again like they had the first day. He'd done so many goofy things to lift her spirits. When she closed her eyes, she seldom dreamed of Stephen, and even then it was about walking away. But her dreams of Kyle were filled with hope and plans. The future.

If she could see it so clearly, why did she fight it so hard?

Fear, of course. Same old story. Mama had been quick to point it out. She'd been afraid to try for a job in her degree field and kept working at the bank. Why? Because who'd want to hire her? She'd lived at home until she started dating Stephen, and then she'd moved in with Lizzie so she could keep the hours she wanted instead of listening to Mama nag.

Fear sent her racing to the top of the billboard, and fear kept her pinned to the deck. Paralyzing fear. So, how could she let it go?

Take a chance.

The words rang so clearly in her head, as if the woman on the billboard had spoken. Take a chance on what? Kyle? A new job?

She squinted at the letters against the white plastic, which nearly blinded her in the bright sun. God? Maybe tomorrow, when this was all over, she should climb down and talk to the preacher. He'd offered prayer for her on his radio show. Maybe he'd have some advice on how she could start to live again.

It couldn't hurt. Nothing else she'd done in her life seemed to be working.

Kyle couldn't shake the ominous feeling that had plagued him since leaving Melanie last night. He sent her food up at regular intervals without a word and sailed through all the farm chores like a pro.

She didn't even flinch at his presence, but rather sat in a huddle staring off into space. He did see the empty food containers and wrappers, so at least she'd eaten. And the last time, he'd left her enough nonperishable stuff to get her through the rest of her time. This was "Day Thirteen," but he didn't know if she'd come down today or tomorrow morning.

The only thing left on Pa's list that he hadn't touched was mending the broken fences. He still hadn't found any places that needed mending. And with Stephen's threat hanging on the horizon, he needed to make sure the louse couldn't sneak in from the back of the property. He'd driven Pa's truck around the entire perimeter of the farm a couple of times. For hours. Everything looked intact.

Pa was getting up there in years. Was he starting to lose his mind? Calling his wedding a funeral might be a sure sign, but no one had mentioned anything about Pa being crazy.

Here it was already Thursday morning, and Kyle had about given up. As he sat at Pa's kitchen table with the checklist, his cell buzzed. A number he didn't recognize. Hmm. He tapped the screen. "Kyle Casey."

"Kyle. Glad I caught you. I was afraid you might not be awake yet." Paul Mitchell sounded like he'd been running. "You've got a cow trying to escape."

"Escape?" Kyle tapped his forehead against the table. Now, what?

"The fence by the fellowship hall. You know, of church. This is Paul."

"Ah. That's the one. Pa said there was a fence out. I was sitting here trying to find where it had broken down."

"Fence is fine, Kyle. At least in that spot." Paul laughed. "The cow keeps head-butting it. Like she's mad at it or something."

"I'll check it out."

After ending the call, Kyle headed out in the truck, squinting at the bright morning rays. Sure enough, there stood Gertie, banging her head against a fence. He hopped out, squared his shoulders, and faced her. "Okay, look, Gertie. I don't know what the problem is, but this is ridiculous. I don't even know how you made it out this far."

She cocked her head toward him and backed away from the fence. Wait a minute—were those footprints? Fresh mud from the early morning showers?

"Who was it, Gertie? What did you see?"

Maybe reporters. It was nothing to see vans parked in the church lot these days. Some had approached him in town, but he mostly avoided them by sticking to the drive-thru windows and taking Pa's truck into town instead of his sports car. Could it have been Stephen?

Kyle pivoted, facing the rows of corn behind him. It would be a challenge to get to the billboard from here. Thick trees and thorny brush separated the front field from the clearing that opened to the church lot. Whoever came in this way must not have known, because they apparently wandered into Gertie's field while looking for Melanie.

Kyle walked a semicircle around the fence. Maybe whoever it was dropped something.

Three minutes of searching proved fruitless. He patted Gertie on the head. "Whoever it was, you chased them out, didn't you girl? I bet it was that rotten old creep our Melly girl tried to marry. Wasn't it?"

Gertie nudged him in the arm. More of a love pat than a head butt? Kyle couldn't say, but he'd take it. He went back to the truck and brought Gertie an apple. "Here you go. Now, let's get you back to your sisters."

When he drove back across the farm, Gertie followed close to the tailgate. He rewarded her with a couple more apples then headed to the house.

He'd seen a tent in Pa's garage. Maybe he needed to camp at the base of the billboard. Order food and have it delivered to the church gate. And maybe... not that he knew how to shoot one, but maybe he needed to pick up a gun.

He drove around to the other side of the thorns, walked across the clearing, and passed through the gate to the church parking lot. Paul's truck sat in its usual spot, but he was nowhere to be seen.

The double-oak doors loomed at Kyle like something from a horror movie, but he shook it off. He'd already been inside a couple times and it hadn't killed him. Mom had wanted him in church more than anything. He'd spent half his life hoping to make her proud of him through baseball, but what she'd wanted was for him to love the Lord like she did.

He knew what she'd say. That sense of dread when he approached the door—guilt. And it would pass. To be honest, Kyle didn't know what he was running from.

His hands trembled as he reached for the door handle. Why? Such deep emotion welled within him. He half-stumbled over the threshold then across the foyer to a heavy wood door labeled Office.

"Paul?" Kyle reached through the crack in the door and gripped the polyurethane-covered wood. "You in there?"

"Hey, Kyle." Paul waved through the crack. "Come on in and have a seat. I'm running some copies. I'll just be a minute."

Kyle fell into a deep leather chair and leaned forward, resting his elbows on his knees as his heart rate slowed. Maybe he was worked up over the footprints. Should he have called the police? Or at least Wayne? Maybe they could set up a watch to make sure Melanie was protected.

"Okay. All done." Paul set the stack of papers catty-cornered on a solid oak desk that matched the doors. "How's the fence?"

"It's fine. No damage, except for the muddy footprints. You didn't happen to see a person walking around in the area, did you?" Kyle peeked out the window toward the fence, where Gertie still stood guard. "Covered in mud?"

"No. You think someone tried to get over it?" Paul came up behind him and pressed his forehead to the glass.

"Melanie's ex-fiancé threatened me. He told his cousin he was coming to get her back. I'm afraid he might be trying to hurt her." Kyle twitched his jaw. "I guess I should call the police. At least have them check things out."

"You should." Paul nodded and poked his head through a door at the back of the office. "Susan, can you get the sheriff on the line and have him come by and meet us in the parking lot? We think there may have been an intruder on Kyle's property."

"On it!" The sixty-something lady with a pixyish cut whisked into the room and sat at the desk. She dialed a number and waited.

"Let's go check things out from our side before he gets here." Paul nodded to a side hall. "Those people sitting out there might have spotted someone. Have you checked on Melanie?"

"I saw her a couple minutes ago before we came in here. She was sitting in a huddled pile, so obviously upset, but I haven't seen any evidence that anyone's approached her." He followed Paul past doors opening to kidney tables and brightly colored posters. "We're not exactly speaking at the moment."

"That's a shame." Paul frowned. "You've been a good help to her."

"What do you think about love, Paul? Do you believe that two people can fall in love in a short span of time?"

Paul scratched his chin and cleared his throat. "You know, Kyle. I'm not sure I believe that bit about falling in love. You heard my sermon the other day. I'm more of the opinion that people choose to love each other. That love is obedience to Scripture, not something you fall in and out of."

"So I can choose to love Melanie and it would work out. If I wanted, I mean."

"You could." Paul raked his fingers through his silvery hair. "But Kyle, before you can love anyone, you have to love yourself. And before you love yourself, you have to make peace with God. Anyone can see you walking around with guilt hanging over your head. When you walked onto that baseball field the other night, I thought your shoulders were going to drag trenches in the ground."

"I don't feel guilty when I'm with her. I feel peaceful. Happy." Kyle laughed. "Well, except when she tells me we can't try to be together."

Paul took out his wallet and fished through receipts and cash for a worn 1x2 photo. "Here you go. Mrs. Mitchell. Natasha. I call her Tash and she hates it." He laughed. "We've been married for twenty-four years."

"No way. You look younger than that. I can't imagine you being married twenty-four years."

Paul shook his head. "Could have been longer. Tash is not the mother of my sons. I was married to another woman, long before she ever stepped in the picture." He stuffed the picture back in his wallet. "It's a funny story. Most people go to Vegas to get married. I fled the place and met Tash in the unemployment line."

"No kidding."

"I'd lost custody of my boys by then, and my wife had moved in with one of our best friends. Apparently they'd had an affair the entire time we were together. I was so depressed that I'd considered ending it all. But there Tash stood in front of me, dressed in bright blue with a fiery red ponytail I kept wanting to touch. When I sort-of-accidentally bumped into her, she turned around with a wide grin on her face and bright eyes. I was smitten. Forgot about everything bad in my life and—I never looked back." Paul approached the fence line. "I see some footprints here on the pavement. Looks like whoever was there parked across the street. There's a little mud on the edge of the road there, and they could have easily parked in that lot across from us and not been noticed."

"Yeah." Kyle knelt by one of the prints and rubbed the dried mud between his fingers.

"So anyway, Tash was a Christian. She promised if I'd go to church with her—faithfully, mind you—we'd get the boys back. I went with her, met the Lord, was baptized, and my life was transformed. We both got jobs, found an apartment we wanted, and got married soon after that. We've made the choice to love and serve each other every day, and we're still going strong." He grinned.

"Wow."

A police cruiser whipped into the parking lot and rolled to a stop a few feet from where they stood. He lowered his window and leaned out. "Got a problem, Paul?"

"Seems like Kyle's had some trespassers."

"They weren't the first." Kyle recounted the visit from Bart Handley. "But I think Stephen, Melanie's ex-fiancé, might be the culprit. He's threatened us. I thought I'd scared him off, but he may be trying to hurt her."

"Hmm." The officer lifted his wrist, twisting his watch face toward him. "Brenda and the girls are out of town, and I have free time after my shift ends. I could sit and watch the lot for a while if you want. I'd hate for anyone to vandalize the church or harass Melanie."

"Weren't you going to the game?" Paul glanced at his watch. "It's starting soon."

"They aren't playing tonight." The officer pointed to the soggy ground. "Field's too muddy."

Kyle shook his head slowly. "That's a shame. I was thinking about heading out to see if there was a game myself before all this happened."

"Not today." Paul crossed his feet in front of him and leaned against the fence. "Doesn't feel quite the same when Chip and Micah's team isn't playing." He laughed. "I know that's terrible, isn't it? Preacher being a bad sport."

Kyle shook his head. "Shows your human side."

The officer interrupted. "Let me wrap things up downtown and grab a bite to eat, and I'll make my way back over."

"Here." Kyle snatched a twenty from his wallet. "Let me buy. It's the least I can do."

The officer grinned. "So, I guess you thinking about taking off to a baseball game means you're not headed up a certain billboard." He lifted his gaze toward the sign. "Looks like your girl's in a rotten mood."

Kyle shrugged. "I pushed her to come down and eat with me last night. Tried to put on the romantic moves. Told her that…" He scratched his temples. "Well, I guess it doesn't matter. She's coming down tomorrow anyway."

"See you soon, Kyle." The officer waved and whipped out of the lot.

"Thanks, man."

The sky darkened as a thick charcoal-gray cloud passed in front of the sun. Kyle pulled out his phone and tapped the screen to open the weather app. More rain coming. Surely there was some way to convince her to come down before the storm.

Chapter Twenty-One

Melanie peeked between her fingers at her phone screen. Kyle. Girls. A Milton bar. Not even a week ago. She recognized the place. It was the same place Stephen frequented, and Kyle had been honest about going there to meet him. But had he been honest about everything?

The pictures sure did seem to tell a story, but for them to come from Stephen's Twitter account… How could she ever know that she could trust either one of them?

She dabbed sunscreen on her nose and rubbed it under her eyes, across her forehead, and over the tops of her ears. By noon, it would probably be in the nineties. Lunchtime was always the hottest time of day for Milton. But only one more lunchtime on the billboard after today. She was staying up here till two tomorrow. In twenty-seven more hours, her thirteen days would be over.

And then what?

All this time sitting up here, and she'd not reflected on her life. She hadn't considered her accomplishments of the past and the hopes she had for the future. Had she done anything worthy? Did she truly have hope beyond working a low-paying job and finding some small-town chump to share her life with?

As long as she could remember, everyone in town had called her an obstinate country girl. They'd say things like, "Ain't nobody else gonna win that shootin' contest. That girl's got enough stubborn in her to take 'em all down." At the bank, she was the classy, no-nonsense teller. Better have that check signed right, and if those amounts don't match, watch out. Persistence. Grit. Fiercely independent. But who was she? Both personalities fit.

Gaping, Melanie palmed her cheeks. "Oh, no. I'm Mama made over!"

Well, at least before she met Stephen… Had she been that much of a doormat since then? Sitting at home waiting for him all those nights while he went out and did who knows what?

He'd always picked the locations and times of their dates—home early, of course, because she had to get up for work. And here she'd thought she'd been courteous.

She sat taller, leaning back into the small shadow cast by her shower-curtain shelter. Again, just like Mama. No matter how many times Daddy betrayed her, Mama kept coming back. The gambling, the disappearing, the months without working, the rumors of affairs—Melanie had seen it all over the years. Sure, there was something to be said about loyalty, and Mama did love Daddy. Maybe she was too loyal. But the difference between Stephen and Daddy was that Daddy loved Mama back. Every time he failed, he tried to make things better and succeeded at it for a good, long while. It was easy to forgive Daddy and trust him again.

What was that old saying about love covering a multitude of sins? Daddy had sure cashed in on that one.

But not Stephen. Never Stephen. So many humiliating memories flashed before her. The night he followed her to the bowling alley to meet friends and her car broke down on the way. He drove right past her and left her there—didn't even notice she was missing! The night she was so sick she needed to go to the emergency room, and he wouldn't wake up from napping on the couch, so she drove herself. She'd always done all the cooking and the dishes when he came over to her apartment to eat, and she'd always paid for all the groceries to feed him.

And even worse, he'd arranged things so he'd have total control of her after their wedding.

Her heart sank as the scope of it all came crashing down. She'd given up her apartment to move into the house he'd rented on the outskirts of town. She'd sold her car, with his promise to buy her a new one. She'd quit her job because he said he'd take care of her, and that she'd never need to work again. Homeless, carless, jobless, and completely reliant on him. How could she have been so stupid? Why, why, why?

Because she wanted to stop dating at number thirteen. Well, maybe she should. Part of her wanted to give up dating altogether anyway. To shy away from anything that could ever lead to more pain. But another part of her wanted... Kyle.

As the tears streamed, she dug through the small tote he had fixed for her to put her belongings. The tiny tiara she'd chosen in lieu of a veil had tangled in her long diamond earrings, a present from Sadie, the aunt who'd taken her and her cousins on the walk that fateful day when she'd encountered the mystic palm reader who'd set the course of her life.

Melanie scooped the earrings with her right hand and dangled them into her left. Maybe she should give Aunt Sadie a call. If anyone would cut her some slack, it would be Sadie.

With a hopeful sigh, she tucked the earrings back into the tote and dialed the old number, which she recalled by heart.

"Hello?" Sadie spoke over wind whistling into the phone speakers. Working in her flowerbed, no doubt, probably trying to save her perennials from the overabundant insects.

"It's Melanie. I know it's been a while since we've talked. I was... I need..."

Melanie's cell beeped, and Sadie appeared on the screen with a request for a video chat. She tapped the icon, and winced at her teary face in the top right corner.

"Advice?" Sadie chuckled. "Girl, I was wonderin' how you were doing. Sorry I didn't make it to the wedding. It was such short notice, and I was out of the country. Then, when I heard about this billboard business, I called your mama. She demanded I keep my nose out of it. Said I was the one who got you into this mess in the first place."

"What?" Melanie scratched her scalp. "How did you get me in this mess?"

"Well, Stephen's dad and Jimmy are brothers-in-law. You know, that man I dated back two Christmases ago who turned out to be such a fraud? She said I was the one who brought him into the family. Lyle, Stephen's dad, was married to Jimmy's sister. Not Stephen's mom, of course. His stepmom. And if I hadn't met Lyle, you wouldn't have met Stephen. I'm the one who told him I had a beautiful niece."

Melanie wrinkled her nose. Sadie always had some story about twenty people she'd never met. Somebody's sister's cousin's aunt. "I didn't know. But Stephen came into the bank all the time before that, Sadie. I'd have met him whether you introduced us or not."

"Well, it's no matter now, I suppose. Anyway, your mama told me to mind my own business. Said if I talked to you, I'd make things worse." Sadie wrinkled her nose. "And I would have. I usually do."

"I don't see how things could get any worse. I have no job, no car, no home, and definitely no husband." Melanie popped the cap on a water bottle and took a long swig, letting some of the water dribble down her chin and onto her neck. The tiny hint of cool made her want more. Maybe she should give it up. "Do you think I should come down? Everyone says I need to because of the storm. But I said thirteen days, and it's only been twelve. I don't want to be a quitter. Not with all those people watching."

"A quitter?" Sadie snorted. "Why do you think you'd be a quitter? Don't you think you've made your point?"

"Well, I know it's silly, but I've built my whole life around thirteen. You remember what that woman told me all those years ago, right? And how many times it's worked for me. Stephen was number thirteen."

"Oh, Melanie." Sadie's sigh lasted a whole twenty seconds. "You were marrying this boy because of thirteen? Maybe this is my fault after all. I should have never let you girls stop and talk to that looney psychic woman. I never realized how far you'd carry her words."

"You didn't believe her?"

"Of course not. And you shouldn't have, either." Sadie waggled her finger at the camera. "I told your mama she needed to nip that in the bud years ago. I didn't realize you were still obsessing over thirteen."

"I'm trying not to. I guess I thought if I waited the whole thirteen days we'd be able to fix things and still get married. Except…"

"Except?" Sadie pulled the phone close to her head, filling the screen with her scrutinizing eyes as both brows shot upward.

Melanie bit her lip. "I don't want to fix things. I don't want to get back with Stephen anymore. I don't want to rule my life by a stupid number."

"You shouldn't want to. That's ridiculous."

"I knew it was ridiculous, but it kept working out. Thirteen brought me luck so many times." Melanie's cheeks stung. How much more could she cry over this? It had to end. "I just kept riding the wave. It felt right."

Sadie moved the phone back and shook her head. "Remember that just because something feels right doesn't mean it's so. Your Uncle Bill used to say that even a broken clock was right twice a day. But it would be a disaster to set your path by that clock, just as it was a disaster to set it by the number thirteen. There's only one right way to set your path."

Melanie wiped her face with the back of her hand, holding the screen where Sadie couldn't see. "What way is that, exactly?"

" 'Trust in the Lord with all your heart, and lean not on your own understanding. In all your ways, acknowledge Him, and He will direct your path.' " Sadie cleared her throat. "Child, have you prayed about this?"

"No." Melanie ducked her head. "I don't even go to church anymore."

"I know that." Sadie rubbed her nose under her glasses. "I was told to keep out of that, too."

Melanie glanced down to the parking lot where Brother Mitchell sat in a semicircle of men and women engaged in lively conversation. "The preacher who was going to do our wedding ceremony seemed nice. I was thinking about talking to him when this is all over."

"That's a good idea." Sadie leaned forward and attacked a patch of dirt with a spade.

"Maybe I'll even visit there one Sunday."

No response. Was Sadie listening? She wasn't even looking toward the screen. Melanie flicked her glaze to a fluffy white cloud hovering just above the church. "Sadie, what do you think I should do? Mama keeps texting me that she wants me to come back home. But I don't want to live at home."

A beautiful Monarch fluttered next to Sadie's cheek as she offered a kind smile. "Baby steps, sweetheart. Step one is climbing down off that board. You'll never know until you take it." Sadie's voice stiffened. "Storms are coming in a few hours, Melanie. Don't make other people risk their safety to protect you. Come down from that billboard and do the right thing. Please."

Melanie chewed off a hangnail. Come down. She had to. And soon. Maybe in the next couple of hours. But how could she face everyone? "I'll think about it. Thanks."

"No problem, kiddo."

As her cell screen darkened, Melanie set the phone aside and buried her face in her hands. What a fool she'd been. Aunt Sadie was right. She needed to clean up her mess and get off the billboard. And she'd do it as soon as her thirteen days were up. Or… as soon as she finished this last good cry. Agh! What should she do?

She gritted her teeth, arced her body, and peered behind the billboard as Kyle's sports car raced to the end of the driveway. Guess he wasn't coming back. Why was she surprised? After all, wasn't that what she'd told him she wanted? She tore a granola bar opened with her teeth and bit off a big chunk of it.

She sighed as Kyle made the two right turns into the church parking lot where the crowd had tripled. Maybe a cry wasn't such a good idea with everyone watching. She needed to go down with dignity and hold her head up high.

She rested her back against the billboard, wrapped her hand around the PVC pipe supporting her shower-curtain shelter, and slid it to the deck.

"Ow." She'd struck her wrist on a sharp corner, but what was it? A box?

Sure enough, a small wooden box had been wedged between the billboard and the pipe. She inched the box out of the space and pried off the lid. A message was written on a piece of paper in Sharpie. *Some things to make you laugh when you feel sad. –Kyle.*

Her entire body slumped as she fisted the pile of papers contained within, like she could melt over the edge of the scalding steel deck. Jokes. Dozens of them. Corny and goofy, just like Daddy's. What a sweet gesture. But when? And why hadn't he mentioned them?

Was she out of her mind to push him away?

Kyle set the box of autographed caps and photos on the ground next to Paul's chair. "I got your message, Paul. Sorry, I'd left my phone in the truck. If you really think anyone wants any of this stuff, I have tons of it. Not sure why I kept it."

Paul picked up one of the caps and examined the bill. He folded it then rested it on his head. "Thanks, Kyle. I'm sure there would be lots of people in this crowd who'd like one. I know it doesn't always feel like it, but this town rallies behind their own. Don't feel like you have to be buried under your shame forever."

"I know." Kyle dropped into the seat next to Paul. "It's just a little weird coming home, that's all. Humbling, I guess."

"Tell me about it." Paul sat forward and rested his elbows on his knees. Tell me everything. Start at when things first went wrong. Clean your conscience."

"You want the whole story? All of it? Like you haven't heard any of it?" Kyle scrunched his forehead. Did Paul live behind a rock?

"I've heard bits and pieces." Paul smiled and tore a piece of barbecue-smothered bread from his sandwich. "Tell me everything from your point of view. Besides, if I'm going to be sitting here a while waiting for this crowd to clear, you need to do something to entertain me. I get bored easy."

"I doubt that." Kyle scanned the front corner of the fence line, where several members of the church had gathered—not gawking at Melanie, but rather rallying around her. Praying for her. On intervals. Someone had the idea to reheat the barbecue they'd frozen the other night. They'd even volunteered to sit in a couple places on the farm and keep an eye until the police could track Stephen down and make sure Melanie wasn't in danger. No one could ever accuse this church of not being hospitable and caring. "Okay. Sure. The whole story."

"All of it." Paul winked. "Purge your guilt."

"Ha ha. As if I could." He turned as someone tapped his shoulder. "Oh. Thank you, ma'am." Kyle accepted a plate from a middle-aged woman and plunged his fork into the leftover baked beans. "When I first got the call that I'd be playing in the major leagues, I thought nothing would ever go wrong in my world. That I was invincible. Infallible. And I didn't need help from anyone."

Saliva caught in Kyle's throat as he tried to swallow the sweet, mushy blend of pork, ketchup, brown sugar, and vinegar. He picked up the Coke the lady left with him and washed it down. "My parents tried hard to keep me focused on God. But I guess I kind of became my own god. I mean, I've been taught right, I think. We didn't attend the same church as yours, but we read the Bible every night. Mostly the Psalms. I never felt like it clicked. Then, when I left home, I tried several other churches, and they didn't click, either. And now, I'm such a loser that there's probably not any point."

Paul set his plate in his lap and wiped his fingers on a napkin. He removed his folded pocket Bible and fanned through the pages. "Kyle, God didn't establish a set of churches. He established *His* church. The one Christ died for. Have you ever truly read the Bible? You might be surprised at how many people you'd find who relate to your situation." He stopped at the book of Psalms and traced his finger over the crease between the pages. "King David messed up royally. Pun intended."

Kyle chuckled. "You and your jokes. I never realized a preacher could be so funny. Dad used to tell me some of the same ones."

"About half of them are your Pa's. I'm sure he passed them down to your dad." Paul plucked a chip from his plate, inspected it, and plopped it in his mouth. He smiled wider as he chewed, like something had just come to his mind. "Have you ever heard the story of David and Bathsheba?"

"Yeah. He had an affair with a beautiful woman. But weren't the kings allowed to have a bunch of wives back then?"

Paul flipped back a few pages and pointed to the text. "I'm reading from the book of second Samuel, chapter eleven. Notice verse three here says Bathsheba was the wife of Uriah, the Hittite."

Kyle squinted at the small black words. "Yeah, I see that."

"Well, listen to verse five here. Or, well, you can read it for yourself. She became pregnant. King David's child."

As Paul read on, Kyle traced his finger over the onion page. "So, after she got pregnant, King David had her husband killed." His mouth twitched. "I was in church all the time. How have I never heard this part of the story before?"

"Let's focus on you hearing it now. Kyle, I want to read you another verse. This is Acts, chapter thirteen, verse twenty-two. 'He—God—raised up for them—that's the nation of Israel—David as king, to whom also He gave testimony and said, I have found David the son of Jesse, a man after My own heart who will do all my will.' "

"So you're saying then that David—who had another man killed because he got his wife pregnant—was called 'a man after God's own heart.' Was that before or after... wait, he was already king. Did God take David off the throne after that?"

"No, He didn't. David had to suffer the consequences for his sins, but he remained king of Israel until his death."

"Hmm..."

"But David repented sincerely and turned back to God with all of his heart. That's why God commended him. And that's how King David is remembered—a man after God's own heart. You know, there are a couple verses where there's an exception clause, like in I Kings 15:5. Let's read that one." Paul flipped the pages. "See, here? It says David 'did what was right in the sight of the Lord, and had not turned aside from anything that He had commanded him all the days of his life, *except* in the case of Uriah the Hittite.' "

"What does that mean?"

"David wasn't perfect. It means that no matter what you've done, God still loves you. He still wants you to become a Christian and to serve him. To follow his plan of salvation, including baptism for the remission of sins, like it says in Acts 2:38. A handful of mistakes doesn't negate that if you live a life of repentance and obedience."

Paul turned to another passage. "Psalm 51. David wrote this after confessing his sins of adultery and murder. 'Have mercy upon me, O God, according to your loving kindness; according to the multitude of Your tender mercies, blot out my transgressions. Wash me thoroughly from my iniquity, and cleanse me from my sin.' Do you hear that, Kyle? That's called contrition. When you are washed in the blood of the Lamb—that's baptism—your sins are washed away. Here." He passed Kyle the Bible. "Read the rest of it for yourself."

Purging with hyssop. He'd have to Google that later. But Paul was right. That was about the most apologetic thing he'd ever heard. "So I think I understand." He handed Paul the Bible back. "If I become a Christian it will be blotted out. The whole thing will be erased."

"Well, not completely." A firefly landed on Paul's leg, and he let it crawl into his hand. "You can find peace in your life. But there may still be consequences. I doubt repentance would help you play pro ball again or erase those not-so-flattering pictures that surfaced on Twitter this week."

"Yeah." Kyle winced. Why had Paul had to go and bring that up? Peace sure did sound great, though. He stole a glance at the billboard. If… if he had someone to share his life with.

Chapter Twenty-Two

Melanie gripped the upper railing of the billboard sign and lunged forward with the thick branch she'd snapped from a nearby tree.

"Whoa, Melly." Strong arms circled her waist and sporty cologne wafted closer as Kyle's husky whisper sent chills to her core.

"I didn't hear you come up." She retreated, dropped the stick on the deck, and landed on her knees, her back pressed against his chest. "You did come." But the distance between them remained.

"I brought your lunch." He gestured over his shoulder with his thumb to a white Styrofoam box. "Now, what are you doing? Trying to get yourself killed? I swear, between you and Gertie…"

"Just wanted to get my dress back." She sighed. "Not that it's salvageable."

"You never know." Kyle's voice deepened. "A wise preacher just pointed out to me that most broken or damaged things are salvageable with a little TLC." He rubbed his hands over her arms. "Are you coming down tomorrow? Or maybe… now?"

Now. The very word pierced her heart. She faced him and swallowed. Those pleading brown eyes. Those full, kissable lips. "I don't know. I don't want to be a quitter. I mean, there are national news trucks in town. This mess is viral, Kyle. If I quit now, then—"

"Then what?" The slightest scowl flickered across his face.

"If I give up with so little time left, what will people say?"

"Who cares?" Kyle planted firm hands on her shoulders. "I want you to come down with me. Let's start over. Both of us. Together. I'll give you the money to get back on your feet."

"I don't want your money." Her jaw set in that firm line Mama always chided her for.

Kyle released her and backed away. "Give it some thought. I'm going to see your dad. He's coming home today. Bet he'd like to see you. Give it some thought."

Melanie's throat ached like sandpaper as she cleared it. "I will."

Those words, barely choked out, hung in the air between them. Kyle brushed his fingers across her forehead and touched her lips. "I'll be waiting."

As he climbed down the ladder, her fountain of tears opened again. Maybe she'd have that last good cry after all.

From his spot in the front lot of Milton Memorial Hospital, Kyle had a clear view of Melanie's billboard. She only looked like a huddled speck, of course, but he couldn't shake the feeling that he should be there. Should he have stayed and waited it out with her?

He rubbed his hand over his growing stubble and rested it on his chin. Paul's words still played in his mind from their conversation at lunch.

"Ask yourself if you've ever truly felt guilt over what happened." Paul gripped Kyle's shoulder. "Sure, you've had some embarrassment. A little twinge over it. Maybe some indignation and even a hint of remorse for disappointing people. But, have you been truly contrite? Are you sorry from the depths of your soul?"

Kyle's face slacked. "The baseball, not so much. You're right. I'm mad rather than sorry. Indignant is a good word choice. But for how I've treated women…" He gripped the bottom of his plate with white-knuckled hands. "Watching Melanie grieve Stephen has been eye-opening to me. It's like a window into the heart of every girl I've ever hurt. I don't ever want to hurt anyone like that again."

"But are you truly emotionally moved? Deeply sorry? Pricked to the heart?"

"I think so. I can't sleep at night for feeling guilty, if that's what you mean. Here, want me to take your trash?"

While Kyle carried their plates over to the serving table, he'd watched all the elderly ladies putting together the meal of reheated barbecue for their husbands, who were keeping watch over Melanie. When the men walked by, they teased and smiled at their wives with that simple, easy comfort that comes from loving someone for decades. Maybe that could be him and Melanie someday.

When he returned to his seat, he'd interlocked his fingers and brought them to his chin. "I want to love Melanie, Paul. I want to heal her and make her forget all that pain. I want us to grow old together like all these couples have. It's like retribution."

"Retribution?" Paul shook his head. "That doesn't seem like a very good reason to love someone. Do you realize the commitment?"

"I know it's a commitment." Kyle took several deep breaths. "And, well, it's not the only reason. But I guess you're right. I feel so compelled to—"

"Can I give you a little advice? Not preacher to the man in the parking lot, but brother to brother?" Paul scooted his chair around to face Kyle. "Fix yourself first. Figure out a way to feel truly convicted for your sin and give your life over to God. If you truly repent with all your heart, you can be forgiven. He will take all your guilt, sin, and regrets, and give you forgiveness, peace, and a new start in life. He transformed me, and I know He can do it for you, too. Study with me for a while. Let me show you the path to salvation as given in Scripture. Then see where things stand with you and Melanie. You might be surprised where it leads."

Kyle turned his chair slightly as well. He leaned forward, pressing his fisted hands against his knees. "Transformation sounds great, but how?"

"For starters, you need to repent. That means to turn around and walk in an entirely different direction. I'm not convinced that you see what you've done as something to truly repent of." Paul stretched his legs out in front of him and crossed one black leather shoe over the other. "Yes, you've lost baseball, but how have you changed as a person?"

Kyle sat straighter. "I have changed. I haven't been to a bar or party for months." Well, except the other night, but he hadn't gone after a woman and he hadn't had a drink.

"Okay, there's a start."

"And I've come to church."

"You've come once. I mean this in the nicest way, Kyle. Your problem, and Melanie's, is that you're both selfish. Every choice you make is about making yourself feel better or satisfying something you think you want. She's sitting up there being stubborn because it makes her feel like she's doing something about her hurt. You're taking care of her because it makes you feel like you're compensating for hurting your ex-girlfriend. But have you been generous with your money? Have you used it for Christ-like service?" Paul lifted his sunglasses from his nose and rubbed underneath them. "Kyle, if you—"

"I get it. I still have all that money in savings." Kyle patted his wallet through his pocket. "I didn't take advice from many people, but I did listen to a financial expert about how to invest and grow my wealth. And I say I want to help other people, but sitting on this money only helps me."

Paul nodded. "Well, it's not only about giving your money away. What do you give of your time, Kyle? Of your heart?"

Kyle, of course, had no answer. He was about to protest that he spent a lot of time taking care of Melanie, but he knew that the motivations in his heart were selfish. Paul had stood up and told him to think about it, so Kyle took Melanie lunch. Now he was here to visit Wayne. Still thinking about it.

As he walked from the parking lot to Wayne's hospital room, several random strangers smiled and spoke. All friendly. Maybe staying in Milton wouldn't be so bad, at least for a while.

"Mr. Casey?" A petite blonde nurse stood from her seat behind the station. "Mr. Turner has been asking if you've stopped by. Go on in."

"Thanks." He leaned closer and squinted at her name tag. "Sarah. Thanks, Sarah." She flashed him one of the flirty grins he'd become so accustomed to, and he shook his head. Melanie was his girl now, whether she knew it or not. No matter how long it took to win her over.

He strolled into Wayne's room and tossed him the autographed ball cap he'd brought. "Wayne, you're looking a little peaked, man."

"Nah. Just tired of this place." Wayne sat straighter. "Good to see you, Kyle."

Kyle set a Styrofoam box on the tray next to the bed. "I also brought you some leftover barbecue from the other night. They'd kept it in the church freezer and reheated it all today. Having a sort of come-and-go luncheon while people at the church keep an eye out for Melanie. You wouldn't believe the people. First responders, local politicians, little old ladies…"

"Good to know the community's watching out for her. I'm doing fine, except this little blip in my heart." Wayne slipped the cap on his head. "What do you think? Too sporty for this old country hack?"

"Looks great on you. Maybe you can wear it on your next tour. Let me know when it fades or gets dirty, and I'll give you another. I have boxes of the things." Kyle grinned then frowned. "Tell me about the blip. What's going on?"

"An irregular heartbeat. Showed up after my surgery. They didn't want to let me go home until they watched me a few days, but Doc says he'll free me in an hour or so. And I've got to do one of those stress test things next week. My heart rate's been constant all morning. Driving me crazy, these nurses." He winked at Kyle. "Speaking of crazy, how's that daughter of mine?"

"Obstinate as usual. I took her lunch and asked her to come down. Said I'd give her time to think about it." Kyle stretched out his legs, brushing the cables under the bed. "I'm worried about Stephen and the coming rain, but she seems fine other than that."

Wayne pushed himself higher in the bed. "Melanie's a good girl. She is. But she has a single-world viewpoint. She's never once had to want for anything, and I think it would do her some good to use her talents for others like Brother Mitchell said in his sermon the other day. She used to volunteer at this hospital, you know. Took care of small kids and older people. And you should see her with wild animals. She's like a squirrel master or something. Birds, deer, elk— she could tame them all."

"Tame them?" He snickered. Maybe when Melanie came down, he'd let her have a crack at Gertie. "Can she tame Pa's cows?"

Wayne guffawed. "I don't know that anyone can tame Pa's cows except Pa." Then he wheezed and he clasped his chest, gathering up the plastic tubing that hung from his breathing apparatus. "I've got to get out of here. They're killing me with this oxygen. I think it's poisoned. Anyway, did you tell her about the weather?"

"No, but I'm going to try to talk her down before the storm. I'll take care of the cattle first and run some water bottles out to Paul. There's a whole crowd waiting for her to come down, and this heat is raging." Kyle poured ice water from a plastic pitcher into Wayne's Styrofoam cup. "Can you think of anything else? Anything that might work to convince her?"

"When they send me home, I'll have Louisa bring me by the church. Maybe if she sees me... You're falling for her." Wayne grabbed the cup and trembled as he brought it to his lips. He spilled water down his chin as he sipped it.

"Here. Let me get your straw." Kyle reached for the tray.

"Don't ignore the question." Wayne clamped his free hand on Kyle's arm. "You *are* falling for my daughter. Answer me."

"I didn't hear a question. Besides, it's too soon for that." Kyle jerked, but Wayne's weakened grip outdid him. He needed to get out and train again. For what, he didn't know, but it was a shame to lose all that muscle and strength. Although, farming could certainly pack on the brawn. If he stayed...

"I fell in love with my wife in one day." Wayne's dimples punctuated his goofy grin. "Spent sixteen straight hours together on a tour bus, and I asked her to marry me the next day. And she said yes."

Kyle's eyebrows shot straight up. Louisa Turner? The classy, somewhat scary woman who'd backed him up against a drink machine had fallen in love in a *day*? She certainly shared Melanie's tenacity and spirit, but she seemed way too together for what Wayne was claiming.

"You've had how many days?" Wayne winked. "And a sweet dance up there in front of God and everybody."

"I thought you were upset that I—"

"Well, that was before I realized you were falling for her. Don't think I don't know your reputation, son. Keeping yourself detached and hiding yourself away. I can read the Internet, and I know your Pa's cell phone number."

"You talked to Pa?"

"For almost two hours the other night. Made those nurses half batty I laughed so loud. Serves them right."

"Well, what did he say?" Kyle jerked and bumped over a stack of Get Well cards on the table beside him. He chewed the skin off his lower lip as he straightened them. "Is Pa coming home anytime soon?"

Wayne gripped the rails of the bed and pushed up. "He'd kill me if I told you where he is, but he said to give you another chance. That maybe you could be trusted again if we all believed in you. So here I am. Believing in you."

"He is coming home soon." Kyle shook his head. "Stubborn old man."

"Like his grandson." Wayne chuckled. "And this old coot. But he honestly didn't say when or if he'd see you. And as far as trusting you, if anyone knows about needing change, it's me. I can't judge you for anything, Kyle. Especially not gambling. I battled that beast for five years. It was a low point for my career and my marriage. But a good man helped me change. And I can see you're changing, too. Little things, but still change."

"Big things." Kyle dropped back into the chair and folded his hands in his lap. "I haven't touched a drop of alcohol since my last press conference. Didn't drink that much, anyway, but I don't want anything to cloud my judgment. Not anymore. The gambling only happened that one time, and I have no desire for a repeat performance. I haven't partied, and I haven't taken a fistful of money to a club to spend on chasing women. Being away from all that has brought clarity. My life was so empty then. Hopeless."

"What will you do?"

"Paul Mitchell's boys talked to me the other day about some private coaching. Says the boy's baseball team at the high school is desperate. And I believe them. I've seen the team play. Paul was telling me the last coach quit mid-season, and his son and son-in-law jumped in and took the team. They've learned everything they know from Internet videos and their own experiences with high school ball, which were limited."

"You going to do it?"

"I'm thinking hard about it." Kyle held one of the cards in front of him and traced his finger over the glittery balloons on the cover. "Of course, I have to finish dealing with a certain um… issue on the farm."

"Go sit with her, Kyle." Wayne pointed to the clock. "There's not much time before the storm tonight. Talk to her. If you can't get her to come down, then do what you can to protect her. Give her a better shelter. Stay with her so she won't sit up there scared. Do whatever it takes."

Sit with her. Kyle twitched his nose. In the rain. And a massive flash-flooding thunderstorm. Wayne was out of his mind. It was time to just drag the girl down and make her stop being so stubborn.

"Mr. Turner?" A red-haired woman poked her head in the door. "Dr. Mason is on his way down the hall and I've messaged your wife to come back from the cafeteria. We're going to get you out of here in the next few minutes."

"Sounds good." Wayne raised his cap. "See you at the church, Kyle."

On the muted television screen, a weatherman waved his arms frantically over a green, red, and yellow map. Moving circles covered purple triangles. Was that Milton? And tornadoes? He hadn't seen anything about them earlier. And… what was that street? Looked like the storms were closer than he'd thought. He needed to hurry if he was going to protect her. He swallowed and patted Wayne's arm. Probably best to not worry him about it right now. "Okay. I'll see what I can do. Get better, man."

In the hospital parking lot, he pulled up the weather app on his phone. That was odd. The radar looked completely different. Heavy rain, yes. But no tornadic activity. What was up with that?

Gritting his teeth, he searched the number to the local weather station and dialed.

"Hello?" A chirpy female's high pitch blasted through the speaker. "How may I direct your call?"

"This is Kyle Casey."

Silence.

"You know, the pro baseball player?" He gulped. "Well, former. Anyway, I'm worried about the weather because—"

"Kyle Casey! That girl." She gasped. "The billboard."

"Yeah. The girl and the billboard." He polished a spot off the windshield with his thumb. "Is there any way I could talk to the weather guy? Make some sense out of this forecast?"

"I'll get him. He's on a break now, but I'm sure he'll be glad to talk to you. I mean, you are Kyle Casey." She giggled.

"Yes, I am." He shook his head. If that's what it took to talk to the news guy, then fine.

"Dave Cline, here. I'm a big fan, Mr. Casey. Even with your troubles." The deep television voice boomed through the speakers. "Heard you wanted to talk to me?"

"The storm. All those tornadoes. How much time before they get to Milton? I saw rotation on the TV a few minutes ago, but when I pulled up my weather app—"

"You didn't see rotation a few minutes ago."

"But I did." Kyle creased his brow. "On Channel 3."

"There's no way…" Dave laughed, a deep, guttural laugh that clearly stated he thought Kyle was an idiot. "Oh. No wonder. There's a tornado in this soap opera that's airing right now. That map is of some fictional place in south Florida. We aren't having tornados. Not in Milton, anyway. Not today."

"Are you kidding me?" Kyle joined in his laugher. Had he been away from Milton so long that he would confuse the map? He *was* an idiot. No wonder the guy seemed so nonchalant. "But we are expecting a storm, right? Is there any danger there? Heavy rains? What about lightning?"

"Well, we're lucky. The front's coming in later than expected. Think it will arrive from the north shortly after daybreak in the morning. So even though we're expecting a lot of rain, there's a good chance you won't see any lightning."

"Oh. Well, that sounds good." Kyle's shoulders relaxed. "That stubborn girl says she will not come down until her thirteen days are up, and that's not until tomorrow afternoon around two."

"She'll get wet, and it will be muddy getting her out of there." Mouse clicks and keyboard strokes sounded in the background as Dave breathed heavily into the phone. "We're expecting quite a bit of flash flooding from this setup, but not the storms like we had a few days ago. I'd still try to talk her down. Haven't the police been involved?"

"Her dad told them to leave her alone, and let her be stubborn if she wants to. And since she's on my property, I get the say to let her go through with it. If I told them to remove her, they would. But it's better if she comes down on her own. I don't think anyone thought she'd make it this long."

"Good luck to you, Kyle. Great talking to you. Maybe one day you could come out and join us on the air. We could do a little segment on how wind impacts the ball speed or something." Dave disconnected before Kyle could respond.

Kyle shaded his eyes and scanned the skyline. The Lowe's sign across the street from the hospital blocked a patch of fluffy white clouds. Judging by the afternoon sky, it might not rain at all. How could Dave look at such a bright blue and see flooding? He shrugged. If he did as Wayne asked and stayed up there with her, it might be a long twenty-four hours.

Chapter Twenty-Three

Melanie opened the weather app on her phone and cringed. The pit in her stomach deepened. She had to give it up. It was time.

She wadded the napkin and stuffed it in the Styrofoam box. All those people would be waiting. Should she walk to the farmhouse? Surely Kyle would come back.

Her trash bag rustled in the waxing breeze. She untied it and dropped the box in, then loosened it from the deck. It would be a real hassle to get all this stuff down without Kyle's help.

With a grunt, she squared her shoulders. Might as well go ahead and get started.

The clouds shifted to the right, exposing a piercing beam of sunlight. Melanie raised her hand to her forehead to shield it, her gaze dropping to the church parking lot. Wait… was that… Mama? And Daddy? He looked fantastic for someone who'd just spent days in the hospital.

Great. Just great.

She ducked behind her curtain, new tears welling. She couldn't hide up here forever.

But to face Mama right now? No way was she ready for that.

Kyle set a case of water bottles on the table where a group of local police officers sat devouring the last of the leftover brisket. "Any news on Stephen?"

"No." Officer Parker scrubbed away at his mouth with a worn napkin and stood. "Looking like he may have skipped town again at this point. It's doubtful he's going to surface during the storm, so we'll come back by tomorrow."

"Well, hopefully I'll talk her down before then." Kyle pointed up at the billboard. "I guess Wayne's given you guys the go-ahead to force her down if she doesn't do it on her own?"

Officer Parker shrugged. "He said you could pull it off."

"I'm working on it. Getting ready to go back and drag her down if I have to." Kyle moved on to Wayne's table, where Louisa sat rubbing her temples. "Are you sure you're okay to be sitting here, Wayne? You're welcome to rest at the farmhouse if you need to. I'm getting ready to head up to talk to Melanie, but I can give you the key."

"Nah. I've got my ice pack." He patted a plastic cooler by his feet. "And Louisa's got me all set up in this wheelchair."

"Louisa looks tired." Kyle sat and pushed the key across the table toward her. "Here. Take this just in case. The front bedroom is a guest room, and you're welcome to it."

"How did we fail Melanie so much, Kyle? I took her fishin' and shootin' and huntin' from the time she was old enough to walk. We tried to keep her grounded. We taught her how to take care of herself. The girl could survive in the woods for a decade. I'm sure of that." Wayne picked up a thick, juicy rib and ripped into it with his teeth. Barbecue sauce dripped from his chin, and Louisa sighed.

She handed her husband a thick, brown napkin. "You spoiled her, Wayne. Made her think she was the center of the universe."

He faced his wife. "Oh, no you don't. You can't pin all that on me. Those pageants when she was little? Prancing her around in dresses and makeup like she was a princess?"

Louisa squared her shoulders. "Wayne, those pageants gave her confidence and grace. They gave her half a chance, at least, to still maintain a hint of professionalism with all that redneck—"

"No!" Wayne slammed his fists against the table. "If you hadn't supported her in the obsession over that stupid number she'd have never—"

"It's not about that. Not about any of that. Don't you understand? Stop it! Just stop it right now!" Kyle scooted his chair back from the table and stood. "You're talking about her like she's dearly departed. Like there's no hope of reaching her. But honestly, have you tried?" He pointed at Louisa. "Do you realize that she's dodged your every call because she's scared to death of what you're going to say to her? That you'll nag and make her feel guilty and offer no emotional support?"

Wayne gave Louisa a smug grin. "See, I told you."

"And you." Kyle pivoted and met Wayne's gaze through slivered eyes. "Why can't you have a direct conversation with your daughter? You gave a bridesmaid some pictures on Melanie's wedding day because you're scared to death to tell her yourself about her lying, cheating fiancé. *Here, Kyle. You climb up and get her down for me. And let me sing her a song—that'll get through to her. Go sit with her in torrential rain, even though it could put you both in danger.*" He shook his head. "No, Wayne. What Melanie needs is honesty. She needs real, true conversation from anyone. She needs you people to stop treating her like she's some fragile flower who can't know the truth. Will somebody..." He swung his hand over the crowd to where all Melanie's friends sat in a wide-eyed huddle. "Will anybody *please* start being honest with this girl?"

"What about you?" Wayne shoved the table so hard it moved a foot. He stood and squared up against Kyle. "You love my daughter. Have you told her?"

"Sit down." Louisa swatted at him. "You're going to hurt yourself."

"Melanie doesn't want me, Wayne. She made that loud and clear. I offered, and she chose to sit up there and wait this out instead of climbing down to be with me. I know you have this dream of her raising strapping boys on that farm so you can teach them how to hunt like you did her, but you're going to have to find some other guy and some other farm. I'm not going to force somebody into a relationship they don't want to be in."

Someone cleared their throat behind them. Kyle spun toward the parking lot, coming face to face with Paul Mitchell.

"If you fellas want to kill each other, that's fine, but not in my parking lot." Paul stepped in the middle of them. "You're here supporting your daughter today, Wayne. Sit down and talk this out like men. Whatever you two are arguing about, this day is about her." He pointed to Melanie's huddled shadow behind the shower curtain against the billboard. "Now I've tried to stay out of this as much as I can, but if it were my daughter, knee replacement or no knee replacement, I'd find a way to get up there and talk some sense into her. I'd have the police help get her down. Something. You can't let her run from her problems forever."

"She's twenty-six, Paul. I can't do everything for her." Wayne slammed his hands against his thighs and grimaced. "If I force her down, I'll lose her. She'll never come back home."

"I've had about enough of this." Louisa leapt to her feet and stalked around the table to Kyle. She dropped the silver key into his hand. "I don't want the key to your house. Give me the gate key."

"Give you what?"

"Give me the gate key, Kyle." Louisa thrust out her palm.

"The gate's unlocked." He pointed to where it stood slightly ajar. "I just came through it myself."

"Good." Louisa marched across the parking lot while Kyle followed. When she reached the gate, she kicked off her shoes. "It's been thirty-five years since I've walked barefoot in grass. But believe it or not, I'm more than capable of getting to the top of that billboard to talk to my daughter."

"And how long since you've climbed a tree?" Wayne rolled his chair after her. "Somebody help me walk to that billboard. This, I've got to see."

Sweat poured down Melanie's forehead, and she wiped it off with the hem of her shirt. The humidity was getting worse. Leaves rustled in the pine tree next to her, and something clinked against the ladder. Heart pounding, she peeked out from a crack in her shelter. Someone was coming.

"Melanie?"

Chills spread through Melanie's veins, pinning her to the deck like she'd been frozen with ice. "Mama?"

Perfectly manicured fingers wrapped around the top rail of the ladder. A few seconds later, Mama's tight bun rose over the deck, tiny leaf fragments poking out of it. She pulled herself to stand in front of the billboard, looking so regal she could have been plastered to the sign.

Melanie lifted the curtain and shielded her eyes from where the sun glinted from the metal covering the billboard lights. "I guess you've come to yell at me."

"No." Mama walked closer to the curtain and held out her hand. "Come out, sweetheart. Sit by me."

No force on earth could have stopped the flow of tears that emerged when Melanie slipped into Mama's arms amidst cheers from the church parking lot. She cried against the lace collar, holding Mama's shoulders like she was in danger of losing her forever. "I'm so sorry. I'm so, so sorry."

Mama's shoulders shook and tears streamed down her own cheeks. "No, Melanie. I'm the one who's sorry. I've been too critical. Too unrelenting. And somehow, I've made you feel like you couldn't talk to me." She drew in a deep breath. "I love you more than anything in this world, and it breaks my heart to see you in so much pain. Raw and vulnerable, and I could only sit at home helpless. I should have climbed up this billboard that first day. Instead, I spent all day being embarrassed and worrying about the money."

Melanie ducked her head. "I should have come down the first day. I know I should have. But the truth is, Mama, I don't know my next move. I go down, and then what? It's like you've said. I have no job. I have nowhere to live except home, and what twenty-six-year-old goes back to live with their parents? Lizzie's the only friend who's still texting me. What am I coming down to?"

"Life." Mama pointed at the trees. "You have always been full of sunshine and life. Bright smiles, good heart, and unwavering courage. This is paralysis by fear, that's all. You got so scared that you couldn't move. But Melanie, your father and I will help you through this. I know moving back home is the last thing you'd want to do. You've been on your own for so long. We can swing a couple months' rent in an apartment if you'd like that. It would give you some time to find a new job and get back on your feet. And if you look into that crowd of people in the church parking lot, you'll see all of your friends. Even that Billings girl who claims she feels terrible. She's apologized to me six times and wants to apologize to you, too."

Tricia? Melanie wrinkled her nose. How could she face Tricia? How could she face anyone? "What about Stephen? What if I see him in town?"

Mama snickered. "Did I ever tell you that Mr. Beaumont at the bank was my first true love? We shared so many laughs about that when he hired you. He was hoping you might go on a date with his son."

"But you're friends with him."

"I am. But I sure wasn't when we broke things off. It was sheer nuclear war." Mama winked. "If you asked for your job back, I'm guessing he'd say yes. He loves you like a daughter, and he'd do it as a favor to me. But... I don't want you to go back to the bank. You've worked that job since your senior year of high school. That was only meant to be your part-time job when you were young. And if you'd tried to move into a higher-level job there, I'd give you my full support. But I raised you to dream. And I'm not convinced that being a teller is your dream."

"You've worked at Carter Realty since you were young."

"About that." Mama rubbed her thumb over her pointer finger. "I was like you. Got a job straight out of high school and stuck to it like glue. You remember how many years ago that was?"

Melanie swallowed back the wave of emotion dammed up in her throat. "Twenty-six years ago. When I was born. When you were supposed to be going to college."

"Yes." Mama wiped away her tears with her pinky. "We've all made bad choices here and there, you know. Stephen was a bad choice. But I should have stepped in. Intervened and told you my misgivings."

"I don't know." Melanie brushed a loose hair from Mama's eyes. "Maybe I needed this to happen. I needed the time. To put my life on pause and think. To understand why I held on to numbers for so long."

Mama chuckled. "Does this mean you're finally finished with that awful number thirteen?"

"I am officially retiring thirteen."

"Oh, Melanie. I'm so sorry for not being the mother you needed me to be these past two weeks." Tears caught in the corner of Mama's eyes. "Will you please forgive me for leaving you up here alone?"

"It's fine, Mama. I had Kyle."

"Kyle." Mama rubbed her chin. "What happens next with him?"

Melanie forced a shrug. "Nothing, I guess. I climb down, and we part ways. Isn't that for the best? I don't think I'm ready to date anyone."

"You don't want to part ways. He doesn't want you to."

"Have you read all those stories about him? Seen the pictures of him with all those girls? How can I be sure I'm not getting mixed up with another Stephen?"

Mama held up her palm. "He's not Stephen. Kyle's mom and I go back a long way. We were good friends in elementary and high school, up until your daddy swept me away to all those bluegrass concerts. When we came back to town, they'd moved away, but you played with him all the time when you were a toddler."

"I did?"

Mama nodded. "I have pictures somewhere. Kate and I always said we'd arrange a marriage for you two."

"What happened? Why didn't you reconnect when we moved back to town?"

"She met Denny and immersed herself into that church. They started doing mission trips and never had time for anyone else."

"Ah. The church thing again." Melanie scrunched her nose.

"Yeah. We still talk on the phone quite a bit. She misses Milton. She misses Kyle."

"I could see that." Melanie grinned. "It's hard not to."

Mama glanced over her shoulder toward the billboard sign. "She's always after me to get into church. Seems like it's always in my face lately. The suggestion of going, I mean. Maybe I should."

"I've been thinking a lot about it recently. Wondering if that preacher could help me find my way back to something normal."

Mama reached for her hand and squeezed. "I don't know much about the Bible, but it had its good influence on me and your daddy more than once."

Melanie leaned closer and dropped her voice to a near-whisper. "Did Daddy really cheat? All those rumors, and I refused to believe them until I was sitting up here thinking about it. And I know you forgave him, so it seemed like they might not be true. But now... were any of them true?"

A long pause. Mama tilted her head to the sky and pressed her lips tight.

"They all were. Oh, Mama. I knew it."

"Some were true."

"And you stayed. How could you stay?" Melanie cupped her forehead and closed her eyes.

Mama brushed her hand over Melanie's chin. "I stayed. I did leave your dad once for about six weeks when you were a toddler. Most miserable six weeks of my life—and his. We realized that at our worst, we were both still better together."

"Why?" Melanie couldn't help but gape. It made no sense.

"Kate told me something profound that I should have taught you. She said, 'Love is an action. Love is a choice. And love is a command.' The woman had those words stenciled overhead in their living room. When you walked into their house, it was the first thing you saw."

"Wow." That was exactly what Kyle told her the preacher had said. They *could* choose to love each other. Couldn't they?

"Kate said that if I chose to show your dad compassion, kindness, and forgiveness, I might just save my marriage. And it worked."

"Do you think it would have worked with Stephen?"

"I don't know, Melly. I..."

Melanie's breath hitched. Mama hadn't called her Melly in years. "It's okay. I don't think I want to know the outcome of anything with Stephen."

"It worked with me and your dad. And it might work for you and Kyle. But I doubt it would have worked with Stephen."

Melanie grinned. "Kyle *is* pretty handsome, isn't he? And funny like Daddy. That's the top of my list. I want someone who makes me laugh."

"Your daddy certainly makes me laugh. Although recently, we've had nothing but serious conversations. Speaking of church, that man is bent to get into it. Paul Mitchell visited him every evening in the hospital. Prayed with him, played bluegrass for all the nurses while Wayne sang gospel songs. He's a different man since this happened, and Melanie, that's a good thing."

"I should have gone to the hospital."

"Can't say that I approve, but I do understand why you didn't. To bear the thought of being without love is too much for a lot of people to handle. You know, I only went to church a handful of times my whole life, and those were mostly funerals and weddings. But, there is one passage about love that I committed to memory. The one Kate used in her wedding." Mama unpinned her hair and let it fall to her shoulders. She closed her eyes and rested her head against the billboard. " 'Though I speak with the tongues of men and of angels, but have not love, I have become sounding brass or a clanging symbol.' "

A deep whistle sounded from Mama's throat as she drew a shaky breath. " 'And though I have the gift of prophecy, and understand all mysteries and knowledge, and though I have all faith, so that I could remove mountains, but have not love, I am nothing. And though I bestow all my goods to feed the poor, and though I give my body to be burned, but have not love, it profits me nothing.' "

"Wow. That's amazing."

"I'm sure you've heard the next part before." Mama gave her a sad smile. "We had it on that photo board hanging in the den above the couch. The quote is on a lot of greeting cards. 'Love suffers long and is kind; love does not envy; love does not parade itself, is not puffed up; does not behave rudely, does not seek its own, is not provoked, thinks no evil; does not rejoice in iniquity, but rejoices in the truth; bears all things, believes all things, hopes all things, endures all things. Love never fails.' "

Melanie clutched her collar. "I remember that, but I didn't realize it came from the Bible."

"I hope you know that's how your daddy and I love you. And how we should love each other. You see, Kate told me this was not a list I should demand Wayne do for me, but rather what I should do for him. She told me to trust God. If I put my time and effort into being this kind of woman, Wayne would respond with the change I wanted to see. If I kept bucking him, we'd just go farther and farther apart until the relationship crumbled." Mama sniffed. "I've gotten away from that advice over the last few years. I need to start treating your daddy better again. I haven't been the best wife. Or mother."

Melanie dove for her, wrapping Mama in her arms so tight she was sure the poor woman couldn't breathe. "You are a good mother. You are. You push me to be better, and I just push back instead of changing. I've never doubted how much you love me."

"And yet you wouldn't come to the hospital because you were afraid to face me."

"I'm so sorry." Melanie clutched Mama's sleeve. "What do you think I should do next?"

"Things will all work out." Mama freed herself and stood. "My advice is to wait for Kyle, and come down with him. I just left him talking to the preacher and your daddy. Wayne's convinced that boy's in love with you, so there's no doubt he'll be getting a pep talk. I'm sure Kyle will be up here in a few minutes ready to try again. I'm not saying to jump into a relationship, but you might at least get your feet wet. He comes from a good family. He got lost a little on the way, but he's been honest with me and your dad about all his mistakes. I hear contrition in his voice." Mama laughed. "And every eye in town will be on him to make sure he doesn't hurt you like Stephen did. Every friend I have."

"And then what?"

"Start living your life again."

Chapter Twenty-Four

Kyle wrapped his fingers around the roll of dimes and squeezed. "I'm not so sure, Wayne. I've already tried pouring my heart out to her. I don't think there's any point. Stephen called it. If Melanie wants me, why hasn't she come down? And I can't see what a roll of dimes has to do with anything. How could this change her mind?"

Wayne trilled his lips and slapped his thigh. "You're not trying hard enough. Melanie used to collect dimes when she was a kid. She has a huge milk jug full of them in her bedroom closet. Probably a thousand dollars' worth. When I first started touring, I'd give her a handful of change. Told her it was her salary for accompanying me on the road. She'd always take the dimes and quarters and hand me back the rest."

Kyle laughed. "Why not keep the gallon jug full of quarters?"

"Well, she liked to spend the quarters on chewing gum. You know how they always have those dispensers at restaurants and such? She'd buy herself a big ol' hunk of gum and stuff those dimes in her pocket."

"Dimes, huh?"

"Dimes. She gives them as gifts sometimes, too. A little card with a dime glued to it and a note."

"Hmm. What should I do with them? Wrap them with a bow or something?"

"Use them to tell her how much you love her. Just try it and see." Wayne winked at him. "Can't hurt."

"Well, looks like her mom's back now. I'll see what I can figure out. First, I have to get those aggravating cows to move to higher ground."

"Apples. And cucumbers."

"Apples?" Kyle's brow shot skyward. That was right. Melanie had said that, and it had worked on Gertie once before. In fact, he still had the bags he'd bought in the barn.

"Cut them so she can taste the juice at the first bite."

"Melanie, or the cows?" Kyle grinned.

"You'll figure it out."

"I'm on it."

Shoulders squared, Kyle returned to the farm. He loaded the apples in the truck bed and drove straight into the middle of Gertie's cow posse.

She flicked her tail with an angry snap and marched closer.

Kyle hopped out and lowered the tailgate. "Okay, girl. We've got to talk. Rain's coming tonight and I've got to get you and your sisters to higher ground. I don't know why you're all just sitting there in the mud, but I need you to move." Kyle sliced three of the apples in fourths and dropped the pieces in a white plastic bowl. He nudged the bowl under Gertie's nostrils and chuckled. Her face—was it his imagination?—softened.

Juice ran down her jaw as she chomped the apples. She ate until they were gone then butted the empty bowl.

"Oh, I brought more." He grabbed a couple more apples and sliced them with his pocket knife. "Just have to save a couple for my other girl."

Gertie scrambled to her feet and inched closer. She nuzzled the bag, snatching a whole apple and chomping it in half.

"Oh, Gertie." Kyle laughed. "That moo sounded an awful lot like you said, 'heavenly.' "

She cocked her head sideways as he stroked beneath her ear. A couple of the cows next to her got up and wandered closer. He gave them a piece of apple then patted Gertie once more.

"Maybe you and ol' Kyle will get along after all." He chuckled and pointed to the open gate. "So here's the deal. I need you to lead your sisters to that hill over there, where there's no danger of high water. So I'm going to leave the rest of these apples right here in Pa's truck bed, and as soon as we get up that hill and closer to the barn, I'll give you all another piece."

He hopped in the truck and drove forward at a turtle's speed.

Gertie flicked her tail a few times and inched forward. It was working!

He drove a few more feet and two of the cows in the pasture started after her. The rest of them took turns standing and joining the line. Laughing from his chest, he poked his head out the window. "C'mon Gertie girl, lead the pack. Pa Casey's got nothing on me."

Melanie zoomed in on her cell camera, her lips curling upward in spite of herself. "Kyle Casey. Cow Whisperer. Who could have guessed that one?"

It made good sense to move the cows to higher ground with the threatening sky.

And… it made good sense for her to climb down. Give it up, admit defeat, and walk away with whatever dignity she had left. But how could she? She'd said thirteen days and she needed to finish it out.

Daddy would go back to his shows, and Mama would go back to nagging at her about everything. And since she didn't trust any of her friends anymore, and she didn't have Stephen, what did she have left?

Kyle. His name pierced her thoughts like he'd shot an arrow her way. The trailer. The promise to work with him on the farm. But

222

for how long? Did she have Kyle for the long haul, or until his soft spot for her wore off? His reputation brought doubts greater than she'd ever carried for Stephen or anyone else. But Mama trusted him, and Mama never trusted anyone. No way could she trust her instincts. Her intellect said run far from the guy, but her heart told her unconditionally to not worry.

Hadn't her heart told her to trust Stephen? How could she know if trusting Kyle was the right choice?

And now, she'd hurt Kyle deeply, though she wasn't sure why. Since she'd refused to come down for the dinner, things had been off between them. And when she'd reaffirmed that they couldn't date, his texts had been abrupt at best. Hadn't he said he understood that she had to finish out her time on the billboard? Hadn't he realized she couldn't jump from one bad relationship straight into another? But then today, it seemed like there might be hope. That he might be willing to try, anyway.

She pressed her fingers to her lips. He'd be back for her soon, wanting her to walk away with him. Together with him. Dare she hope things could work out? But what if they didn't?

Through her camera lens, he bounded out of his truck, closed the gate behind him, and ran to the tailgate. The cows all swarmed him. What was he giving them? She zoomed closer. Red things. Apples?

She laughed out loud. She should have known. He'd listened to her advice. No wonder they'd all followed him. He was so much like Daddy. More than once, Daddy had offered carrots to the neighbor's goats to bribe them to his fence line so they'd eat his weeds. And, Kyle had wanted her to follow him, too.

In her heart, she already had. If only she could convince her mind it wasn't too great a risk. Daddy would tell her if she never jumped, she'd never know. Maybe she should climb down and help Kyle. Though... he seemed to have it covered.

She sighed. She'd do what Mama wanted. She'd come down early go back home and help Daddy until he recovered. And she'd climb down with Kyle, but after that, she'd leave him behind. It was better that way.

Unless… what if she did agree to a date with Kyle? And what if it went great? What if they forged a relationship based on trust and turned out happy?

What if she was smarter this go around? Maybe if she had focused on the moment instead of the outcome, she'd have seen some of Stephen's flaws.

Her cell buzzed. She dug it out of her pocket and frowned. A number she didn't recognize. Should she answer?

"Hello?"

"Melanie?" The deep masculine voice gave her chills.

"Um… Stephen?" Her heart skipped something like eighty beats.

"I want to come see you. Casey's banned me from the farm." Stephen's voice carried a hard edge. Almost like he spat the words.

"What do you mean he banned you?" Melanie's jaw clenched. Was Stephen telling the truth? Why would Kyle do that? "Where are you? Why are you calling from this number instead of your phone?"

"Let's just say if you look over the horizon you'll see police cars all over town looking for me. Seems rumor's gotten out that I'm armed and dangerous or something. Casey's got people from that church all over his property. I can't even approach the gate."

"Why would he do that?"

"He wants you for himself, Melanie. He doesn't want me to have another chance with you." Stephen cleared his throat. "And I do. I want another chance with you."

"Then come tell me. In person. Police or no police." She shook her head. She wasn't giving him another chance, but it would be nice to hear him ask for it. "Apologize to me face to face."

"I'm telling you, Kyle won't let me on the property. You're going to have to come to me. He won't let you see me on the farm."

Kyle didn't seem like the kind of guy to be manipulative like that, but then again he did have a past.

But who didn't have a past? Even she had manipulated ex-boyfriends because they didn't match her number scheme. It was time to end this.

Melanie sent a sharp blast of air through the speaker. "If you want to talk to me, talk. Tell me the truth. Did you, or did you not, go away on a weekend with Tricia Billings right before the wedding?"

Stephen scoffed. "You knew I was on the weekend trip. Tricia just happened to be at the same place, same time. She came to me."

"Did you kiss her?"

Pause.

Melanie dug a tiny gravel from a crack in one of the steel beams on the deck. "Did you kiss her?"

"I did. And more."

She bit her lip. What a sting. She hadn't expected Stephen's abrupt honesty. "And more. Was that weekend the first time with Tricia?"

Another pause. "No."

"How many times? When did it start?" The bird that had nested near her wedding dress flew to the deck as though it, too, hung on Stephen's every word.

He gave a low whistle over the speaker. "Tricia and I loosely dated back in high school, Melanie. Just a 'friends with benefits' sort of thing. We never really stopped."

High school. They never stopped. Melanie's entire body tensed and her arm hairs prickled. Burning tears stung the corners of her eyes. "Were there others?"

"Yes." Something clanged in the background. "I was... Melanie, I was *married* before. Another girl, another town."

"Married?" She slammed the phone against her thigh.

"Melanie?" Stephen's voice crackled. "Melanie, are you there?"

With a snatch, she brought the phone back to her ear. "You were married before and didn't tell me?"

"It didn't come up."

It didn't come up. Seriously? "Aaaggghhh!" She stood, her jaw so tight her teeth ached. "How many others, Stephen? How many?"

"Look. I told you all that to be honest. To prove to you that I *can* be honest. We had a dream together. We had a future. I still want that." Stephen's voice wavered. "Believe me." Was he crying?

"No." She stomped her foot on the deck so hard it shook. "No, absolutely not, never."

"If you forgive me, I'll never stray again. I promise, Mel. I've been so miserable without you. Watching you up there with some other guy, acting like you—"

"Oh, no you don't." She sat back down and scooted under the shower curtains, where she'd tucked away a box of tissues. "Kyle has been nothing but kind to me. He's taken care of me when you wouldn't. I mean, you went to Jamaica without me."

"Only for a couple of days." Stephen cleared his throat. "It wasn't the same without you."

She eyed her phone screen, catching a slight glimpse of her reflection. The red circle permitting her to end the call lay just beside her fingertips. She took a deep breath, filling her lungs to capacity. She was in control of this situation. Not Stephen. Not ever.

With an exaggerated tap, she touched the icon and hung up on him. "There. And good riddance. Don't dare call back."

A shiver coursed her spine. She could almost feel Stephen's rage through the air as the cell rang again. He didn't like being crossed, and he didn't like when he didn't get what he wanted. She was pretty sure he'd already tried to fight Kyle at the club. Would he have the nerve to hurt Kyle so he could get access to the farm?

Chapter Twenty-Five

Kyle hooked the side of one of Pa's tarps over the deck railing. He'd already secured it below, fashioning a slide of sorts so they could easily send all her lighter stuff to the truck bed. She was coming down, even if he had to stuff her through the tube.

Stony silence met him as he poked his head over the deck and fished in his pocket for the roll of dimes. Was she angry again? He unfolded the paper at the head of the roll and took out the first coin. He was winging this one, but he'd speak from his heart. Surely that would count for something.

With slow, soft steps, he crossed to the shower curtain, where Melanie sat huddled inside. A thin crack revealed her puffy eyes and reddened cheeks. So vulnerable. If only he could reach her.

"One." Metal clinked metal as the silver struck the deck. It rolled close to the hem of the curtain, almost falling between the steel planks, and Kyle stepped on it. "One dime because you, Melanie Dawn Turner, are a perfect ten. When you are angry, when you are bitter, when you've cried your eyes out all afternoon. When you are old and gray and your teeth are falling out, I, Kyle Douglas Casey, promise I will still count you a ten."

Cheesy, but maybe it worked. A sound falling somewhere between a snort and a sniffle came from behind the curtain.

Kneeling, he dropped a second dime beside the first. "Two. Because two times ten is twenty, and that's about how many minutes it took me that first night to realize I wanted to spend every waking minute with you from now until eternity. Some people say when they meet 'the one,' that person turns their life upside down. Well, my life was already upside down when I met you. Truth is, even in your heartbroken, stubborn state, you've turned my world right side up again."

Another dime, another sniffle. At least she was listening. And so far, so good for winging it. He nudged the coin closer. "Three. Because three times ten is thirty, and I know you were hoping to be married before you turn thirty. Some of your friends told me that's what they think you were freaking out about. That turning twenty-six meant you were close to thirty. Well, that's just ridiculous."

She lifted the curtain and glowered at him. "You don't know anything about me or my friends."

"Let me finish." He pulled himself up and sat cross-legged on the deck, then moved the three dimes in front of him. "So maybe it is ridiculous, but it's your dream. And I'm hoping you might let me get a ring on your finger before then. I want you to give me a chance. Let's go on that first real date. Let me prove to you that I can be the man you deserve."

Her sigh dragged on.

Two more dimes jingled in his palm. What now? He drummed his toes against the tip of his shoes several times. Right. Thirteen. He had to work in thirteen somehow. "Forty, which is the age I'll be thirteen years from now. In thirteen years, Melanie Turner, I want you and I to climb back up this aggravating billboard as husband and wife, and have us a good laugh about how we met."

"I'm done with thirteen, Kyle." She let the curtain fall. Her breath caught, and then she dissolved into sobs.

Okay, so that was a bust. Should he go on? He rolled the fifth dime between his finger and thumb. He had to go on. "Fifty. Five times ten. As in fifty-fifty. A partnership. You meet me in the middle and we start walking off in a completely new direction. A better direction. A fresh start. Both of us committing to each other… helping each other let go of our past hurts and find happiness."

Her snort sounded a little like Gertie's.

Kyle tore off a bit of the paper on the coin roll. Sixty days. Two months. Did he want to go there? The paper fluttered along the breeze to the branches of the old pine. He took a deep breath. Another dime. "Sixty. Sixty days since the commissioner banned me from baseball. Sixty days since I felt like I'd lost everything, but I cannot compare that to the thought of losing you. If I had it to do over, I'd have never left town with my parents. I'd have been sitting right on the front steps of that high school the day you moved back into town and waited to sweep you off your feet." Now what?

"You wouldn't have even spoken to me." She snatched the curtain and tugged it so hard it ripped free from the PVC pipe, exposing the radio he'd brought her. "The only reason you're—"

"You're wrong." Ha. She might be getting fired up, but she was hearing him. "Seven." Kyle flicked a dime with his thumb, and it landed an inch in front of her. "I know you love Ed Sheeran. We've talked about the promises he makes in that one song. You know, about loving you until you're seventy. The song claims that he falls for the girl every single day. You have to believe me that it's true. Every moment I spend with you drives you deeper under my skin. Seventy, eighty, two-hundred and twenty if we could get there—I want to spend every day with you."

She inched out of the curtain and picked up the dimes, her eyes wide and glistening. "Let me guess. Eight, nine, and ten."

"Eight, nine, and ten." He pulled out a wadded receipt. "Eighty dollars. That's how much I spent at the hardware store on your shelter that first day."

She snatched the receipt. "Eighty dollars? That's just stupid."

"I'm not."

She turned behind her and dug through the bin, emerging with a piece of paper waving in her hand. "This says a hundred sixty-seven dollars and thirteen cents. You didn't spend just eighty."

"Oops. That receipt wasn't the hardware store. That was the farm and tractor supply store. I've been looking for that one. Need it back for taxes. Could you just work with me, please? You asked me to pour my heart out, and I'm trying."

"Fine." She stuffed the receipt in his hand, jolting as she touched him. "Carry on."

He cringed. He was failing miserably here. He should have thought it out before coming up to talk to her. Ninety... hmm.

"I'm waiting."

"Why are you so mad at me?" He rolled the coins in his palm. "I've tried so hard to be good to you, and give you space."

Her shoulders slumped. "I'm not mad at you. Not really. Stephen called."

"He called?" Kyle bit back the long list of retorts building on his tongue. He folded the receipt and stuffed it into his pocket.

"Said you banned him from the farm."

"Because he threatened to hurt... never mind. It's my property, Melanie. Actually, it's Pa's property. If you want to talk to your ex-fiancé, it needs to be somewhere besides here. This is our place. Our time. And I'm trying to pour my heart out to you. Can you at least listen?"

"Fine. Ninety?"

"Ninety days. Three months from now. One of my buddies is getting married, and I need a date. I want you to be my date. I can't even think about asking anyone else." He frowned. Lame. He was losing her. But then, she met his gaze, and her frown softened.

Encouraged, he shot her a slight sideways grin. "And ten." He swallowed as she moved closer. "Ten for one hundred. One hundred percent of me. For the first time in my life, I've spent two whole weeks doing things for someone else instead of myself. Dad used to always talk to me about submission and I never understood. He told me I always ended up single because I refused to submit to my girlfriends."

"Submit?" Melanie dropped down beside him and slid her fingers through his.

His heart stopped. Dare he hope? "Dad told me the Bible said people in a relationship—well, a marriage, but he always said it worked for any relationship—couldn't possibly hope for happiness until they both gave themselves fully to each other. He said my problem was I always let the girls do all the submitting. They did everything I wanted, and I never thought about what might make them happy. So eventually they left me. Usually sooner rather than later." He tightened his grip on Melanie's hand and gave her a light squeeze. "I don't want you to ever feel empty again. Not from me, not from anyone. I want to submit to you that way."

"But you can't be a doormat." She stretched out her feet and crossed them over the deck rail. "That's not healthy, either."

"Well, I said that, too, but thinking back and seeing how my parents were with each other made me realize what it really meant. Mom was the first thought my dad had in the mornings. He woke up ten minutes before she did so he could turn the heat up warmer and make her coffee. And Dad was her first thought. She ironed his breakfast and made him pants before work." Kyle snickered. "Well, you know what I mean. We kids used to get so mad because we'd ask for things and they'd put us off. But now I see it. Mom and Dad were just putting each other first. They were submitting to each other."

"That seems so odd."

"I think it was being in church. They read their Bibles together and lived out their faith by serving others. They just weren't selfish like most of us are." Kyle brought her hand close to his chest. "Like I've been. Melanie, I know those Twitter pictures hurt. But I have been nothing but honest with you. I went to that club to find Stephen and stand up for you. I didn't touch a drink of alcohol—in fact, I didn't even sit at a table. He tricked me into that situation. Told those girls who I was so they'd swarm me and then took pictures of the whole scene. Can you please try one more time to believe that I've changed?"

"Kyle, you're a weirdo. Who falls into these kinds of situations?" Melanie leaned her head against his chest.

"Pro baseball players do. It's the celebrity factor. And I'm not that guy anymore. I may be a weirdo, but I'm serious about this. I've decided to put some roots on this farm and make Milton my permanent home. And I want you to be my girl." He reached into the bag he'd looped over his belt. "I brought you an apple, even. Will you please say yes?"

"You brought me an apple?" A sly grin spread across her face as she tilted it up to meet his gaze. "Well, since you brought me an apple, maybe I could manage a date or two. You know, see where things go. But no promises we'll make it to thirteen years. You haven't counted out enough dimes yet."

"Thirteen." Kyle shook the coin roll and spilled out three more dimes. "Now, will you *please* come down off this billboard?

Melanie eyed the coins, pulled her fingers free from Kyle's, and held her breath for a few seconds. "Thirteen." She'd given up on thirteen. Could it work for her this one more time?

As she reached for the dimes, Kyle slid his fingers between hers, catching her before she grabbed them. Goosebumps spread over her. It had been a long time since she'd held anyone's hand. Stephen wasn't interested, and a lot of her other relationships had never made it that far.

Her skin tickled as he massaged the back of her hand with his thumb. "This is not about thirteen, Melanie. I could give you a hundred dimes and a thousand thoughts. You've built your whole life around a number. I'm asking you to consider building a life with me instead."

"Life. With you." Her pulse beat wildly against his palm.

"We both have a chance for a new start. A chance to do things right from the beginning. To walk together in the right direction. To make our lives about serving other people instead of being selfish. I have the money to do a ton of good for this community, but it would sure be easier with someone by my side. Melanie Dawn Turner, will you please, please come down from this billboard and start a new life with me?"

A growing breeze tickled her nose as it swept across the billboard and set her trash bag rustling against the edge of the deck. The storm would arrive soon, but no way could it mask her thundering heart. She wanted to say yes so badly. To trust that things could be right again.

She tugged his hand to her heart and rested her chin on his knuckles. "Okay."

"Okay? You're just going to make it easy on us and tell me okay?" His grin reflected in his deep brown eyes. "Just so you know, I'm going to kiss you as soon as we get to the ground again. Not in front of all these people, but it's coming."

Her cheeks warmed. "If you say so." She waved her hand over her massive accumulation of stuff. "I guess we should get all this down, right?"

"Got it covered." He laughed and pointed to the hooks on the deck railing. "Pa had these old tarps. I tied them together. Thought we could treat them like a trash chute."

Melanie laughed. "Kyle, you are such a tinker. You'll make a great farmer. You don't even know it."

"A tinker?"

"You know, like Tinkerbell."

"What?" His brows shot up and he twisted his face in mock protest. "You think I'm a fairy? How's that supposed to help me farm?"

"Tinkerbell was a tinker fairy. Seriously, Kyle." She giggled. "She would get screws and flowers and stuff and build neat things from them. A good farmer is kind of a natural tinker. A problem solver, I guess."

"A problem solver." His jaw twitched. "So, here's a problem for you. How are we supposed to get your wedding dress out of that tree?"

Chapter Twenty-Six

Kyle held out his camera. He tapped his phone to snap the selfie with him and the tangled white satin. "Captioning this one 'Say Yes to the Nest.'"

"Kyle Casey, stop Tweeting. You're going to fall out of the tree." Melanie faced him from her spot on the billboard, her hands planted firmly on her hip.

He laughed. "I'm a pro at climbing now, Mel. Besides, I told you. I'm tweeting your return to society. We're going to give the news outlets a documentary of what really happened. If I've learned anything from baseball, it's that the more you try to be secretive and hide things, the more they twist your words. If I do this, we tell our story our way."

She shook her head. "I know you're right. But you falling out of a tree isn't the story I want to tell."

He inched up to the next limb and slid his phone into his pocket. Carefully, he loosened the threads from the branches and slung the dress over his shoulder. As he eased his way down, the weight of the burden struck his heart. He carried the dress she'd worn for another man. Even if it was only for a while, and she hadn't married the guy, the dress represented a past he hadn't been a part of. A past he didn't belong in. Did he belong in her future?

When he reached the ground, he spread the dress over the plastic he'd placed over the truck bed. It wasn't too bad, really. Some leaves and a little dirt. A few loose threads. He'd run it by the dry cleaner's later and see if it could be salvaged.

He carefully folded the dress, rolled it into the plastic, and started back up the ladder. Other than the shower curtains and PVC pipe, which Melanie had probably disassembled by now, they'd brought down everything. And now, the moment of truth. Would she stick to her word? Would she go through with it? Could he have another chance at loving someone and having love in return?

He closed his eyes, picturing her as he'd seen her that first day. Vulnerable, beautiful, and angelic. When he opened them, laughter bubbled in his chest. A shower curtain draped over her shoulders like a queen's cape and secured with duct tape. Scissors in her teeth, and her body twisted in an awkward angle as she twisted apart two pieces of the pipe. More like a handyman than a princess, but beautiful as ever. And his. Hopefully, his.

She turned and grinned, letting the scissors fall to the deck. "What are you gawking at?"

"The girl of my dreams." He crossed over to her and took the loose pipe from her hands.

"If you like sweaty hot messes." She snorted.

"Love them." He kissed her forehead, and cheers erupted from the parking lot.

Wayne bellowed a whoop that could have been heard across the world. Kyle grinned and gave him a thumbs-up.

"You should have tweeted that." Melanie loosened the tape holding the shower curtain over her shoulders and let it fall.

"Wait. Let's do it again." He took out his phone, held it in front of them, and took a selfie while kissing her forehead.

"You're out of control." She giggled. "What are you captioning that one?"

"I'm not tweeting this one." He stuffed the phone back in his pocket and freed the next piece of PVC pipe. "I just want to remember this day. That moment. So, I have evidence to believe you really told me yes this time."

235

"You're silly." She carried the pipe and curtain over to the rough-hewn chute and let it fall to the truck. "I think that's about it. Maybe we should take a selfie and announce to everyone that the Billboard Bride is finally coming down."

He draped his arm over her shoulder and posed beside her to snap the picture. "I'm not sending this one out just yet." With a wink, he linked arms with her. "We have business when we get to the ground, and then we can announce whatever you want."

Business. Melanie's heart skipped a beat. The promised kiss. Tingles. Excitement and pure joy. And hope for a future of happiness. How could she have ever debated taking this leap with Kyle? "Maybe we'll hold off on that announcement for a while. If business is good, that is…"

She chuckled, pulled away from him, and dashed down the deck ladder. As she hopped across to the tree, his brown eyes twinkled. He followed, reaching the ground seconds after she did, and spun her back against the tree.

"Melanie Turner, I know you already said okay, but I'm going to ask this one more time and make it official. Now that you're down from that wretched billboard, will you please *finally* agree that we belong together? I want more than a date. I want a lifetime."

"I want that, too." She held her breath as his face crept closer. She closed her eyes as his hand cupped her cheek. And then… bliss. Soft lips offering promise. The hardening kiss revealing their hunger for an insatiable love that left them both full instead of empty.

It rendered her even more breathless, if that was possible. Why had she resisted him for so many days?

Sharp whistles and catcalls disrupted their merriment, and she pried her fingers loose from his arms. He spun, a scowl distorting his features as the faces came into focus. Guys she didn't recognize, but clearly he did.

"Looks like Casey's at bat again." A tall redhead sneered. "Going for another homerun this time?"

Kyle hulked over to the guys as the crowd thickened behind them. Someone had fashioned a makeshift bridge over the narrow part of the creek with one of the heavy wood tables from the church, and people trekked through the gate, snaking along the creek like ants until they crossed.

Rage pulsed in Kyle's veins. She could see it as he folded his muscular arms across his chest and faced up to them.

"You have no reason to be here other than to start trouble." Kyle waved to a couple officers who stood at the edge of the crowd. "I want these guys off my property. Off Pa's property."

The redhead leaned, his gaze drifting past Kyle and meeting hers. "I want to talk to the girl, Kyle. To warn her."

"Daylen. Lacey was a different time. A different situation, and Melanie knows the whole story. I'm not the same person I was back then."

"That's why you're making out with her in the forest two weeks after meeting her." Daylen tried to sidestep Kyle, but Kyle dodged him. "Let me talk to her."

Melanie darted to Kyle's side. "You need to leave. He asked you to leave."

"If you know what's good for you, you'll leave, too." Daylen shoved Kyle, and the officers moved closer. "He destroyed my sister. Crushed her and stomped on the pieces. If you know all about that, then—"

"Sir, you need to leave." The officers stepped closer. "We're going to escort you back to the gate."

"Fine." Daylen gave Kyle another shove before heading back to the makeshift bridge, his cronies in tow. The crowd paused, letting them cross back over.

When they reached the other side, one of the officers blocked the bridge. "You folks need to go back to the church. This is private property."

With frowning faces, the group dwindled, leaving a handful of Melanie's friends and a redheaded girl she didn't recognize. Her heart stopped. Was that Lacey?

Mari Beth cornered the officer, but he didn't let them pass.

Melanie puffed her cheeks. "I'm going to have to go talk to them, Kyle."

"Okay." He moved to the center of the group who'd gathered on his side of the creek. "We do appreciate you all coming to support Melanie. The prayers and waiting while we sorted all this out, especially. And on behalf of... Pa?"

A wisp of a man in his eighties shuffled to the front of the crowd, a grin spanning his brown-spotted cheeks from ear to ear. Tufts of wayward white hair jutted in all directions, and the collar of his short-sleeved plaid shirt gaped around a thin, wrinkled neck. Beside him, a peppy woman with graying blonde hair clung to him.

Pa waved his arm. "Hello, Kyle. I hope you don't mind. I invited some friends over to see my new place."

"Your new place?" Kyle's gaze darted over the horizon. "Oh." He laughed. "The trailer? The footprints on the fence the other day. You've been here all along, haven't you?"

Pa snickered. "Since Tuesday. You just about caught me, son. Meet my wife, Sharon. Your new grandmother. She didn't want to live in your grandma's old house, so we decided to remodel the trailer. It's plenty for the two of us anyway."

"I met her, Pa. At the wedding. Remember?"

Pa slapped his thigh. "That's right. At the wedding. Well, son, it's been an interesting two weeks. I'm glad to see you're managing the farm well."

Kyle's chest swelled. "Better than I'd hoped."

"And you must be Melanie." Pa stepped forward and grabbed her hands with both of his. "More beautiful in person. No wonder my idiot grandson is smitten. I hope he knows what a treasure you are. It's not every day a man snags a Turner. Does he know you're the state archery champ?"

Melanie wrinkled her nose. "Not the champ. Second place. But that was a long time ago."

"Hey Perkins," Pa called to the officer. "Let Brielle Collins cross over."

"Can you let the rest of those girls come, too? They're my friends." Melanie gritted her teeth. Well, except for Tricia Billings. But no sense in making a huge deal of that now.

The girls all crossed over, but instead of swarming Melanie, they swarmed Kyle. Gush, gush. Eyelid flutters.

Melanie shook her head.

"See, it's already happening." Daylen's face had reddened to match his hair. "You're always going to come second to his fame."

The breeze carried his taunt as the officers escorted Daylen toward the church gate. His words swarmed her, echoing in her ear and piercing her heart. Doubt flooded in. Was Daylen right?

The red-haired girl hung back from the rest of them, just a couple feet from Melanie. Her profile didn't match Daylen's, so maybe it wasn't Lacey? But she looked vaguely familiar. What had Pa called her?

"Brielle. Used to be Masters. Now Collins. Nice to see you again, Melanie."

Brielle Masters. A new wave of emotions washed out her doubt. Envy, shame, and rage. "Brielle. The girl who crushed me at state."

Brielle brushed a perfectly curled tendril behind her ear and grinned. "You held your own pretty well if I remember. Didn't it come down to one point? You had a perfect run except for that last target."

"Yeah." Melanie allowed herself a tiny smile. She had been an awesome archer in her tournament days, and had even improved since then. "What brings you to Milton? Coming for a rematch?"

Brielle reached into her shirt pocket and retrieved a business card. "Any time you want, Turner. Anyplace, any day, and I'll still win." She laughed. "But I'm here for a proposal, actually. I've started a new business in Milton. It's kind of a CrossFit meets martial arts. Hard to explain, but I want to offer training for youth athletes in any number of sports. Archery being one."

Melanie glanced at Kyle, who was writing on Mari Beth's sleeve with a black sharpie. "And let me guess. Baseball."

"You two would be a godsend, I'm telling you. I can't keep up with the clientele and I need experts. You wouldn't believe how archery has boomed in the area."

"Hmm. I'll have to give it some thought."

Brielle pressed the card in Melanie's hand. "Just say yes. I'm counting on you. Show up next Monday and check things out. If you don't like it, walk away. If you do, I'll have clients for you on Tuesday. Benefits and everything. This company is a franchise with room to grow and eventually manage your own. You can fill out the paperwork Monday afternoon. But I know you'd make an awesome teacher. Your technique is flawless."

Teach archery? Melanie's trigger finger itched just thinking about it. It sounded kind of fun. And for Brielle to seek her out and offer… "You know what? I think I'm in. I need something new and different, and this sounds awesome."

"Great." Brielle winked. "Bring your best bow. We'll face off at noon on my lunch break. If you win, I'll buy your lunch for three months. If I win—"

"I'll win." Melanie accepted Brielle's handshake then faced her friends again. "And if I can pry these fangirls away from my man, you can ask him about it, too."

"Don't put too much stock in what that redheaded creep said back there." Brielle leaned closer. "I've known Kyle since grade school. Our dads were on the same high school team. He's not a bad guy. He just lost himself for a while."

At that moment, Kyle waved, and the swarm of girls broke away. Melanie winced as she saw them coming.

Anna Kate reached her first, waggling so close to Melanie's nose she scratched it with her fingernail. "Girl, you've got some explaining to do. You didn't answer even one of my texts."

Melanie groaned as the wind picked up its speed. Anna Kate hadn't sent any texts, and they both knew it. It was time for Melanie to redefine the boundaries in her friendship. In all her friendships. They'd better get this conversation started if they were going to finish before the storm.

Kyle breathed clearer the moment he broke away from the giggly girls Melanie called friends. How did she stand these goofy, overgrown twenty-something teenagers? They'd smothered him with their gushing and excitement. It was making Melanie uncomfortable, he could tell. And then stupid Daylen had to yell out his comment about her coming second. He resolved right then and there that Melanie would never again come second to his pseudo fame.

When he reached her, he placed a light hand on her shoulder, and she jerked away. But then, her face softened, and she stepped closer again. Reflex? At least he hoped so.

"Hey, Brielle. I see you and Melanie have met." He hugged the tall, slender redhead, careful to not hold on too tightly. Would Melanie be jealous? Living in fear of making her uncomfortable would be a rough strain on their relationship.

"We met a long time ago." Brielle flashed her stark-white teeth in a wide grin. "I envied her talent a long time until I finally beat her."

Melanie gaped. "You envied me? Seriously?"

Brielle drew her arm back and released a mock arrow. "You do know that wasn't the only tournament we competed together in, right? That I lost to you several times before winning? That my coach made us watch videos over and over to study your methods? I told you. Your technique is amazing. You were my motivation." She passed Kyle a business card. "So I have this new gym in west Milton. We specialize in training athletes, and I'd love to have a new baseball coach. Already talked Melanie into taking some archery clients. Maybe you could come on board, too?"

Kyle turned the card over in his hand. "I'll give it some thought. I was thinking about doing some private coaching. Maybe even opening my own place."

Brielle shrugged. "The building next door to me is empty. It would be a great place for a batting cage. There's even an upper deck that could be converted to a track."

"Sounds cool." Kyle tucked the card in his wallet and hugged Melanie closer. "We'll come and check it out sometime next week. Thanks for thinking of me."

"My pleasure, Kyle. See you guys." Brielle walked over to Pa and Sharon and hugged them then crossed the creek and headed toward the church gate.

One of Melanie's friends, a buxom blonde, sauntered closer. "Hey, Melly. We're going clubbing tonight if you want to come with. Bring Kyle, too."

A slight frown flickered across Melanie's face, and she gripped Kyle's waist even tighter. "I think I need to rest tonight. It's been a long two weeks."

"K." The girl giggled. "Or you just need to hang out with your man candy."

Melanie rolled her eyes. "You girls have fun."

Another girl, a somber toothpick with raven hair, approached. "You must be Kyle." She gave him a shy smile. "Nice to finally meet you. My dad is a huge fan."

Thunder rumbled in the distance, and Kyle glanced toward the sky. They needed to wrap this up. "Great to meet you, too." He extended his hand for a shake. "What did you say your name was?"

Melanie shifted her weight and blasted a burst of air from her nostrils. He turned to her, finding fire blazing in her eyes as the raven-haired girl cleared her throat.

"Tricia Billings."

Kyle's breath hitched. No wonder Melanie was freaking out. He'd just shaken hands with the enemy.

Chapter Twenty-Seven

Melanie clenched her jaw and tried to loosen her grip on Kyle's arm. *I will NOT be jealous of Tricia Billings. I will NOT be jealous of Tricia Billings.* The words to Dolly Parton's "Jolene" flashed through her mind. *Please, Tricia. You've already taken Stephen. Let me and Kyle have some peace.*

She swallowed twice and still couldn't find words to speak.

Tricia tapped her hand against her thigh and chewed her lip. Finally, she sighed. "Melanie, can we talk?"

Talk? She wanted to *talk*? A thousand words of fury planted themselves on Melanie's tongue. She choked them back and managed to squeak out a small "Okay."

Kyle left her side, and Melanie followed Tricia to a group of old stumps several hundred feet away.

"It's beautiful here." Tricia sat on a stump and picked a fistful of clover from the grass beside it. She laid the clover on the stump and separated one, holding it out in front of her. "Before my mom died, we used to sit in the field outside our house. I'd pick clovers while she read me poetry. I miss her so much." She blinked several times. "You never know what you have until it's snatched away."

Melanie forced herself to breathe. Why had Tricia gone and said that? It was so hard to hate her when she'd reminded Melanie of her troubled past—the past Melanie had watched unfold with the rest of Milton. Tricia's mom had been a community sweetheart and died in a horrific tragedy. Raped, stabbed, and the house burned to the ground, and the police didn't catch the guy. She lived through all that, spent months in the hospital healing to a disfigured state, only to be shot and killed by the creep the weekend she moved into their new home. Tricia had gone from a bubbly, peppy cheerleader to a dark, friendless soul. How could she blame the girl for becoming an isolated misfit? And how could she deny her own shame in refusing to reach out to a girl who so obviously needed a friend?

A dismal day ten years prior resurfaced its ugly face. Tricia standing by herself next to the girl's restroom at prom, her tear-streaked cheeks painted with black, red, and gold tints from the makeup job Melanie had envied. Everyone had talked about Tricia's non-existent boyfriend. The boy who she'd claimed was coming to the prom, but never showed.

Tricia had grabbed Melanie's arm before she went in. "I can't go in there," she'd said. "Too many people who want to see me fall on my face. Can you please bring me out some tissue paper?"

Melanie had snorted. "I don't speak cheerleader," she'd said, and left Tricia standing there to cry. Raw, exposed pain.

Melanie cringed. She'd been there. "Yeah, Pa's farm is beautiful."

Tricia carefully tore off the three leaves and stacked them on top of each other. Then, she removed the leaves from another clover and twisted the two stems together. "I'm so sorry about Stephen. It was dumb and selfish of me."

Tears stung Melanie's already aching eyes. "I really don't know what to say. It was dumb. And it hurts. A lot. But I haven't always been the nicest person to you. I can see you wanting to hurt me."

"I didn't mean to hurt you." Tricia tied on a third stem then caught her hair in a ponytail. She looped the stems together and secured at her nape. "I've been in love with Stephen since the sixth grade. It wasn't really about you."

"Really?" Melanie bit her tongue. Was Stephen the no-show prom date? It certainly fit his MO. She didn't need to cut this girl any slack. Relationship breaker. Homewrecker. But how could she not? Tricia's face echoed nothing but torment and misery.

"Really." Tricia covered her eyes with her hands and rubbed her palms over her brows several times. "I guess I've always believed that one day he'd give me a fair chance. He always promised, you know. Always said he'd figure out a way to break it off with whoever he was with and find a way to be with me. Always came around when he was newly single or bored in a relationship. And then…" She sucked in several rapid breaths. Her shoulders shook as she released them. "Then, I'd call and he wouldn't answer. It would be months before he'd talk to me. But this last time, I thought it would be different. He gave me a ring."

Melanie sat on the stump opposite Tricia. "A ring? When? Why?"

"Two months ago. He needed money and I loaned him some." She slumped her shoulders and lowered her clasped hands between her knees. "Of course, he never gave it back. He said the ring was his grandma's and it was worth a lot of money. Later, he told me I could sell it to make back the loan. But I didn't keep it. I gave it back to him and told him to forget the loan. Stupid, I know."

Two months ago? Why would Stephen have needed money two months ago? The week he proposed? "Do you know what for?"

Tricia shook her head. "He said it was a tricky situation and he couldn't tell anyone."

A good slap to her forehead held back Melanie's tears. "That's when he asked me to marry him. I'm sure it's the same ring." Her chest constricted, and her neck and face warmed. "That's when he talked me into selling my car and we opened the joint checking account together. I pretty much handed him that money. Who knows what he did with it. I bet if I go to the bank, the account will be drained."

"You sold your car?" Tricia flung her hand over her mouth. "You had that car for years. Everybody knows you loved that old thing."

"I did."

Tricia frowned. "That's awful. Well, maybe Kyle will buy you a new one. At least you've lucked out to find someone who has money instead of someone who's always conning money. I tried to warn you about Stephen, you know."

"I know. I'm sorry I didn't listen." Melanie winced as the wind slapped loose hairs into her face. Maybe this should be a conversation for another time. The storm was getting closer. "Did you know he'd been married?"

"I did. I'm the reason they split up. I kept calling him, and he eventually started meeting up with me. She caught us." Tricia cast her gaze toward the ground. "I'm a terrible person. I mean, look at me. I live alone in a dump of an apartment. I have no friends. I've spent my entire life chasing a dream that's never going to happen. I'm seriously starting to wonder why I even bother with anything." She sighed. "I guess you hate me. And you should."

Melanie reached for Tricia's hand and squeezed it. "I can't explain why, but I don't really hate you. I want to. Believe me, my first reaction was to run instead of talking to you. But all I can think about right now is how hard your life has been. Even though you did what you did on purpose, I think maybe Stephen's more to blame for jerking you around all these years."

"I want to be a better person, but I don't know how." Tricia sniffled. "I just keep falling into the same rut over and over again. My dad and stepmom changed jobs and moved us to a new city to get me away from Stephen. That's how bad it's been. And then, when I graduated, I followed him place to place in the hopes that each time would be the one where he decides I'm the girl he's wanted all along. When he said he was leaving town the weekend before your wedding, I found a reason to be with him. I'm really sorry for that."

A clap of thunder sent Melanie's friends skittering across the bridge and back to the church gate. Kyle waved to her, and she held up her hand. "You know what, Tricia? It's getting ready to dump buckets, but we need to finish this talk. Maybe we could meet for lunch tomorrow." Her cheeks warmed. "Um… I'll have to borrow money from my parents I guess. And you might have to drive us. But I think maybe we could work together and help each other heal. I sure don't want to fall back in with that crowd." She giggled. "Is that weird? Me reaching out to you instead of hating you? You and me deciding to be friends. Everyone will know we're crazy."

Someone coughed from behind a nearby tree. Melanie pivoted, finding Paul Mitchell standing behind them.

"You're not crazy, Melanie. Maybe a little melodramatic," he winked, "but not crazy."

She couldn't deny it. Mama used to say that melodrama was her middle name.

"Sorry. I was over here taking pictures of these lichens for my granddaughter. She's been working on a science project and… well, I couldn't help but overhear your conversation." Paul adjusted the strings on his jacket, loosening the hood. "There's no reason you girls can't work this out peaceably. It's not written in stone that you have to hate each other. Melanie, if you forgive her, it will go a long way toward your own healing."

"I think I can forgive her." Melanie nodded. "I almost feel relieved that it happened. Life with Stephen would have been miserable, and she's saved me from that." She smiled at Tricia. "Maybe you can start over, too. Kyle and I have decided today is the first day of our new lives. It can be the first for you, too."

Huge tears rolled down Tricia's cheeks. "I don't know how to start a new life. I can't figure out where to begin."

Paul knelt in front of them. "Maybe this is bigger than you. Maybe you could start with God. And, with a peer group of imperfect girls who are working hard to put their lives back together after experiencing some sort of shame. Every third Thursday night, we have a small group of twenty-something women who meet for a ladies' Bible study. This coming week, they're studying about God's top five priorities. The things that need to come first in your life when you're rebuilding. They eat, too. The elders' wives put it together and provide a home-cooked meal. Why don't you both come?"

Tricia arched her brows. "Come where?"

"Church." Melanie pointed toward the fence. "Who else comes?"

Paul chuckled. "Brielle Collins. I heard you girls have a history, too. Kirsten Craft and Leanna Tracy, if you know them."

"Maybe we will." Leaves rustled behind them. Melanie turned to find Pa and Kyle punching at each other and laughing.

"We'd better find our way to shelter." Pa pointed through the trees to the darkening sky. "Storm's almost here. My cell's been lit up with warning notifications for the past half-hour."

Paul nodded. "I'll see you, Pa. I'm going to make sure no one's lingering out there by the church."

Melanie turned to Kyle. Now what? She didn't want to walk away from him. Not without a good, long conversation about their future. But she still had to reckon with Mama and Daddy.

Kyle hugged her and planted a kiss on top of her head. "Go home and rest. Call me first thing when you wake up, and we'll talk over breakfast."

"Okay." Her hand lingered on his arm. "I'll see you then. Bye, Pa. It was nice meeting you."

"My pleasure, Melanie."

Tricia started toward the bridge after Paul, and Melanie hurried to catch up.

"Hey. Where are you headed tonight?"

Tricia shrugged. "Back to my apartment. I'm off work the next two days and then work the next ten."

Melanie caught her hair in a ponytail and let it fall back to her shoulders. Since everyone already knew she was crazy, might as well prove it. "I have a thought. Come home with me. Stay there tonight. We have an extra bedroom, and Mama might not spend the next twenty-four hours nagging me if we have company. You won't have to be alone in the storm, and we can finish our talk."

Tricia bit her lip. "I… well, I guess—"

"Just say yes." Melanie winked. "Say yes before I change my mind about hating you."

"Well, when you put it that way…" Tricia shook her head.

They laughed together as they crossed the creek and made their way over the tree roots and grass to the gate. When they reached the church parking lot, Mama was loading Daddy into the car.

"Hey, Mama. If it's okay, I'm having someone over tonight." Melanie bobbed her head toward Tricia as Mama's eyes widened.

"Already bringing company." Daddy winked. "But I thought you'd be bringing Kyle over first. Louisa, get in my wallet and give her some money to pick up snacks."

Whistling, Mama sucked in a deep breath. She released it to a monstrous boom of thunder, then slammed the car door shut behind Daddy. Melanie dodged her gaze—the one that said, "that brazen hussy is not welcome in my house."

"How are you getting home?" Mama's snarky rose about twelve notches. So much for apologies and feel-good conversation. Things would be back to normal for them.

Tricia stepped forward. "I can bring her, if that's okay."

Everything about Mama's posture indicated that it wasn't okay, but she stalked around to the other side of the car, reached in, and brought out Daddy's wallet. She handed Melanie a fifty-dollar bill. "Pick up a couple pizzas and some chips. And get some of those turtle brownies your dad likes."

"Okay." Melanie folded the bill and tucked it in her jeans pocket.

"And be home before the storm." Mama spun to face Tricia. "You hear that?"

"Yes, ma'am."

They walked over to Tricia's old-but sleek black Camaro and got in as the first drop of rain hit the windshield. As Tricia turned the key in the ignition, her jaw flinched. "Are you sure this is okay?"

Melanie nodded and giggled. "She's really more bark than bite. And you owe me. You're my layer of protection tonight. Now let's go hit up Janey's Pizza and stir up some real town gossip."

Kyle backed Pa's truck into the barn and parked it next to an old white freezer. When he got out, the mechanical hum drew his attention. He walked over, lifted the door, and laughed from his belly. "I knew there were steaks."

Pa patted his stomach. "I didn't want to make things too easy for you. Figured getting you out in public at the grocery store and such would help you want to settle in Milton. So, what have you decided? Will you stay?"

"Think I will, Pa." Kyle closed the freezer door and followed Pa out into the rain. They raced to the farmhouse and hurried inside.

"Now, boys, don't you get mud all over the entry." Sharon called from the kitchen, where savory spices drifted from several saucepans on the old gas stove. "Supper will be ready in about thirty minutes if you want to wash up." She wiped her hands on her apron and walked in to join them, her gray-blonde ponytail swishing from side to side. "Will Melanie be joining us?"

Kyle grimaced. "Not tonight. I told her to go home and sort things out with her parents. Don't want to push her too hard to come around."

Pa slapped him on the shoulder. "See, I knew you were a smart boy. Just take things slow. There's no reason to be in a hurry when you have a lifetime ahead of you. Now. Would you like to explain to me why all my towing gear is shiny like it's never been used? And my tractor?"

Kyle covered his eyes with his fingers. "Nope. But you might ask a certain bovine."

"Let me guess." Sharon sat on the corner of the couch, her bright green eyes beaming as she smiled. "Gertie."

"That aggravating cow." Kyle lifted his hands in surrender. "I suppose it's all going to come out anyway. Gertie knocked the tractor into the pond, and Melanie helped me get it out with the come along."

Pa scoffed. "That's a little ridiculous. How did she knock a tractor into the pond?"

Sharon slapped her hand over Pa's thigh. "Give the boy some credit, Pa. I believe you, Kyle. Gertie has pulled her share of pranks on me."

"Well, I think I finally won her over with some apples, so we're all good now." Kyle pointed to the three bags sitting by the entry. "And I bought more today just in case."

Still chuckling, Pa disappeared into the back of the house, so Kyle went into the kitchen to help Sharon with the cooking. A half hour later, Pa returned with a manila folder and a black ink pen.

"Let's look over this paperwork, shall we?" Pa passed over the folder. "I've had my accountant examine everything and try to find us the best tax scenario. We have a couple different options."

Kyle sat with Pa at the kitchen table, but Sharon came over and snatched the folder. "You boys are going to visit and eat before we talk any business." She swooped over to the counter and traded the folder for a stack of white ceramic plates. "I want you to tell me what it's like standing on the pitcher's mound in Wrigley Field."

Chapter Twenty-Eight

Stephen Mullins swished the last drink of his amber concoction in the bottom of the tumbler glass and then downed it. Rain pelted the window beside him, like driving nails into his chest. Why had he been so careless and let himself get caught cheating before the wedding? Stupid, stupid, stupid.

In a few minutes, the not-pretty-enough waitress would trudge over and offer him another drink. But what was the point? It wasn't working. Nothing would drown these sorrows. Not even the high-dollar whiskey.

Melanie had grown on him. The tough-as-nails brunette with ten ounces of spunk for every ounce of reason—but then, she'd changed.

They always changed. Every girl he'd ever dated had changed for the worse. Who knew why? Maybe he had a contagious fungus that altered their brains and turned them into doormats. Not that he didn't like when they did whatever he told them. He just got bored with them.

But—watching Melanie up on that billboard—he could see some of the tenacity that had drawn him to her in the first place. A hint of that spunk returning. If he could just get her to listen to reason, they could start over, and he'd figure out how to keep her from losing her personality.

If he could get her away from that stupid baseball player long enough to talk to her.

Threatening Kyle had been an idiot move. And Kyle had been smart enough to involve the police. So now what? How would he ever convince Melanie to take him back if he couldn't get to her to have the conversation?

"Mister Mullins." The smooth, deep voice came from nowhere.

Stephen scanned the empty restaurant and arched his back to look behind him, seeing no one.

A few seconds later, Bart Handley popped around from the next booth and slid into the red leather seat across from him.

"Well, if it isn't the five-o'clock loser." Stephen caught the waitress's eye and held up his empty glass. "What do you want?"

"You're a tough fellow to find, Mullins." Bart dumped the mixed-up sweetener packets on the table and sorted them by color. "I was hoping you might help me out with a little project. You know how Marvin Vanovich has that daily talk show?"

"I don't watch garbage." Stephen snatched the red stirring straw from his empty glass and chewed the end of it.

"Marvin's retiring this fall. I've auditioned for the job and it's between me and two other people. If I can pull this off, it's mine."

Stephen flicked the straw across the table, laughing as it landed in Bart's lap. "Pull what off?"

"Reunite you and your fiancé on national TV. I have to submit a video showing that I'm up to the task of filling Marvin's shoes. I've got some footage of Kyle Casey pouring his heart out. We can chop up that confessional and make him sound like a real loser. All I need to do is talk him into another interview with Melanie and then you come onstage and ask her to take you back. What's he going to do on live TV?"

Stephen picked a banana pepper from his half-eaten nachos and popped it in his mouth. "Two problems with that. One, how will you get Kyle to agree to go on live TV, and two, he's got people watching his property. How do I get there?"

Bart cackled. "Duh. News van. We'll just smuggle you in."

"And then what?"

Bart leaned forward, gripping the table with both hands, his eyes dancing like he'd just won the lottery. "Well, I have it on good authority that she's a little miffed at you over selling her car." He withdrew a keyring from his pocket. "How's she going to feel when you hand her the keys to her new Prius and tell her it was a surprise you were planning to give her after the honeymoon?"

Stephen balked. "You're just going to give me a car? Are you out of your mind?"

"My dad has a dealership." Bart shrugged. "He gives cars away all the time. Tax write-off or something like that. Considers it advertisement. We'll get a couple good shots of the car from an angle that shows his dealership name, and he'll be happy to give it away.

"What if she says no?"

Bart slid the keys across the table. "You get to keep the car and I still get the fame. Win-win."

Stephen palmed the keys and rolled them over in his hand. Melanie Turner did love her some drama, and this would be the perfect opportunity to say what he needed to say without interruption. If he had any shot, that would be vital. "Okay. I'm in."

A wicked smile spanned Bart's chubby cheeks. "Great. I'll just need you to sign this release form, and we'll do the title transfer in the morning if you'll meet me at Dad's office around ten. Thanks, man. You won't regret this."

Melanie stretched and yawned, dragging her widespread palm over the stiff, new navy sheets. Mama had redecorated the whole room. Nagging or no nagging, Melanie had to give Mama credit for effort.

Tricia, too, actually. Melanie sat up in her childhood bed, resting her head against the intricate oak headboard. Imagine! Her sleeping so soundly next to the "enemy" in the room next door. They'd talked until four in the morning. They'd laughed and cried and laughed again, and Melanie couldn't shake the sense of guilt for treating Tricia so badly over the years. With a new start on the horizon for both of them, it seemed that maybe they'd both found the friendship they'd been missing all those years. And best of all, it had nothing to do with the stupid number thirteen.

Melanie slid out of the covers and made the bed. She crossed to the window and opened the blinds, letting sunlight flood the room. Mama had outdone herself. And the pictures! Ten frames, in an asymmetrical pattern on the wall. Melanie with Daddy, up on stage holding a mic. Maybe age three. And in kindergarten, Melanie with Mama, holding a pair of scissors to cut the ribbon for the groundbreaking of Milton Community Park.

In the center, a toothless boy and toothless girl. Two mostly-bald brunettes, barely over eight months old and dressed in identical plaid shirts, grinning from a porch swing. Pa's porch swing. Kyle and her.

She darted to the dresser, snatched her phone, and snapped a picture of the photograph. Within seconds, she'd texted the picture to Kyle. *Look at these cuties.*

Her phone dinged immediately. *See? Told you. We were meant to be.*

Her heart fluttered and warmth surged through her. Could she have really gone from such devastation to sheer happiness in days? Was it possible? *I know.*

Get ready. I'll pick you up for breakfast in thirty minutes.

K.

She opened her bedroom door and followed the scent of cinnamon to Mama's bright yellow kitchen.

"Oh. Hey, Melanie." Tricia grinned behind a dusting of flour. "I hope you don't mind me not waking you. I never went to sleep. Couldn't. I came in to the kitchen for a drink and your mom found me. We had a good, long talk, and now she's teaching me how to make homemade cinnamon rolls. Your dad's still asleep."

Melanie dipped her finger in Mama's cinnamon and butter blend and licked it clean. "I don't mind if you don't mind me heading out to have breakfast with Kyle in a few minutes."

Mama beamed. "You do what you have to do. Go meet that boy, and say whatever you have to say. I'm going to let this girl rest a bit and give her another cooking lesson if she'll let me."

Tricia gave Mama a shy grin. "I'd really like that."

Melanie poured herself a cup of coffee and headed toward the hall. She paused by the doorframe. "Thanks for everything, Mama. The room was perfect. I think everything will turn out alright."

Kyle pulled in the Turner's driveway and started to open the door.

Melanie rushed outside and raced to the truck. She poked her head through the open window. "Hey."

"I was going to meet you at the door." He tossed her a mock-pout. "Now get back in that house, and let me court you the right way. Both of our mamas would have my head on a platter if I didn't treat you like a lady."

Melanie flashed him an eye-twinkling smile and ran back to the house. Carrying three vases of roses, he walked along the sidewalk to the front door and raised his fist to knock.

Louisa swept the door open. "Mr. Casey."

"Brought you flowers, Mrs. Turner." Kyle passed her a vase. "Peach roses. Winna Marie at The Basket Case said they were your favorite."

"Oh, Kyle. How thoughtful." Louisa brought the vase close to her nose and whiffed it. "Melanie, get in here!"

Kyle grinned. "If it's okay, I'd like to see Tricia, too."

"Tricia!" Louisa sniffed the flowers again. "Girls, you have company."

When Tricia stepped into the living room, Kyle walked forward and handed her a vase of white roses. "White. Pure, for your new start."

A lovely pink covered Tricia's cheeks, softening the effect of her stark black hair against her porcelain face.

"I figured you might appreciate flowers, too." He winked at Melanie, who came in behind her. "Now, don't you be getting jealous, Mel, because these red ones are for you. And we all know what red roses mean."

Melanie gasped. "Are you serious? How did you arrange this overnight? It's next to impossible to get flowers in any reasonable time in this town."

Kyle handed her the vase, brushing the baby's breath against her cheek. "Winna called and offered."

"That's awesome." Melanie set her vase on the coffee table. "Are you ready? I'm starving."

"Let's roll." Kyle held out his hand, and Melanie took it. "See you later, Mrs. Turner. Bye, Tricia. And tell Mr. Turner I hope he's feeling well today."

"Will do." Louisa patted his shoulder as they walked out the door. "You guys have fun."

She closed the door behind them, pressing her face to the glass as Kyle beat Melanie to the car door to open it for her. "Your mom is going to call my mom before we even pull out of the driveway."

"Yep." Melanie slid into the bucket seat and buckled her seatbelt. "Where are we headed?"

Kyle reached across her to the console and handed her a handwritten menu. "It's called Pa Casey's Kitchen, and you wouldn't believe the spread of food."

"Oh, my." She turned the paper over in her hand. "This is a lot of food."

"Well, you know Pa. Um… I guess you don't really know Pa, but if you did, you'd understand it's typical. It would make sense that he insisted."

When they reached the farmhouse, Pa greeted them in a crisp white shirt and bow tie, and Sharon escorted them in to the dining room like the hostess at a fancy restaurant. They'd covered the table with a black tablecloth and two elegant place settings flanked by flickering candles.

Sharon pulled back a chair for Melanie to sit, then folded her napkin in her lap. "Coffee?"

"Please." Melanie lifted a crystal goblet containing ice water. "I'm not sure I've ever been to a place as swanky as this."

After seating Kyle, Pa and Sharon took turns bringing in dishes filled with grits, bacon, sausage, fried eggs, hash browns, fried apples, homemade biscuits, and fruit. Finally, Pa brought in an iron skillet filled with steaming white gravy topped with cracked pepper. "I hope you like Southern cooking, Melanie. But then again, you are Wayne Lee Turner's daughter."

"I like it fine, thank you." She picked up a biscuit, knocking flaky crumbs to the tablecloth. "This all looks wonderful."

Sharon brought out butter and assorted jellies, and set a pitcher of coffee in the center of the table. "Cream or sugar?"

"No thanks." Melanie gave Kyle a sly grin. "Black as night for me."

"Me, too." He raised his mug to hers. "To our new beginning."

"To our new beginning." She brought the mug to her lips and took a sip while Pa and Sharon backed out of the kitchen.

"If you two lovebirds need anything else, it's all in here on the counter." Sharon hooked her arm around Pa's elbow. "C'mon. Let's leave these kiddos alone and check out the flood damage."

"Flood damage?" Melanie frowned as she set her mug on the table.

Kyle pointed out the window. "It's not too bad. Just a little overflow by the front pond that maybe washed out some of the fence line right next to the creek. Water's supposed to go down by this afternoon, and I've got the cows contained in the back field." He laughed. "Thanks to you and your apples."

"I saw that, actually." She dug her fork into the fried apples and held one up. "Wow. Cinnamon crusted and everything."

"Sharon's an awesome cook." Kyle helped himself to a hefty serving of eggs and gravy.

"Speaking of Gertie, how's she doing?"

"I'm not sure." Kyle scooped out a generous amount of butter and spread it over the center of a steaming biscuit. "When we finish up here, we'll go check things out."

An hour later, when their plates were empty and the dishes were washed up, Kyle led Melanie out to the barn. He kicked an old rusty can of WD-40 out of the way and stepped over trash and equipment to the bucket Pa used as a stool in his shop. This place needed some serious attention. Pa used to keep it immaculate, but being in his late seventies must have slowed him considerably. Although, seemed like he'd been pretty spry in the last week. Spry enough to climb over a fence, at least.

Loose nuts and bolts lay strewn across the rough concrete floor and assorted empty aerosol cans littered every corner. And yet, one small area bore very little dust.

"What is that?" Melanie pointed to a silvery item on the counter.

"I don't know." Kyle crossed to the clean spot on the hand-built counter, where an eighties-style boom box sat lonely with its duct-taped antenna. Beside it, a plastic tub held several packs of D-cell batteries and a crate boasted stacks of cassette tapes.

Tears welled in Kyle's eyes as the shaky black lettering came into focus. Kylie—Milton Dodgers vs. Arlington Sting Rays. "Wow. These are my old little league games. Broadcast by a local ham radio guy who started his own station." Had Pa recorded all of them?

"We have to listen." She chuckled. "I can't wait to hear about Kylie's game."

"You hush that or I'm going to start calling you Melly like your friends do."

"Ex-friends. No room in my new life for girl drama and silliness."

Kyle popped a cassette into the player and pressed the rewind button. The thing still had good batteries. Pa must have listened recently, reliving the good old days, no doubt. His heart sank. How much sorrow had his mistakes caused Pa? Surely not more sorrow than his being estranged. When Pa came back, Kyle would have to start being around more. Kyle pressed play. Milton's own Bobby Lucky's rich baritone eased in through the static.

"We've got us a stiff game tonight, fellas. Those Dodgers have made Milton little league history by not giving up a single run in two games. Now, some might say bad coaching is the cause of that, but I say Greg and Lefty, you boys have gotta teach those boys how to hit."

Bobby cackled. "Okay, I know. I'm saying the same thing. But when coaches don't know what they're doing, everybody suffers."

Kyle shook his head. Good ol' Bobby didn't care who he upset. Pa had sent Bobby's obituary in the mail a few years ago, a long piece Lefty Green had written about how Bobby helped him become a better man and led him to his job as a college coach. And Bobby had always sung Kyle's praises. What would the old man have thought if he'd learned of Kyle's suspension. Poor guy probably rolled over in his grave.

"Now I know," Bobby droned on, "You mamas and daddys and pappys and Pas might have a different idea. Don't think I haven't heard what you're all saying in the grocery aisles about that Casey kid. Is he a tall drink of water? Yessiree. Does he have freakishly long arms for a fifth grader? You betcha. But say what you want to say. Somebody's taught that boy how to pitch a baseball. That's why you all keep losing."

261

Kyle held his arms straight out in front of him. "Freakish? Bobby, you don't know what you're talking about. My arms were never freakish."

Melanie gave him a light pinch in his arm muscle. "I don't know about that…" She dodged him as he took a mock swat at her.

The cassette squeaked as it played on. "Sure, that boy can throw a perfect game. Ain't nobody questioning that. He's already done it twice. But—"

Crunching sounds from the cassette player intensified as his voice turned into something more like alien communication. Kyle lunged to stop it. He pulled it out of the player and twisted the ribbon back into the cassette.

How incredible was this find? He should get one of those devices that turns the cassette into an mp3 file. That might be a good gift to give Pa for Christmas.

Melanie hummed to herself as she dug through the rest of the cassettes, and he wrapped his arm around her shoulder. She was another incredible find. Maybe life could be good again after all.

Chapter Twenty-Nine

Melanie swirled the last bite of apple-smothered biscuit in her mouth and washed her hands in the deep stainless-steel barn sink. "Sharon is going to have to give me this recipe. Or maybe not. I'll be big as Gertie if I don't cut back."

Gertie grunted and plodded closer.

Melanie stroked the cow's honey brown chin and grinned. "Not that you're oversized, girl, but you and me both have had more than our fair share of apples today."

"I can't believe you brought them with you." Kyle chuckled, poking his head out the side door of the tractor. "They were tasty, though. I do understand." He tossed a shop rag toward her, missing by a few inches and striking Gertie square on the forehead.

Gertie's resounding moo came out more like a growl.

"I thought baseball players were *good* at throwing things." Melanie snatched up the shop rag and tossed it back to him.

"You hush." He caught the rag in his left fist without looking. "See, I haven't lost my touch."

As their laughter faded, gravel dust stirred up in the distance at the end of the farmhouse driveway. A white van barreled toward the house.

"Now who on earth could that be?" Kyle hopped down from the tractor and moved to Melanie's side.

"Oh, that's Bart Handley's van. The station sold him an old news van and he thinks he's some kind of roving reporter. Wonder what he wants?"

"To bug us." Kyle stalked over to the truck. "Reporters are all the same. Good or bad."

Melanie walked around to the passenger side, dodging Kyle as he hurried to open the door for her. "Well, it's time to stop for lunch anyway. Pa and Sharon will be back soon, and Mom's bringing Dad and Tricia by to meet them for lunch. Don't know if I remembered to tell you that."

"You didn't." Kyle planted a light kiss on her cheek. "But it's fine. Gertie, we'll be back later to fix the rest of that fence. Stay out of trouble and don't you go getting any ideas."

Another moo-grunt.

By the time Kyle pulled Pa's truck in the farmhouse driveway, Bart and Christian had set up cameras to film the front porch. Kyle hopped out and rushed to them, his fists swinging at his sides. "What are you doing? Who gave you permission for this?"

Bart pivoted, dropping the lens wipe he was holding, and met Kyle in the too-tall grass. "Please, Kyle. I'll lose my job."

"For trespassing?" Kyle snorted "I can see that."

"I lost the footage from the other day. It was ruined. And I'm up for a promotion." Bart folded his hands together in front of him. "Please. Just one more small interview. You can rethink what you said and give America the apology they deserve. The one everyone's been waiting on."

Kyle grimaced as Melanie walked up beside him, and her heart ached for him. People on Twitter had been merciless to him about the apology. Maybe if he took advantage of Bart's offer, he could get some peace about the whole situation.

Bart lurched forward. "Melanie Turner. Milton's own Billboard Bride. If you'd like, you could make a statement, too. Don't you want to tell everyone how you're doing now that you've climbed down. The whole world is waiting with baiting breath."

"Abated breath, Bart. You should remember that one. We learned it in senior English. Sometimes people drop the A." Melanie shook her head. "You know what, I'm fine with making a statement. I think I do have a couple things I'd like to say."

Bart tripped over the stump from an old forgotten tree in his haste to get back to the camera. "Great. Give me a few minutes to get everything settled and we can let you both sit on that rocker swing. Shouldn't take more than ten minutes or so of your time."

Kyle shoved his hands in his pockets and rocked on the balls of his feet. "Is there a release to sign?"

Bart rolled his eyes. "I'll find one. Think I've got some in the van."

"Well, get it and we'll see you out front in a little while. I'm going to run in and clean up a bit while Melanie works on lunch." Kyle tipped his cap at Bart and headed into the farmhouse.

Melanie followed him, pausing in the doorframe long enough to steal a glance at the noon horizon. She could get used to this life. Funny how things seemed so much easier when she quit worrying so much about planning around a number.

Kyle stifled a belly laugh as he crossed the porch to the canvas swing and took the spot closest to where Bart sat behind a sawhorse covered in plywood and wood grain contact paper. The guy had literally brought a talk-show desk with him, and even had a button he pressed that played audio applause. He wore a purple sports jacket with a yellow shirt and tie. He was taking this gig way too seriously.

It had required some convincing to get Pa, Louisa, Wayne, and Sharon to humor him, but he'd done it. There they all sat in lawn chairs applauding when Christian held up a sign. Tricia Billings had even agreed to be an "audience" member, and the girl looked completely at ease leaning close to Louisa and sharing a chuckle.

He stretched his feet out in front of him and crossed them at the ankles, his toes landing an inch from the edge of the concrete porch. He'd put a railing up when this was all over. Maybe extend the deck to the back of the house and build a seating area out back where he and Melanie could share the sunset.

A frown crept its way across his face. Was he jumping the gun? Was it too soon to relax and believe that everything was as it should be and it would stay that way? Too good to be true, some would say. Don't believe it until the dust has settled. All those old adages filtered through his mind, shifting into doubt.

"Ladies and Gentlemen." Bart brought his adjustable microphone closer to his lips. "Let's give a big welcome to former pro-baseball player, Kyle Casey!"

Kyle gave the camera a small wave and sat straighter. What was the harm in playing along? Wasn't the whole point of his renewal to serve others and help people? Maybe he could do some baseball tip segments or something one day and help Bart grow his viewers. Get the station to take him more seriously. He grinned. "Great to be here, Bart."

"Viewers, as you all know, Kyle Casey was a hometown star who worked his way up to the pros. He had come a long way since his graduation from Milton High School ten years ago, and never intended a homecoming. But following his..." He lifted his lens-less, made-for-television glasses, and directed his gaze over the bridge of his nose. "...his idiot decision to bet on baseball..." As the glasses dropped, he shot the camera a wink. "No offense, bro."

"It was an idiot decision." Kyle shook his head. "No offense taken."

"Good." Bart steepled his fingers then pressed his hand together as if he were about to pray. "Now Kyle, my understanding is you've got something you'd like to say to America, to the commissioner of baseball, and to everyone who was hurt or affected by your decision."

"I do." Kyle looked the camera dead in its eye. "With all my heart, I'm sorry. My actions were selfish and mine alone." He swallowed. "When everything first happened, I wanted to throw blame in every direction but my own. Baseball gave me a dream and an opportunity, and I sneezed in its face. Instead of taking the game seriously, I met my own arrogant desires and satisfied my own ego. I realize that an apology made of words is a weak thing and could never be enough. So, I ask your forgiveness. And, I ask God's forgiveness. You see, my biggest problem is that I ran away from Him years ago. I stopped listening to my parents and others who gave me good advice, and I became the sole judge of my own character. I quit going to church and tried to find happiness in people who patted me on the back and gave me compliments for my sports achievements and appearance." He pushed with his toe, sending the swing backward a few inches.

"That's good." Bart gave him a toothy smile. "Go on."

Kyle tapped his fingers against his thigh as Pa nodded to him. Confession *was* liberating. But Paul Mitchell had been right. He needed to figure out how to have a more contrite heart. "Well, when Melanie climbed up that billboard, it forced me to stop wallowing in my embarrassment for having made the mistake, and to face the emotion head-on. I saw through her eyes the pain in every girl whose heart I've broken, especially Lacey Robbins. She did not deserve to have her despair made public on every social media channel, and neither did Melanie."

He stood, hooking his thumbs in the hem of his pockets. "I apologize to everyone whose heart I've broken with my flawed decisions and pursuit of my own sinful lusts. To my parents and to Pa Casey, I apologize for tarnishing our family and bringing shame to us all. And to all of Milton. I apologize for my betrayal, for compromising your trust. And I promise I will work on giving back as much as I can to make retribution for all my poor decisions."

Bart waved him on. "Great stuff there, Kyle. Keep it coming."

"Oh, I have plenty more apologies to go. To the coaches, who put so much time and effort into helping me become a great talent. I'm so sorry for squandering the opportunity. I apologize to the young players, who dream of following in my shoes. I should have been a better role model. And from now on, I will. I promise that I'll speak to high school and middle school players when I have the chance to help them avoid making the same mistakes. And I apologize to all the hard-working men and women who put so much time and effort into bringing baseball to the fans. To the commissioner, for dishonoring you and the sport. To the trainers, owners, even down to the super-nice people who work all the vendor booths. Please, accept my heartfelt apology."

"Anything else?"

"I just want to say one more time how truly sorry I am." Kyle again looked directly into the camera, "And to plead for your forgiveness."

"There you have it, folks." Bart cast a dramatic wave to his right. "Kyle Casey wants forgiveness. Should we give it to him?"

He nodded to Christian, who swung the camera toward Pa, Sharon, Wayne, Louisa, Paul, his wife, and Tricia. When they all sat in stony silence, Christian swung the camera back toward the house.

"And Melanieeeee Turnerrrr!" Bart pointed toward the farmhouse door with both fingers as his fake applause sounded.

Kyle's breath caught in the back of his throat. This woman, this beautiful, spunky, tough-as-nails but fragile-as-a-kitten woman was his? Suddenly baseball dwindled to nothing.

Melanie's heart thundered as she crossed the threshold to the farmhouse porch. She eased the screen door closed behind her. Was she crazy to agree to this interview? Nobody ever watched Bart's show, but featuring both her and Kyle should get him a few viewers. It couldn't hurt anything. She'd already put herself out there by climbing on the billboard.

Kyle's eyes lit up as she met his gaze, and her pulse quickened even more. Not one of her past thirteen boyfriends had ever set it racing like that. Or given her such a receptive, welcoming smile when she came into a room. Or, well, onto a porch stage for a public confessional.

She took her seat in the canvas swing next to Kyle and promptly took his hand. And then… she cringed. Live TV. All of Milton would have something to say about that. Too soon. Too forward. Too stupid to fall into the same trap so quickly. She squeezed his fingers then planted her fisted hands in her lap.

"Thanks for joining us, Melanie." Bart took a sip of air from the empty coffee cup he'd borrowed a few minutes before filming Kyle's interview. "Now, I've known you since kindergarten, way back when the boys would tease you and call you…"

Melanie groaned. "Smelly Melly. Good one, Bart. And then, I'd knock them flat on the ground. Haven't heard that one in decades."

Bart waggled his finger in her face. "Ah, but the nickname has resurfaced since you climbed up that billboard. Everybody figured you must smell real good after sitting up there for two weeks. But you didn't, did you?"

Melanie furrowed her brow. "Smell bad?"

"Stay." Bart reached behind him to the windowsill where a piece of white foam board set propped against the glass. He turned the board around, revealing a photo of Melanie climbing down from the billboard.

She wrinkled her nose. What a weirdo. Bart had always been a little strange, even back in school, but to put so much effort into a little community segment that nobody watched… "No, I climbed down a few times a day, actually. In the early mornings, I washed my hair and stuff, and of course I climbed down whenever nature called. Which, thanks to Kyle bringing me a ton of water and keeping me hydrated, happened pretty often."

Pa guffawed, triggering an explosion of snickers, even from Mama.

When the laughter died down, Bart took another fake sip of coffee. "The question that's been on everyone's mind from the get-go is why did you climb up that billboard in the first place? I mean, we all know how tough you are. That jilted bride thing has happened to a lot of girls weaker than you and they haven't done anything so drastic. Why the billboard? And why stay up there exactly thirteen days?"

Melanie let out a long sigh. "Fear." She caught a loose tendril of her wispy brown hair and let it tumble to her shoulder.

"Fear?" Bart scoffed.

"Fear." A sweat bee buzzed around Melanie's sandal strap, and she wiggled her foot to shoo it away. "Well, and rage."

"Because…"

Fury bubbled under her skin as Bart faced Tricia. No. She couldn't let him make her feel uncomfortable. Tricia already felt bad enough. That slimy weasel, he knew the because…

Tears filled her eyes. "Because my world had just been crushed by someone I thought I loved."

"Thought?" Bart swung back toward her. "Oh, we all know it was more than thought. Everyone in town could see how much you *thought* you loved Stephen Mullins. Why, you were practically—"

"Obsessed?" Melanie shook her head, letting the loose tears spill to her collar. "You don't know the half of it. But it was really stupid of me."

Daddy raised his fist. "Amen!"

More laughter.

"Then tell us." Bart gave her a wicked grin. "Follow the good preacher's advice. Purge. They say it's good for the soul."

Melanie frowned. Had he eavesdropped when she and Kyle had talked to Paul about that? "For thirteen years, I've ruled my life by a superstition. On my thirteenth birthday, a fortune teller told me that thirteen would be a special number in my life. So, I made every decision on it. Stephen Mullins was my thirteenth boyfriend. He proposed when we'd dated thirteen months. Our wedding date was thirteen weeks later. I thought it was in the cards that we married."

"Can you list them?" Bart cackled. "Your thirteen boyfriends, I mean."

"List them?" Melanie's fists clenched and her eyes narrowed. "No, I will NOT list them. Look. I climbed up that billboard out of sheer, passionate anger and hurt. I sat up there to think. To figure out my next move since Stephen had backed me into a corner. I had no car, no apartment, no job—and I didn't want to face the thought of moving back home. But you know what I've learned?"

She stood. "I learned that family is valuable, and more than willing to help me get on my feet. I learned that I gain more by listening to others than being stubborn. And, I've learned that true friendship isn't about what club we can hit up on Friday nights or shopping. It's about conversation, loyalty, and forgiveness."

"Forgiveness?" Bart stood as well. "I guess that's why Tricia Billings is sitting in this very audience." He nodded to Christian, who swung the camera toward where Tricia sat.

"Stop it!" Pa bellowed and stepped in front of Tricia. "You can stop your cameras right now and get off my property."

Bart reached back to the desk and held up an envelope. "Kyle signed a release, Pa Casey. We have an hour here. Guaranteed. Now, sit down, and we're going to finish this."

Chapter Thirty

Stephen poked his head out the back door of Bart Handley's van and took a deep whiff of the damp farm air. Ugh. The stench of earthworms. He fought off an incredible urge to sneeze and planted his brand-new sneakers into the plushy wet grass.

As he quietly closed the van doors, a loud, angry moo came from behind him. He pivoted to a sour-faced brown cow, just feet from where he stood. Behind her, a section of the fence separating a nearby field lay splintered on the ground.

How had she done it? He hadn't heard her approach. But more importantly, she stood between him and his stealth entrance to the farmhouse porch. Everyone would be watching now. Bart hadn't given the signal yet, but maybe he should go on out before someone saw the cow and found him. Why did Melanie have to bring the whole family anyway? Wayne and Louisa wouldn't have anything good to say about him being there. That was for sure.

A shout rang out from around the porch. Melanie's country twang in full force, of course. As Wayne would tell it, she was madder than a wet hen. It didn't bode for great odds for him. Maybe he should just get back in the van and forget about it all.

"You leave her alone, Bart Handley! Tricia Billings is my friend!"

Melanie's words pierced the air between them as Stephen's realization dawned. That beat-up black Camaro he'd seen in the drive belonged to Tricia. This would be a disaster.

And what did Melanie mean, "her friend"? Stephen shoved past the cow and stormed to the front of the house, stopping just shy of a sunken spot where water had pooled in the grass.

There, a whole group stood in a semicircle in the gravel drive, surrounding the farmhouse porch, poised in various angry stances. Louisa, with fisted hands on her hips. Wayne, gripping the edges of his walker with white knuckles. Pa Casey, waggling his finger in Bart's face. And Melanie... full of passionate, adorable rage.

Stephen cringed. He was such an idiot to have thought Bart could pull this off. Maybe he should wait until they all calm down.

He stole a quick glance toward the van. Or, maybe he should just run before they turned their fury on him.

Stephen! How dare you show your face here?" Melanie stomped down the porch stairs and marched over to where he stood, the soggy ground squishing beneath her feet. "What do you think you're doing here? I thought I told you to leave me alone."

"I messed up, Melanie." His shoulders slumped. He knelt before her and wrapped his arms around her knees, resting his head against her thighs. "I'm so sorry. I heard what you said a minute ago about forgiveness. Is it too much to ask that you'd extend some to me?"

She wriggled free from his grasp as Tricia and Kyle came up beside her. "Are you out of your mind?"

Stephen bumbled to his feet. His gaze darted between hers and Tricia's, and his eyes twitched. After a few long seconds, he shook his head and reached into his pocket. "I bought you a car. A Prius."

The key ring slipped from his grasp, and he knelt to retrieve it.

With a monstrous moo, Gertie darted in from nowhere and head-butted him into the large pool that had collected in the front yard after the storm. "Gertie!" Melanie raced to the cow and hugged her neck.

Kyle followed and gave Gertie a good pat. "You go, girl!"

Paul Mitchell approached the rain pool and extended his hand to Stephen, who waved it away. He slipped, falling face-first into the water again. As he came up, water dripped from his thick black bangs and rolled down to the tip of his nose and chin.

Gertie grunted and charged between them, splashing Melanie's pants as she made a bee-line for Christian and his old-school amateur video camera. She knocked the tripod to the ground, stepped over it, and knelt to munch on a patch of thick grass beside it as the cassette popped out of the camera.

Christian reached for it, but Gertie swatted her tail at him. He scrambled backward, landing at Tricia's feet.

"Eww, Gertie." Kyle laughed and pointed as Gertie dumped her pile directly on the cassette. "Good to know you've always got my back. Although, I suppose I'm going to have to apologize again."

"It's ruined!" Bart caught his hair in his fist and tugged at it. "Now my audition's ruined. Thanks a lot, you guys. Thanks a lot."

"Audition?" Kyle's eyebrows jetted upward. "What do you mean, audition?"

Bart gripped his head in both hands. "My one shot at doing something noteworthy with my life. My only chance of having an audience bigger than six or seven people. And you've ruined it." He swung around to point at Kyle. "You, and your stupid cow."

Kyle winked at Wayne. "Cows aren't stupid, Bart, but people sometimes are."

Stephen stood and hulked over, squaring up to Kyle.

"Are you serious?" Kyle backed away from him. "I'm not going to fight you, dude. Just leave. Get off the property, leave Melanie alone, and don't come back."

"She's mine." Stephen stepped closer to him. "Melanie, walk away from this loser, and we can start our life together just like we'd planned. We can go to the courthouse and get married next week if you want."

Melanie sighed. "Stephen, I don't want a life with you. I want you to leave."

Tricia came up and draped an arm over Melanie's shoulders. "I want you to leave, too."

Stephen slapped his arms at his side, sending a spray of water droplets flying. "How can you two can be friends after all this? I don't like it. Not at all. How can you hate me and not hate her?"

Melanie shrugged. "I don't know, either, Stephen, but I don't hate her. And, I don't hate you. But we can't be together. Not after everything that's happened."

She pointed to Bart and Christian, who'd accepted a roll of paper towels and a trash bag from Sharon and were cleaning off the camera and cassette with crinkled noses. "What were you guys planning? For you to ambush me on live TV? Stephen, I don't think you understand how to be in love. And maybe I didn't either. You can't just coerce people into doing whatever they want and expect them to be happy."

She reached to rest her fingers on his arm, cringing as Kyle cleared his throat from behind her. "You cheating on me was a blessing in disguise. It gave us both an out for something we knew in our hearts wasn't right. I'm at peace with this, Stephen. I want you to be at peace with it, too."

Stephen slammed his folded arms against his chest. "So that's it, then. You're choosing the baseball player. And everything I did for you over the past year and a half is for nothing." He spun to his right. "What about you, Tricia?"

Tricia rolled her eyes. "Melanie's being too nice. You're an idiot. Just leave."

Paul Mitchell strolled over and extended his hand to Stephen. "Can I give you a ride somewhere?"

Stephen sucked in a deep breath, puffing his chest like a blowfish. "Yeah. Anywhere but here.

Kyle drove the last nail into the fence then stepped back from it. It had been two weeks since Melanie had come down from the billboard, and it seemed that all he'd done was build fences. Well, and a few other things… "How 'bout that, Pa? Does it meet your high standards?"

Pa let out a whistle. "Beauty, Kyle. Best fence work I've seen out here since your dad was a teenager."

Kyle tucked the mallet into his borrowed tool belt and gathered the loose nails back into their box. "What about me? Think you could ever forgive me for what happened with the baseball and stuff? I know I let you down, and I'm truly sorry."

With glistening eyes, Pa put his arm around Kyle's waist. "I've always been proud of you, Kyle. A few bad decisions don't negate that. And forgiveness isn't necessary because I already have. But I do want you back in church. Every time the doors are open. Active and involved. Promise me that."

"I'll go. I've been a couple times already." Kyle draped his arm over Pa's shoulder. "And I'm ready to learn whatever you need to teach me about the farm. I'm in this for the long haul. It's actually kind of refreshing to come home."

"I'm counting on that. Now, about that girl…" Pa turned sideways, freeing himself from Kyle's grasp, and tipped his chin up, his eyes narrowing.

"You don't approve of us jumping into a relationship so soon."

Pa shook his head vigorously. "No, not that at all. I think she's got a lot of spunk and she's good for you. She's got a Christian's heart. After all, what kind of girl would offer friendship to someone who'd just caused her a broken engagement. Melanie's almost protective of Tricia. You can see she's got a true heart of a servant. Those girls are like sponges around Sharon. I think they'll both be fine women. I was thinking maybe if we could get one of your two crazy brothers to come home, Tricia would make a fine match."

"Then I don't understand. You're looking over your nose at me like you always do when something's wrong. What's the problem?"

"Melanie needs to be in church, too. I don't want you two to go building a relationship on the wrong foundation. I had a beautiful forty-five years with your grandmother before God called her home. Let Christ be your cornerstone."

"You're right, Pa. Mom and Dad tried to tell me that so many times over the years. I'll do everything I can to make that happen." He glanced at his watch. "I'd better go wash up. Told Melanie we'd watch the sunset together before I drove her home."

"If you can pull her away from Sharon." Pa snickered. "Those girls have been quilting for the past four hours."

"Oh, I'd say I know what'll do the trick." Kyle winked.

"And what's that?"

"Cinnamon apples." Kyle pointed back toward the farmhouse. "Sharon made us up a batch this morning and I'm going to heat them up and pack us a little picnic."

"Well, if that doesn't secure her heart, I don't know what will." Pa patted his stomach. "They've sure secured mine."

Melanie peeked through the blindfold at Kyle's worn-out sneakers. He'd driven her all over creation, but she knew exactly where he was taking her. And she'd smelled the cinnamon apples, too. Who knew how many amazing dates they'd have sitting on top of that billboard? Maybe decades' worth.

She let him help her down from the truck and tried to act confused as he walked her along the path to the base of the sign.

"Now, careful here." He guided her up a small step.

What was this? A wooden floor? Some kind of stage? Maybe they weren't near the billboard after all.

"And a few more paces directly in front of you... then pivot... then..." He nudged her to a soft leather seat.

"Where are we?" She giggled. "What have you done, Kyle Casey?"

He sat next to her, leaning close to her ear. "Built us a paradise."

That husky voice. His firm grip on her shoulder. And the synchronic pounding of their hearts. She, tough-as-nails Melanie Turner, couldn't hold back the tears. They soaked into her blindfold as he loosened the knot at the back of her head.

When he lifted the fabric from her eyes, she gasped. "Oh, Kyle. This is amazing. What is… a gazebo? And… that sky!"

He kissed her temple. "I thought you might appreciate the view behind the billboard for once. I mean, this is kind of our place, but you really don't get any privacy up there."

"No, you don't. But this is amazing." She fell against his chest, taking in the long, painterly streaks of crimson and purple that crowned the horizon. The trees and buildings in the distance had already turned into dark shadows against the fading sun. All this time, she'd missed the truly breathtaking view. Hopefully, she'd never miss it again.

"Brought you apples." He reached into a small backpack and brought out a foil pack of apple-stuffed biscuits.

"You sure know your way to a girl's heart." She took one out and held it to her nose for several glorious seconds before savoring a bite. As she licked the stray cinnamon away, he turned to her, sliding his hand through her hair.

"Yep."

Their lips met to the first notes of "The Marriage of Figaro," and her shoulders shook with laughter as a black remote slipped free from his hand. When she pulled back from him, she spotted the CD player in the corner of the gazebo. Kyle's eyes twinkled… just like Daddy's.

"Wayne Lee Turner put you up to that."

Kyle jutted a mock pout and ducked his head. "Guilty as charged."

Her dream come true. A man who treated her great and made her laugh.

The music played on as he kissed her again, her heart rejoicing with every resounding note. Finally, it all made sense. Life wasn't about numbers at all. It was about moments, and choosing to live them the right way.

From now on, she'd do exactly that.

Epilogue

Kyle tugged at the collar of his crisp, white shirt as beads of sweat rolled down his neck. "Can't believe it's so hot for September. Hey, careful, Paul. That lower branch is weak."

"I know." Paul clamped a fist over the fourth lowest rung of the billboard ladder and swung over to the pole. "You sure you want to do this up here?"

Kyle laughed. "We wouldn't have it any other way." He waved down to the church lot, which mirrored an inauguration crowd, stretching all the way back to the baseball field. They'd rented projectors and set up white screens, and it still wouldn't be enough for everyone to see. People had driven from across the nation. Fans. People who'd forgiven him and were willing to share this day. They'd never know how much it meant.

"Besides, it's brought the church some free advertising." Paul climbed up to the deck and stood beside him. "You ready for this?"

Kyle nodded. "Hey, Christian, you ready?"

"Yep. He poked his head in front of the camera. "Best man Christian Wilkins, reporting for duty. And folks, you should know what a privilege it is to stand up for this guy. He's done so much for me over the past year. Also, don't forget that the Wilkins Production Company is always available for your videography needs. Also, welcome to all the website folks joining us for the video streaming. Kyle, we're up to twenty-four thousand hits. That's a lot of fans, dude."

"And I appreciate all of them." Kyle waved to the parking lot. "Now, let's get this show moving. Someone cue that music. We need to get my bride back up on this billboard."

Applause rippled through the crowd as music from Pachabel drifted from the high school band's orchestra. The cherry picker's engine roared to life below them, bringing Wayne and Melanie closer to the deck.

"Dearly beloved, we have gathered today in the presence of God to witness the blessing of the union of this man, Kyle Casey, and this woman, Melanie Turner, in holy matrimony."

As Paul's words floated around him, Kyle studied Melanie's face—the kind and loving face that he'd already cherished for the past fourteen months they'd dated. Her rosy cheeks and fiery-yet-twinkling eyes told of a lifetime of passionate servitude and love stretching before them as they walked together first as Christians and then as husband and wife. It was right, as Paul had promised it would be. How blessed they were.

"Now, cut to the bridesmaids, Bart." Christian waved to the parking lot, where the wannabe-talk-show-host turned videographer turned his camera on the three beauties in navy silk—Sharon and Tricia flanking the beautiful Gertie, whose shiny brown fur perfectly complemented her gorgeous magnolia crown.

The crowd roared with laughter, and Melanie's grin widened.

"You were right, Mel. They love it." He blew Gertie a kiss. "Thanks a million, Gertie-girl."

"Who gives this woman to be married to this man?" Paul faced the cherry picker and held his hand out for Melanie to step onto the deck.

"Her mother, and…" Wayne wiped his sleeve across his eyes. "Her mother and I."

Melanie's non-traditional, short white sundress suited the situation perfectly as she planted her bare feet on the small space behind the ladder and eased over to where Kyle stood. He took both her hands in his, and closed his eyes. *Thank you, God, for my angel—for this blessing. I surely don't deserve her.*

"If any can show just cause why this man and this woman should not be joined, let them speak now, or forever hold their peace."

Gertie's despondent moo burst through the speaker, triggering another burst of laughter from the crowd.

"It's all good!" Tricia pointed at the mic Bart had planted next to her. "She just wants an apple!" She reached into a small pouch and passed Gertie a couple slices, and the hysterical audience applauded.

Kyle shook his head. "Gotta love that silly cow."

Melanie excitedly waved her phone at him, pointing to the calculator results. "That's amazing, Kyle. Almost three hundred thousand dollars."

From behind her, he leaned around and kissed her cheek. "It's insane. All those people came to watch us get married and donated to our cause. All those kids. And their parents. Milton is going to be so lucky to have an athletic training center and those scholarships will help provide so many opportunities. Now, are you finally ready to leave for our honeymoon? That plane isn't going to wait for us, you know."

"Go on, Melanie." Louisa wrapped a large rubber band around several stacks of twenties. "Don't keep your husband waiting."

Melanie's entire soul lifted. Husband. She took his hand and they walked together out the church doors.

As they neared the end of the walk, he stopped her next to a metal feeding trough and reached into his pocket. "I've got something for you."

"What?" She squinted as he planted a handful of dimes in her palm.

"Thirteen." He winked. "For old time's sake. Drop them in the water and make a wish."

"Nah." She passed them back and wrapped his fingers over them. "No more silly superstitions. I retired thirteen a long time ago. Besides," she grinned. "Fourteen has been pretty awesome. And I can't wait to see what fifteen has in store for us." She stood on her tiptoes and planted a kiss on Kyle's upturned lips. "And here's to many more."

THE END

About the Author

Monica Mynk is a high school chemistry teacher and author from Eastern Kentucky. She spent her early years reading books with her mother, acting out plays with her brother and sister, climbing in corncribs, and helping her dad on the farm. Periodically, she loves to tell corny science jokes

Monica comes from a long line of preachers, elders, deacons, and Bible class teachers, and hopes to live up to their example. She clings to the hope that God's promises are new every morning. A favorite hobby is writing devotionals, which can be found on her blog.

In her spare time, Monica loves spending time with family, especially her husband and beautiful children. They've been known to hang out at the soccer field, and they are active participants in the Lads to Leaders program She is an active member of the American Christian Fiction Writers (ACFW).

NEED A SPEAKER?

Monica enjoys conducting ladies days and writing/editing seminars for women. If you're interested in booking, more information is available on her website.

https://monicamynk.com/speaking/

Also by Monica Mynk

Goddess to Daughter Series--Romantic Suspense

Years ago in rural Dreyfus, Kentucky, seven fourth grade girls studied mythology at a small Christian school. Three bore names of goddesses, and the others took on goddess nicknames.

Pretending divinity made them feel powerful until their teacher explained they could only attain true power through Christ. They promised to always be friends, following Jesus together. Then, they went their separate ways and fell deep into sin.

The Goddess to Daughter Series explores their stories of redemption and love. Available in print and on Amazon Kindle. Find more information at https://monicamynk.com

The Cavernous Trilogy—Young Adult Dystopian

A Christian Teen battles for her soul against an extremist leader—her father

In a divided America, several secessions lead to the formation of a new nation, the Alliance of American States. Fueled by extremists who solicit members via social media, the Alliance has one weak point: Callie Noland, daughter of deceptive leader Adrian Lamb. When he snatches her from the man she's always called dad, he forces her into a suppressive life, training to serve in the Alliance military. Can she maintain her faith in God and stand up to the man who calls himself Lord and Master?

Available in print and on Amazon Kindle.

Find more information at https://monicamynk.com

Ungodly Clutter—Ladies Bible Studies

Have you ever been embarrassed to invite someone into your home?
Cobwebs in the corners? Laundry piled to the ceiling? Mile-high
dishes in the sink? If it's true that cleanliness is next to godliness,
does that mean those of us too stressed and over-worked to maintain
a clean home are ungodly?
Perhaps, God would be appalled to enter many of our homes...
but not for the reasons we might think! Today's world is full of
distractions and many litter our living space without us giving them a
second thought.
How can Christian women cleanse their homes of the idols and
temptations that hinder salvation?
Available for print and Amazon Kindle.
More information at https://monicamynk.com

Acknowledgements

As always, there are more people to thank than I have space! I am ever grateful to all my family and friends who've supported me, promoted me, and stood by me as I've lived out my dream of being a writer.

Thank you to my readers and fans. I'm so humbled by your continued support and feedback. It is a joy to share my stories with you, and I hope you keep coming back to read more!

Special thanks to my new best friend from afar, Melanie, for lending me your ear and your name. I cherish our friendship and hope you achieve this dream one day as well.

Also, to Lora, my new amazing editor, who has been an absolute godsend! I appreciate the email hugs, conversation and prayers as much as the edits.

To my beta readers, you'll never know how much I value your loyalty and critical eyes. It's so hard to catch every mistake! Thanks for helping me with that final polish.

To Lane, Matthew, and Dana Kate, my loves. Thanks for making sure I have (a little!) quiet time to write.

And last, but not least, a big thanks to my special parents. You've sacrificed so many things for me over the years, and I love and appreciate you both. To daddy, who taught me so much about farming, faith, and life, this book is for you. You did not share Wayne's failures, but there are so many elements of you in the story, and I had to lend him your name. Mom is my champion, and you are my hero. Thank you for enduring my stubborn days...er...years, and having the patience to see me through to the other side of them.

Made in the USA
Monee, IL
31 July 2023

40177636R00173